SWORDS AND CIVILIZED MEN

"So, Afrianda!" raged the warrior Zaius. "This is how you dishonor me—the designated High Champion of Saditha's Temple! Am I then to wed a tarnished princess—am I to accept, under the Goddess's sacred wedding canopy, the pawed-over leavings of a filthy infidel?"

"Die, wretch!" was Conan's cry as he sprang up from Afrianda's reclining form. As his long knife flicked out of its beltloop, he was stayed only by the extreme desperation of the princess's clutch on his arm. Half-dragging her along with him, he halted some two steps from the motionless, indignant Zaius.

"Conan, you cannot slay him thus!" the princess pleaded on her knees behind him. "He is sacred to the Goddess!"

"True enough, foreigner," Zaius agreed. "This is not your quarrel, so begone. It would be a high sin to soil a ceremonial sword on your unclean pelts and innards."

"The words of a coward," Conan said, "who hides behind a woman—or a goddess!"

"I hide behind none, but I stand before the Goddess," Zaius proclaimed. "How would you, a savage foreigner, know anything of that? I have never seen a northern cretin like you made into a decent offal-slave, much less a free citizen of a pious land—"

Conan sprang at him with a throaty, inarticulate roar.

The Adventures of Conan
Published by Tor Books

Conan the Bold by John Maddox Roberts
Conan the Champion by John Maddox Roberts
Conan the Defender by Robert Jordan
Conan the Defiant by Steve Perry
Conan the Destroyer by Robert Jordan
Conan the Fearless by Steve Perry
Conan the Formidable by Steve Perry
Conan the Free Lance by Steve Perry
Conan the Great by Leonard Carpenter
Conan the Guardian by Roland Green
Conan the Hero by Leonard Carpenter
Conan the Indomitable by Steve Perry
Conan the Invincible by Robert Jordan
Conan the Magnificent by Robert Jordan
Conan the Marauder by John Maddox Roberts
Conan the Outcast by Leonard Carpenter
Conan the Raider by Leonard Carpenter
Conan the Renegade by Leonard Carpenter
Conan the Triumphant by Robert Jordan
Conan the Unconquered by Robert Jordan
Conan the Valiant by Roland Green
Conan the Valorous by John Maddox Roberts
Conan the Victorious by Robert Jordan
Conan the Warlord by Leonard Carpenter

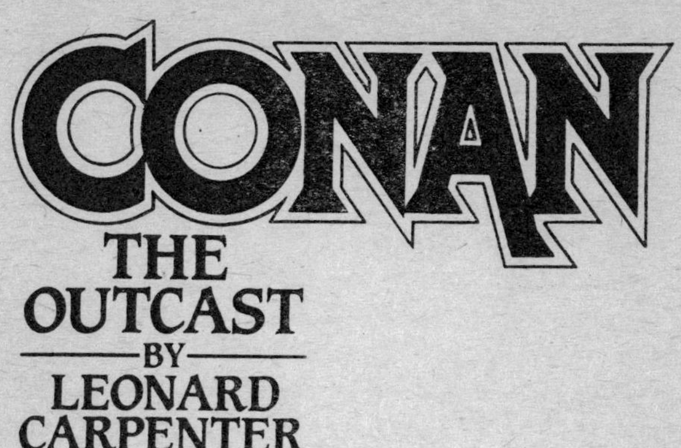

THE OUTCAST

BY

LEONARD CARPENTER

A TOM DOHERTY ASSOCIATES BOOK
NEW YORK

This is a work of fiction. All the characters and events portrayed in this book are fictitious, and any resemblance to real people or events is purely coincidental.

CONAN THE OUTCAST

A Tor Book
Published by Tom Doherty Associates, Inc.
49 West 24th Street
New York, NY 10010

Cover art by Ken Kelly

ISBN: 0-812-50928-5

First edition: April 1991

Printed in the United States of America

0 9 8 7 6 5 4 3 2 1

To Terri & Tom Pinckard

Contents

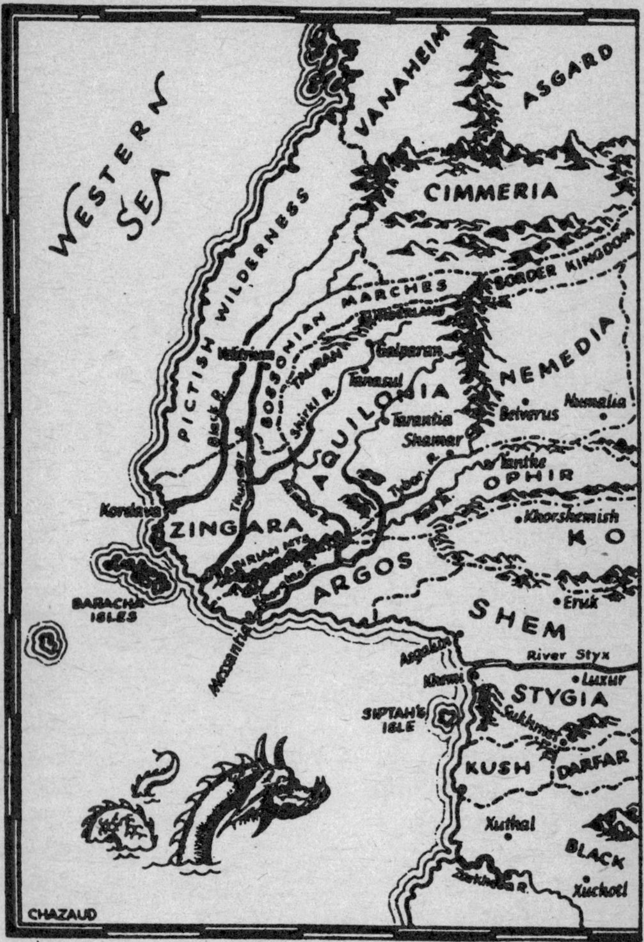

WESTERN SEA
VANAHEIM
ASGARD
CIMMERIA
PICTISH WILDERNESS
BOSSONIAN MARCHES
BORDER KINGDOM
Galparan
Tanasul
Shirki R.
Black R.
Thunder R.
NEMEDIA
AQUILONIA
Belverus
Numalia
Tarantia
Shamar
Tybor R.
Ianthe
OPHIR
Khorshemish
KO
Kordava
ZINGARA
ARGOS
BARACHA ISLES
Eruk
SHEM
River Styx
Khemi
Luxur
STYGIA
SIPTAH'S ISLE
Sukhmet
KUSH
DARFAR
Xuthal
BLACK
Zarkheba R.
Xuchotl
CHAZAUD

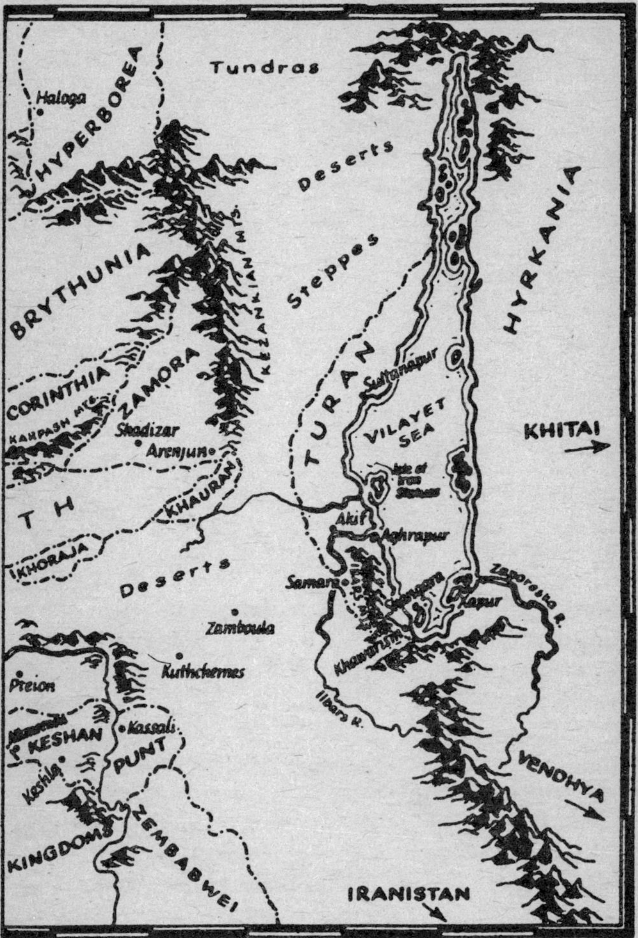

Tundras
Haloga
HYPERBOREA
Deserts
BRYTHUNIA
KEZANKIAN MTS.
Steppes
HYRKANIA
CORINTHIA
ZAMORA
TURAN
Sultanapur
VILAYET SEA
KHITAI
KARPASH MTS.
Shadizar
Arenjun
Isle of Iron Statues
TH
KHAURAN
Akif
Aghrapur
KHORAJA
Deserts
Samara
Zaporoska R.
Zamboula
Khawarizm
Kuthchemes
Ilbars R.
Pteion
KESHAN
Kassali
PUNT
Keshla
VENDHYA
KINGDOMS
ZEMBABWEI
IRANISTAN

Prologue

On the eighth day in the eighth month of the eighth cycle of his reign, during the seventh long year of the drought that had stricken his city, King Anaximander of Sark awoke at mid-morning and saw a vision.

The king came to awareness out of a deep and dreamless slumber. By the bright daylight that already gilded the heavy hangings of his terrace window, he was able to judge the hour as being later than his usual awakening. Anaximander felt rested, with a sense of well-being—in part, no doubt, because of the broad palm fans that waved perpetually at the head of his bed, sending a cooling breeze down the length to his trim, kingly body.

The slaves who plied the fans—a matched pair of comely Zamoran females, honey-pale of skin and bare but ample of chest—had been trained to perform their task in utter silence. The merest rustle of sound, the brush of a rough frond against the king's sleeping form—or, during his wakeful nights, a flaw in the breeze so slight as to cause but a single ringlet of his oiled hair or his long-curled square beard to be displaced—would likely have resulted in one or both servants yielding up their lives to merciless torture. Only thus, King Anaximander assured himself, were slaves induced to perform with perfect efficiency day after day, month upon month.

On that morning, instead of snapping his exquisitely manicured fingers to summon footmen or concubines as was his habit, the king did something unaccustomed. He arose from his firm, cool pallet, draping his regal nakedness in a flimsy silken coverlet. Disregarding the slaves who knelt along the wall of his chamber, he strode with kingly decisiveness to the curtained terrace window. Drawing the draperies aside with his own hand, ignoring the servants who rushed to help him, he stepped out onto his veranda into the full scorching light of day.

He saw, in part, what he expected to see: Below him lay the public courtyard, all but empty of citizens in the rising heat, with just a few pariahs and beggars sprawled in the narrow margin of shade along the palace's northern side. From this height it was hard to tell how many of them were dead of thirst, and how many merely indolent. Beyond the courtyard and a narrow district of tile-roofed barracks lay Sark's outer wall, lofty and thick, notched jaggedly with tooth-shaped crenellations. As always, it was patrolled by city troops in their conical helmets and bronze-scale vests, bearing aloft their long, bronze-tipped spears.

Straight before him, however, out past the fringe of the city wall, his eyes encountered something extraordinary. The view he expected was that of a dry, barren river-plain, brown-furred with wilting crops, its mud cracking and lifting in crazed puzzle-patterns under the fierce desert sun. But instead—there in the plain beyond the city wall, as if reared overnight while King Anaximander slept—stood a city, or the vision of a city.

Broad and sunbright, the scene shimmered more vividly than mere life: A noble town of tiled roofs girdled by a high, straight-topped wall of light-tan firebricks. Inside its gleaming bastion rose stately villas, whitewashed domes and pale stone ziggurats. White birds wheeled above the city, lighting in rooftop pigeon-roosts and dusty green clumps of trees. Front and center in the foreign wall stood the city gate, a broad archway clustered with awakening inhabitants. Through its bronze-faced double portals a long string of laden camels emerged, their drivers guiding them briskly out onto the raised thoroughfare. At one side of the road another caravan stood awaiting entry to the town, its cargo being assessed for tariff by helmeted officials.

Most striking of all was what shimmered before the city: a dappled expanse of blue water. The lush river-course, fringed by bright green shrubbery, ran past the very gate. Robed desert-dwellers filled jars from its rim, and washer-women toiled in the downstream shallows.

Such had been the scene in years past outside Anaximander's own city of Sark . . . until, as the king reminded himself with a pang of bitterness, the great and generous god Votantha had inexplicably turned his back on his city of faithful worshipers, and on the able, efficient servant he had in King Anaximander.

On this fateful morning, the king was not the only one to see the splendid vision; he could tell by the awestruck postures and less-than-disciplined gestures of the soldiers atop his own city wall. He would have called his master-at-arms to deal with the offenders, except that he himself reeled a bit giddily just now. The king blinked and passed a hand over his eyes, which felt seared by the intensity of the mystic revelation.

Already, he saw on looking once again, the image was fading—dimming and receding into the swelter of midday heat-shimmers. Hints of the sun-parched waste that was his own true domain began to peek through the mystic city and eat around its edges.

Rather than face the starkness of his own realm, he turned away from the scene. To the chief guard of his household troop—who stood flanking him just inside the royal bedchamber, his eyes large with wonder at the vision beyond the threshold—he gave an order. His Exalted Priest Khumanos was to be summoned at once.

Some moments later, when the priest arrived breathless, the king sat at ease in a folding chair of gold leaf, already dressed in his gold-threaded ceremonial vest, jeweled kirtle, and flawlessly pleated kilt. In this costume of high state, while fawning servants fretted themselves over the grooming of the royal feet and fingers, he addressed Khumanos. The Exalted Priest was a slender black-skinned man, remarkably young for his high office, with an inquisitive gleam in his eye.

"You heard of the vision that was granted to me by our god? Or saw it yourself?" To the priest's anxious nod and half-opened mouth, the king answered, "It was an image of our ancient trading rival, the heathen city of Qjara—lying leagues to the north and east of here, but transported to my very doorstep by Votantha's will." King Anaximander shook his head in mazed resentment. "The place was sleek and prosperous, aflourish with water and caravans—obviously the city and its folk are much favored by their dearly beloved . . . goddess."

The words must have been a barb to Khumanos. Surely he, more keenly than anyone else, knew how abysmally the priesthood had failed their city and king in recent years—failed to call down rain from the heavens, and to summon the related proofs of divine favor that were the lifeblood and strength of the city-state of Sark. Although Anaximander himself, as Priest-King of the realm, was titular and traditional head of the church, obviously the blame could not repose in him. Therefore it was the priests who had failed, and who, periodically, were called upon to make atonement for their city's shame.

Yet the stern young priest did not try to defend himself nor did he show other signs of unease. Instead he shook his head with solemn concern. "Sire, this is clearly a sending from the great god Votantha, a prophecy or warning. If you wish me and my astrologers to render an interpretation—"

"Nay, Priest. I shall render you the interpretation—which, in any case, should be obvious to all." The king, clearly standing in little awe of the young cleric, frowned in stern reflection past the female slaves who combed his curled, square beard. "Know you first, Priest, that in part I blame my own negligence. In the ease of my kingship, perhaps I have grown too fond of physical comfort and convenience. I may have been blind to the maladies of my kingdom around me, and the decline of our standing by comparison with the neighboring city-states."

The Exalted Priest drew an eager breath and spoke almost too readily. "Why, Sire, to be sure, there are steps that might be taken—"

"But no longer," Anaximander resumed, ignoring his priest's impetuousness. As if to signify his new resolve, he struck the groveling servants away from his shoulders and sandaled feet. "Now, clearly, our city's god demands a sacrifice. Not just the slaughter of a fewscore infants or virgins atop the ziggurat on Midsummer's Eve . . . nor the priming of wells and waterways with the blood of convicts and captive nomads . . . but a true offering, such as the ones our holy legends tell of aforetimes. The god Votantha, by sending us this vision, demands as his rightful sacrifice a whole and prospering kingdom . . . by his divine choice, the city-state of Qjara!"

The king, having arisen from his seat, towered over his cringing slaves. "It is clear to me now that if this sacrifice is carried out, great blessings will be ours. Rain will fall in the hills, replenishing our wells and cisterns, and the rivers will brim over with water for our crops. Caravans will once again ply their routes through Sark instead of Qjara, bringing us rich bounties of trade and tariffs. Votantha will be appeased at last, and his divine favor will enhance our city's power in war and commerce."

"My King—" Khumanos, while not daring to oppose his monarch's visionary ecstacies, was plainly ill at ease. "If it is a war that you are proposing, you must be aware that the city of Qjara is strongly fortified. I am told they are defended by a force of elite warrior-priests sworn to their goddess. Such a siege would be long and costly—"

"Siege? I spoke of no siege. You, Khumanos, should know better than anyone what I am speaking of." The king turned on his cleric with impressive and dangerous poise. "Secrets are passed down in priesthoods, after all, as well as in royal dynasties."

He turned his regal back on the priest and

strolled toward the terrace window, whose curtain now stood open on a barren waste ending in ragged hills. "Our city's ancient traditions tell of empires in these eastern deserts that were stricken by the hand of god—of our god, Votantha, who in those days chose to wear a more fearsome aspect than he now does.

"Those cities of hoary legend—ancient Pesk, Elgashi, and Yb of the Edomites—were stricken as by holy thunder, it is said, blasted from the face of the desert for their sins and blasphemies. Though by my reckoning of history, it must have been in great part for their sins against our own proud city of Sark and the ancestors of my royal lineage."

Anaximander turned against the bright sunlight from the terrace and faced Khumanos, a proud, unreadable silhouette. "In each case, priests of Votantha pronounced curses against the offending cities. They presided over civic exultation and orgy in honor of their destruction. Each bolt from heaven was followed by a resurgence of our holy faith, and a new epoch of prosperity and expansion for our city." The king grew silent a moment. "Methinks, Khumanos, our god is telling us the time is nigh for another such miracle."

"So it may be." The Exalted Priest's voice came back faint and a little husky. "I only hope my king understands that such a miracle would be no mere godly boon or favor, nor an empty display to promote mortal and civic fortune. It would be a millennial event—nothing less than the god Votantha himself visiting the earth, showing his true and terrible aspect."

"Very good, then, priest." Anaximander spoke coldly. "I am glad we both know what is at issue. I would remind you that three former Exalted Priests, all men of vastly greater age and experience than yourself, have poured out their heart's blood atop the Great Ziggurat in the past half-dozen years. All three made the supreme sacrifice in vain, since they failed to break this drought. Therefore I suggest that the time has come for what you describe—a full and dreadful visit by the Living God himself."

The king moved closer out of the glare, showing his subordinate a more visible face. "I understand there are preparations that must be made. A considerable expense of money and labor, too, which I know I can trust you to minimize. I have pondered the matter for some time, as you may have guessed—but now, in view of this morning's sign from the heavens, there is no further question." He moved up to his servant and laid a firm, hard hand on his shoulder. "Priest, I command you to open the way."

"It shall be so."

Bowing unsteadily to his king, Khumanos turned and moved toward the door. He went carefully, struggling at each step to overmaster his own creeping, paralyzing fear.

Chapter 1
The Unclean

The river marsh stretched still and sultry in the afternoon heat. Over the cattails, the golden-tan walls of Qjara loomed in the middle distance; yet there was no alarm or clatter atop them to disturb nature's peace. The air lying heavy on the reedy margins of the pond thrummed with bees, dragonflies and wasps, but this was a lulling sound, faint and continuous in the heat.

A man stood in the pool, his broad back sun-bronzed above the blue-green water. He was intent upon his fishing, and so made no noise—until, with a lightning motion and a silvery explosion of water, he lunged forward, driving a rude three-pronged spear into the pond shallows ahead of him. There followed a brief, splashing chase, until he retrieved what he had pinned to the weedy bottom; when he turned he clutched a long, slippery, greenish-brown thing that wriggled in his two-handed grasp.

He bore it quickly to a sun-bleached snag protruding like a gnarled knuckle from the water's edge. From this rough mooring hung half-submerged a coarse wet sack already bulging with unseen, writhing shapes. Into it he transferred his latest catch, then jerked tight the drawstring at its neck.

He paused then to shake water from his unruly mane of black hair. Taking from behind the stump a ragged loin-wrap, from whose heavy belt hung a thick, long-bladed knife, he fastened it with a single motion around his trim muscle-ribbed waist. Then, looping the squirming sack through the forks of his fish-spear, he levered it up over his shoulder and started back along the shallow edge of the pond.

His camp lay a little way downstream, on a sandy beach shaded by musty-scented bushes. It was within sight and sound of a place where the river played and splashed among stones in a shallow downhill reach. There, among his scant belongings, the forager busied himself for some minutes.

He rekindled a fire, which had sunk to glowing coals and feathery ash in its circle of stones. He fetched clean water in the battered, blackened bronze war-helmet that served him as a kettle. Gingerly he removed some of his day's catch from the sack and did careful violence to it with his overlarge knife on the fallen, bark-stripped log that served as his table.

In the course of these tasks a primal awareness of his surroundings, his hunter's alertness, did not fail him. And so in time, he became mindful of small things—a faint scent of freshly turned swamp-muck wafting unexpectedly to his nostrils, a furtive rustling of leaves and twigs that occasionally made itself heard above the talking of the river—and finally, in the bushes beyond the fire, the shifting of dim shadows that did not correspond to those of branch or bird.

Without showing any concern, the forager arose and ambled to the fire to throw on additional twigs. Slowly, negligently, he turned before it, sweeping the foliage with a glint of steel-blue eyes. Then at once, with a pounce swifter than the one he had made in the river pond, he darted into the brush and emerged dragging a struggling figure, his knife poised near its throat. His victim was slender, nut-brown and near-naked—a yelping, muddy-footed boy.

"Well, what have we here?" the captor guffawed, laying down his weapon. "I thought I had my fill of frogs and marsh-puppies—I certainly didn't mean to catch any more!" He spoke in the Shemitish dialect that was most current in the eastern deserts.

"Let him go!"

This voice, speaking a similar tongue, issued from the edge of the brush, from an older, ganglier boy who stood looking on. The youth stepped clear of the bushes in an adamant, demanding posture. "If you try to eat him, I warn you, we will hang your hide from the city wall!"

He brandished a small flint knife in one fist. Two more children crouched at his back.

"Eat him? . . . why would I want to? Nay, why would I risk the stomach-gripes, unless you urchins steal what food I have!" Releasing the boy from his hammerlock, he nevertheless kept one hand around the lad's wrist, letting him strain and struggle as he wished at arm's length. "Does he really think I would eat him?"

"You are a troll, are you not?" the elder boy demanded. "An evil northern giant!"

"No troll I! I am Conan of Cimmeria—no giant either, for my race, and only evil when my head aches from a night's carouse."

"As I thought—all men know that Cimmerians and such northerners are cannibals." The youth gestured with haughty abhorrence at the helmet-kettle which, braced on stones above the languidly flaming fire, was now boiling and frothing. "At the very least you are a djinn, and an eater of unclean food!"

"Faugh, to eat this young snipe—now that would be uncleanly indeed!" He released the boy—who scampered back to his friends, but soon turned to regard the northerner again in interested suspicion. "What I have cooking here is more than enough anyway—there could even be some to spare." Picking up his knife from the sand, he wiped it on his breech-wrap and used it to stir the bubbling kettle.

"Wha-what is it?" one of the boys sheltering behind the leader asked.

"Why, 'tis a savory stew of crayfish and river

eels." The one called Conan angled his knife-blade flat and lifted out a limp, insectlike crustacean which hung on the tip a moment before slipping back into the cauldron with a plop.

"Unclean!" the third of the watching boys piped up. "The priests of the One True Goddess would thump your head on the altar-stone twelve times if you were caught eating such vermin, or even confessed to it."

"Nonsense," the northerner declared. "You town-dwellers are foolish indeed if you do not consume good, wholesome river-food—or salt it up for the lean times, which must come to your city now and again." He slid his knife through the leather strap of the bubbling helmet and hoisted it off the fire. "Do you boys live within the walls of Qjara?"

"Yes," one of the younger ones replied. "I am Jabed. My father is Japeth, a camel trader, although . . ." the expression on the lad's face grew pensive, ". . . he went away on a camel-buying trip some years since, and has not returned yet. My mother weaves reed baskets for the city market to support us, until father comes back to make us all rich. I will take her some reeds when I go home," he added, displaying a small flint knife of his own, good for cutting through the tough stalks.

"My father was a roof-maker who died in a fall from a roof," the older boy announced. "My mother weaves baskets, too, and I cut river reeds for her—but someday I will be a warrior-priest of the One True Goddess!" He displayed a somewhat longer flint knife; returning it then to a pouch on his belt as if sheathing a noble sword, he stood with a proud, erect bearing. "Someday I may even be as famous a temple warrior as Zaius the Champion."

The Cimmerian laughed. "Your warrior-priests are a well-dressed and well-drilled lot. I would guess their fighting techniques are a bit stiff, though, hampered by more taboos than their diet."

"A dozen of them can wipe out any hundred ragged desert nomads, you can be sure of that!" the boy answered hotly.

Conan gazed back at the youth, taking no issue with him. "And can the son of a roof-maker or a basket-weaver gain entry to their noble brotherhood?"

"Indeed I can," the lad argued belligerently. "Entry to the priesthood is based strictly on skill in temple school . . . and on spirit, and success in games and drills," he finished, as if reciting a lesson.

"Good, then," the Cimmerian nodded. "Maybe there is some hope for them after all. What is your name, lad?"

"I am Ezrel," the elder youth declared. Indicating his companions, he said, "Jabed, Felidamon, and . . ." he indicated the child Conan had first captured, who how hovered at the rear of the group, ". . . Inos."

Conan nodded, saying nothing. He had an inkling that young Felidamon was a girl-child, though she and Jabed were equally bony and wore long, soiled jellaba shirts that made it impossible to tell.

"Are you a fighter?" Jabed asked. "What kind of weapon is that?"

"This," Conan said, taking up the blade from beside him, "is a good, stout Ilbarsi knife, taken in . . . trade from hill tribesmen south of the Vilayet. You can see here, the blade gets thicker toward the end—that makes up for its shortness in . . . chopping firewood. A fine tool, this—it will serve for cutting brush, digging holes, various kinds of skinning and butchery—even as a spit for roasting, and yet it will take an edge keen enough to shave with. A man should keep one by his side at all times . . ." Leaning forward with the blade, he thrust it into the glowing bed of the fire. "You never know what you may catch with it!"

Withdrawing the knife from the coals and blowing off cinders, he showed them that he had speared something oblong and steaming, wrapped in singed leaves—some foodstuff that had been baking under the hot ashes. "Sweet ground-tubers, you see! Here are swamp radishes, too, and leeks."

Digging in the fire he produced more delicacies. Some of these the children were induced to sample after they had cooled. But it took a heart as bold as Ezrel's to lead the way in tasting the fish stew.

"Phoo, it is hot and peppery," he complained. This did not keep him from accepting a sizeable serving on a plate of tree bark that Conan provided. The others followed suit; even timid Inos joined in cracking the segmented shells of the crayfish and sucking out their tender flesh. The children ate greedily, leaving Conan to consume but a modest portion of the stew and finish off their leavings, mainly swamp-leeks.

"You must have traveled far," Felidamon ventured in her piping young voice. "Have you been to cities greater than Qjara?"

"Oh, aye, I have been to Aghrapur, Belverus, Tarantia . . . many such overlarge hives of men. The nearest one is Shadizar, where I may go when the northward passes open, if a caravan happens through."

"Shadizar the Wicked, they call it," Jabed mused. "But they will not speak of it in temple school. Why is that, Conan?"

"Oh, it is a place of great wealth and great misery, all in one. Penniless men and women beg and starve in the streets at the feet of rich, resplendent fops."

"How can that be?" Felidamon marveled. "Don't the priests make them share what they have?"

Conan laughed. "No, the priests are the richest and worst of them. And Shadizar is a slave market—the slaves there live under cruel masters, but many freefolk are even worse off than the slaves! Most of the able, honest men there are thieves—there is even a Thieves' Guild in Shadizar. Fancy that!"

"People in our city say that a lone foreigner like you must be a thief." Ezrel's look was fearless as usual, his words pointed. "Is that why you want to go to Shadizar?"

Conan guffawed. "Well, in truth, supposing that I was a thief, the pickings would be choicest in Shadizar, with its greedy merchants, lotus-crazed aristocrats, and rich, lordly wizards." He gathered up leavings of the meal and tossed them into the fire. "There is much better thieving in such a place than any little camel-bath like Qjara has to offer!"

"You would not want to be a thief in Qjara, in any case," Ezrel said. "The temple warriors would cut you up into catmeat." To Conan's scowl, he added, "But if you promise not to steal, you could come live within the city walls, and not have to sleep on a bed of boughs." He pointed at the shaded warren under a dense bush where Conan's rumpled blanket lay.

The Cimmerian shook his shaggy head. "No, boy, I do not think your elders would want me prowling your city—not beyond the caravan quarter, anyway. And I do not feel like slaying a dozen men to prove the point just now. I will continue to lodge without the city walls."

"But Conan," Felidamon chimed in, "you could settle down in Qjara and learn to ply a useful trade. Camel-breeding, perhaps, or—" she glanced down at the dying fire and the remnants of the meal, "—cookery, at one of the caravansaries!"

"You mean, make food for travelers and accept money in return . . . and do only that, and nothing else?" Conan regarded her narrowly, knitting his brow in puzzlement. "But what would happen when I grew tired of cooking, as I surely would? I am not a slave, to toil endlessly at another's whim!" He shook his black mane vigorously, dismissing the matter.

"And if I would not bow and grovel before your goddess Saditha, why, there would be trouble, too! No, 'tis better that I leave your town to its pious peace." He glanced at the shadows near the stream's edge. "But say, it grows late. Wash off your trenchers in the stream before you go." Ezrel, noting the declining angle of the sun in the western sky, had already risen.

"Yet you will go to Shadizar." Inos, the small fugitive, spoke up unexpectedly. "Which do you like better, Conan—Shadizar or Qjara?"

"For the sort of man I am, Shadizar is the best place." Conan gazed at the little boy with the merest shade of regret in his blue eyes. "But before you go, listen—value what you have, lad!" He clapped a hand on the child's shoulder before hustling him along. "Never desert Qjara for Shadizar the Wicked, and pray that no slave-catcher ever drags you there."

CHAPTER 2
Valley of Fire

Exalted Priest Khumanos trod the desert waste in fear. To an onlooker his mental state would not, perhaps, have shown—but this dusky southerner knew that heat alone would hardly have reduced his young limbs to slack, reluctant obedience. The heavy film of sweat across his shoulder blades, beneath his hooded cotton tunic, was not due to sun; nor was the taut dryness in his throat born of the scorching furnace-breaths of the arid canyons he traversed. As Khumanos trudged onward, the harshness of the land around him went unnoticed. It was a mere faint, heat-shimmering reflection of the mortal dread and anguish that laid waste his own faltering heart.

In the palsied grip of his fear, Khumanos guessed that if anyone could instruct him, or at least point the way, Solon could. Old beyond years, wise beyond knowing, the holy hermit had dwelt in the desert since the time of Khumanos's fathers and before. Not a god, certainly, but not quite mortal either . . . in past times, heads of the Sarkad temple had been known to consult the sage for advice. He was respected as an oracle, a pure wellspring of the parched fanaticism that lay at the heart of true, godly zeal.

Khumanos paused in a rare knife-edge of shade, to rest against the as-yet unheated, northwest-facing wall of a deep, dry wadi. Sparingly he sipped from his lukewarm and already flaccid waterskin. He knew not if he was on the proper path to find Solon—nor if there was such a path, nor even if Solon still lived. But tradition told him that if he placed himself in this part of the barren lands, and followed the central gully towards its source in the nameless hills, he would come to the wise old one's dwelling place.

He thought he must be on the track—for the hermit was said to live in a valley of fire, and the terrain Khumanos was entering certainly looked as if it was carved out of frozen fire. Red sandstone cliffs and ridges rose on either hand, their shapes twisting and convoluting into spires worn ragged as writhing flames. The fiery yellow sand of the dry wash alternated with banks of uneven red cobbles; these, as he tried to cross them, scorched the sides of his sandaled feet like the coals of an open hearth. The few shreds of vegetation, huddled in gully-bottoms or trailing down from narrow crevices in the walls, looked dry and dark, scorched to cinders by the slow, inexorable holocaust.

Ahead of him the gully came to an abrupt end, with no sign of a human presence. He searched the blank walls, hollowed and red-crusted like the insides of a pottery kiln; finally he saw where the way led.

In some primeval flood or avalanche the narrow stone channel of the wadi had been choked with boulders and debris; now, if Khumanos wished to follow the dead stream further, it would mean a hazardous climb up the steep, irregular face of the dam, to a height of a half dozen man-lengths. Not enough of a fall to kill him, perhaps—but enough to leave him broken and helpless, without a chance of survival in this lonely, hostile waste.

Here, then, was the challenge, the test of faith. Compared to the plague of dread that besieged his soul, Khumanos almost exulted at this minor, measurable danger. Slinging his water bag around behind him, he strode forward and made a running leap to the top of the first massive boulder. He placed his sandaled foot on the next, laid his palms on the hot, rough stone edges, and began to climb.

Later, near the top of the precipice, where a large stone had choked the fissure and created a shallow overhang, Khumanos knew that he must die. His fingertips felt raw, his breath came in shallow gasps, and the hot stone—to which he clung as tightly as a babe to its mother—scorched and abraded his chest and chin. The small, protruding rock he had intended to use as a foothold, after twisting loose under his sandal, had skittered away to smash far below. There was no hope of climbing back down—for with his eyes to the cliff wall he was unable to see the precarious, sloping footholds below. Now he knew he must either fall or cling here until the ruthless heat left him dry and brittle as a desiccated insect for the desert gusts to waft away.

Only one small hope remained. It lay above him in the narrow, glaring arc of stone his desperate eyes could scan: from a jumble of debris atop the protruding boulder which he so embraced and cherished, a single twig projected. White, dry and finger-thin, it appeared to have no strength left in it; all that could be said was that it was in reach. In all likelihood, if he shifted his anxious grip and snatched at the twig to sustain his balance, it would start an avalanche that would bear him over backward to his death . . . but just possibly not.

Again, a test of faith . . . with destruction this time only a handsbreadth away. After more hesitation and a long muttered prayer to Votantha, Exalted Priest Khumanos grasped the twig.

It may not have been a twig after all, but a dried root. There may even have been a tough thread of life left in it . . . because it held his faltering weight. A small shower of dirt and gravel bounded down past Khumanos, some of it pelting his eyes and mouth, but he did his best to disregard that. Trusting gradually more weight to his handgrip, he began to inch himself up the curving rock on his elbows and belly. Then, with a heave, he got his knees under him. Creeping breathlessly up the boulder, he came to the top of the dam.

Beyond it lay a level space of dry, silty sand. Further ahead he could see that the canyon continued to branch and twist, cutting more deeply into the crimson flanks of the hills—but here, close at hand, lay something of intense interest.

Partway up a dusty-red mound that projected out into the gully was the shadowy circle of a cave mouth. From it, as from recent digging, darker red earth trailed down, flecked with pale bits of bone and debris. And at the top of the refuse pile before the cave, sitting cross-legged in the sun, was a disheveled man in a dirty white tunic.

Surely this was Solon. Khumanos, feeling doubly blessed by the discovery and by his own survival thus far, fell to his knees in the sand. He spent some time muttering devout prayers of thanksgiving to Votantha. When he looked up again, the figure before the cave was standing, making impatient gestures to one side. The rags of his costume trailed loosely as he waved. Khumanos gathered that he was pointing to a sparse path which ran around the edge of the midden, leading up to where he stood.

Hurrying to obey, Khumanos went in the direction the wise man had indicated. He soon found himself sliding in red shale and leaping from rock to rock, for the trail was ill-made and little-used. As he neared the top of the slide it became more of a garbage heap, littered with gourd-stems and cactus-pear husks, skins and bones of snakes and toads, and other dried offal. Also evident in the heap were larger, heavier bones, some with strange and disturbing shapes. By that route, the priest climbed toward a shelf which lay halfway up to the base of a sandstone monolith that towered and twisted against the blazing blue sky like a pink tornado of flame.

At the cave-shelf Khumanos, coming face to face with its occupant, paused in sudden uncertainty. At close range the old man was a grotesque sight—bent, withered, and filthy in his ragged smock, his clawlike nails untended, his hands and feet knobby with calluses and crusted with grime. His face was a grinning, near-toothless knot of seams and wrinkles; his head was almost bald, with the merest fringe of wispy-white hair in back. Scalp and forehead had suffered grievous overexposure to the sun; they were red and peeling in some places, blotchy in others. Yet his movements had a lightness and spryness that denied any thought of infirmity; the sunburnt, scrawny frame harbored an ageless vitality.

"Elder One," Khumanos ventured, "I come in search of a seer who dwells in the desert—"

"I am Solon," the old man replied, volubly nodding and grinning. "I have watched your approach since midday . . . I could have shown you a safe path around the dry fall," he added genially, "but I make it a point never to aid supplicants. It is well that you survived the climb—it proves you are strong in your faith in Votantha."

The old man spoke volubly and lovingly, as if starved for human company. "Long it has been since a high priest found his way here from the city to homage me. What tribute have you brought?"

"Sublime One, most favored of Votantha!" Dropping to his knees, the Exalted Priest pressed his forehead to the gritty earth at the hermit's feet before sitting upright. In response to the old man's impatient gestures, he reached into his tunic and produced a parcel wrapped in gold-threaded cloth. "I offer you rare delicacies—spiced dates, candied breast of songbirds, soft green figs and honeyed sesame loaf."

Before he even finished speaking, the old man had snatched the packet out of his grasp and retreated with it into the shadows of the cave. Khumanos, half-rising to his feet, crept after him as far as the low, rough archway. But Solon crouched just inside the rim of shade, and did not invite him any further. The priest knelt patiently outside, in the sun's harsh glare.

"Sublime One, I wish I could say that my faith was strong," he continued, "but I am prey to sinful fears—"

" 'Tis good, then, that you have come to the desert." Solon's words were enunciated around greedy mouthfuls of food, which he stuffed into his toothless maw with grimed, crack-nailed fingers.

"Know you," the sage went on after swallowing, "this barren land is a spawning ground of all that is mystic and holy! A pilgrim comes here to face harsh, naked reality . . . only to find that reality wears more cloaks and masks than a troupe of Corinthian mummers. The eastern desert is the country of mirages, hallucinations, starfalls and fever-dreams. Foodstuffs are scarce, and most of those to be found here—the roots, mushrooms, and cactus blooms—poison the brain and open the eyes to frightful inward visions." Solon gnawed and swallowed more as he spoke, which made the sounds of his speech wolflike and difficult to understand.

"And yet," he went on, "the true mystic knows that there are no more powerful narcotics for calling forth demons and spirit visions than pain, fatigue, and starvation. And Votantha Himself knows, this place has a plentiful supply of all three! Here in the desert, the emptiness itself sounds as a mustering call to the demons that lurk in the inner recesses of a man's soul." Having crammed down all the dainty food without offering any to his guest, Solon now wiped his lips on the parcel's cloth-of-gold wrapping. "Here in the lost barrens, the bones and innards of the earth are laid bare, showing the true and savage nature of the beast. Come, follow." With this command he waved a hand and, crouching low, gestured Khumanos back into the shadows of his cave.

The Exalted Priest, his eyes still dazzled by sun, had difficulty making his way inside. Promptly on entering, and then several times again in swift succession, he struck his head on objects jutting down sharply from the already-low ceiling of the tunnel. As his vision ceased swimming from the blows and began to adapt to the dimness, he could see that the protuberances were pale in color: giant bones, as hard and massive as stone, embedded in the softer sandstone walls—which seemed to have been dug away around them to enlarge the place and reveal their shape.

As Solon led the way deeper, the cave opened up somewhat, allowing Khumanos to stand nearly upright. Odd pieces and cross sections of skeletons stuck out of the walls on all sides, representing snakelike fish, lizardlike birds, and other creatures Khumanos had never seen or heard tell of. The place had an eerie, nightmarish aspect, particularly in the bloody dimness of reflected sun which glowed off the apron of red soil outside the cave's mouth. Gradually, by degrees, the high priest was able to perceive more of the details around him—such as, that the hermit had knotted the greasy cloth-of-gold under his chin. He now wore it as a shawl or bandage around his scabrous old head, while he commended the wonders of the cave to his visitor's view.

"As you can see, this hill was once a burial place for dragons—unless these monsters were laid to rest here by some vast avalanche or flood." Proudly he indicated a bony assemblage exposed across the roof of the gallery. It arched up from finlike phalanges, along curving ribs and barbed spine, down a neck which sinuously doubled back along the cave's far wall, to the monstrous, spike-toothed head. One knifelike fang jutted up murderously from the floor of the cave amid a nest of smaller but no less sharp teeth. It was the skeleton of a great long-necked, long-snouted fish, with a stomach cavity so large it almost encompassed them now where they stood. "Such are the monsters that roved these deserts aforetimes," the sage said. "And who knows, they might someday be called back to life by the gods.

"Using these tools, in my spare hours," Solon continued, gesturing to an array of worn, shovel-edged and awl-pointed pieces of bone standing against the wall, "I have enlarged the cave and laid bare the handiwork of the gods. And here, at the very back of my abode, is the source of my strength and the reward of my labor."

Beckoning Khumanos to a covered alcove in the narrowing space, Solon pushed aside a soiled rag of curtain to reveal a natural seep of water. From a glistening white bone that depended fanglike from the ceiling, beads of water plopped slowly into a bowl formed from the lopsided, inverted skull of one of the cave-wall creatures. The old hermit dipped his hand in and slurped noisily from it, taking most of what was in the shallow basin; then he gestured hospitably for Khumanos to drink. The Exalted Priest refused meekly, backing away.

"Sublime One," he said, "I come to your holy shrine to drink my fill not of your scarce water but of your plentiful wisdom! Our great god Votantha, through the mediation of Anaximander the King, has set a mighty task before me . . . yet I know not whether I have the resolution to carry it out."

"I know of your trial," Solon said, pushing past him. "The very heavens are at war. Signs and omens tell us to prepare the way—that the hour again draws near for Votantha to show himself in our sphere. A great thing indeed—it is a rare privilege for a human to confront a god, to cast frail mortal eyes on his living face." Creeping on all fours into a low corner of the cave, the hermit settled his grimy haunches on a soiled mat, where he sat with his callused, spindly legs crossed. "There is, of course, the eventuality of one's own death . . ."

"It is not alone dying that frightens me," Khumanos said, falling to his knees before the sage. "After so great an honor as meeting the Great One, I would hardly expect to cling to my puny life. It is more the dread of the moment itself. . . . What will be the god's true aspect, and how can I, a mere moth before a hurricane, rightly acquit myself? Also . . ." here he bowed his shaven head in shame ". . . there is an unworthy squeamishness in my soul, a weak-hearted reluctance to unleash such terror on other mortals, who after all may be ignorant of our creed—who may, until the last dreadful moment, retain their faith in tamer, weaker gods." The young priest shook his head in embarrassed discomfiture. "If so, they will never truly appreciate the grandeur and glory that is to be theirs—"

"The sacrifices, you mean," Solon prompted him with an air of certainty. "The folk of the city that is to be offered up."

"Yes," Khumanos admitted with downcast

eyes. "Qjara, the place is, a trading station to the north, which Votantha in his wisdom has seen fit to fatten for our sacrifice with plentiful rains and caravans."

"A city of unbelievers," Solon said.

"Yes, 'tis true." Khumanos nodded glumly. "I know nothing of the town . . . but I imagine it is much like Sark, with farmers and merchants, men, wives, and children—"

"An impious waste," the hermit echoed. "I think I see—you would not have them die before accepting Votantha as their lord, and lose the chance to serve at his feet hereafter—that is most pious of you, my child!" Solon cackled a laugh. "But the answer is easy, and is provided for in our holy dogma. Offer the city a mission from your temple, to teach the true way! Give them a chance to convert before the end comes."

Khumanos shook his head. "Many of them would not accept it, at least not in a short while. Most city-states of the Shemitish League have their own gods, you must know—or in this case, a goddess. They cling stubbornly to their beliefs—"

"It does not matter," Solon interrupted curtly, picking food from between his last two adjacent teeth with a grimy, cracked fingernail. "Once you have offered them the choice, it is on their heads. If they choose not to follow, they are unworthy, and deserve an infidel's torment in the afterlife."

"But, Sublime One, do you not see? They are innocent!" Meeting the hermit's eye, Khumanos's sudden tears and breaking voice revealed the full depth of anguish that filled his soul. "Humble, honest men, young women, little babes! Can I really deliver them to the vengeful fury of the Living God without a true, fair opportunity to accept him and make their peace?"

"I understand, Khumanos," Solon said, sternly regarding him. "Your sin is great indeed. At heart you lack the iron faith that is necessary to an Exalted Priest of Votantha." Over the priest's renewed sobbing, he continued calmly. "You are young. Your heart still cherishes idyllic notions of earthly life—nature's plenty, the joys of honest work and family, the carnal love of women—you have not lived enough yet to be burned and tempered fully in the harsh fires of faith." The hermit pivoted on his gaunt shanks and rummaged in a tattered bag of charms and fetishes that lay beside his mat. "A grave failing, but understandable. I have here that which will relieve your suffering."

"You . . . you have?" Recovering somewhat from his sorrow, Khumanos watched the wise old man through wet, blinking eyes.

"I have indeed." From his medicine bag Solon drew a tarnished holy relic; at a distance, it resembled a short, blunt knife. "This can sever the painful ties of youth and cut the cords of your unattainable yearnings."

As the old hermit hunkered up in the low part of the cave and crept forward, ducking beneath the flattened skeletal imprint of a long-tailed bird, Khumanos saw that the object he held had once been a sword or heavy knife, long since broken off near its heavy bronze hilt. The decaying stub of blade was black and jagged with corrosion, and could not have been very keen; yet Solon gripped it between crosspiece and butt as if it were a full-sized weapon.

"What, then, do you intend to do with that?" Khumanos asked him, frightened.

"This?" Solon said, still approaching. "This is the legendary Sword of Onothimantos, a fabled mystic charm. Do you know its power?"

"No." Khumanos, feeling panic leap in his vitals, began involuntarily backing away. "What is it for?"

"Very simple, really. It will kill your youthful soul and release you from its torments." Solon, up on his feet now, slowed with an appearance of maneuvering subtly for position—no great challenge, really, since he stood between Khumanos and the open mouth of the cave. "Do not fear—it will be a great relief in the long run. Your mind and body will be freed for the work that lies ahead."

"What? You mean . . . kill only a part of me? But how can that be? . . . will it hurt?" The Exalted Priest, obviously unwilling to be rushed into a magical rite, moved nervously to avoid the hermit's advance.

"All things are possible with faith in Votantha," Solon said with a wily grin, choosing that moment to strike. "And all things worthwhile . . . hurt!"

Young Khumanos, obviously expecting to be slashed or jabbed by the stubby remnant of a blade, did not throw himself back energetically enough from the hermit's blow. Old Solon, astonishingly, executed a lithe, leaping thrust, as a palace fencer would have done. He struck not with the broken stub but with the whole blade, its main section long vanished—and the young priest, from his bulging eyes and gasp of agony, obviously felt his body pierced by its entire, invisible length.

The ghost-blade struck straight to the heart, true and clean. Khumanos took the blow deep in his fellow feeling; it jabbed sharply through his credulity and, with a skillful twist, severed his noble aspirations. All the earthly human passions in his breast cried out in anguish at the stroke, and his face contorted in searing pain. But by the time the shard of corroded metal thumped against his chest and rebounded without doing visible harm, his soul was already dead.

"I see." Exalted Priest Khumanos spoke coldly and immediately to his attacker, while still brushing away flakes of rust from the chest of his tunic. "You were right, everything is much clearer now." He sank to his knees and waited patiently before Solon. "You must instruct me about the opening of the way."

Solon, putting aside the mystic blade, sat down cross-legged. He then addressed the priest at length, explaining in careful detail the steps which were to be taken. As he spoke on, the hour grew late. Dayblaze faded from the sky outside; it deepened to a sunset of gold and crimson, making the valley resemble a true cauldron of fire. Inside the cave, so that his student might discern the diagrams he scratched in the filth of the floor, Solon was forced to light a flame of turtle oil in a lamp made from an inverted tortoise shell. Its unsteady glow caused the shadows of projecting bones to dance and shimmer on the cave's red walls.

"Thus it must be done, and only thus. Make the least error, and the wrath of the god will be visited on you in ways you could not dream." Solon carefully wiped the last scratchings from the cave floor. "The idol is the key."

"I see," Khumanos said, arising. "How did you, Solon, become the keeper of this timeless knowledge?"

"I was a high priest of Sark, younger than yourself when the city of Yb was visited by our god. I was not the Exalted Priest—he was consumed in the sacrifice. But I served as his assistant, sent to watch the city from afar and carry back word of Votantha's coming. I remember the rituals clearly."

"The city of Yb was destroyed seven centuries agone, Solon."

"Perhaps so. After bearing the news I wandered mad in the wastes for a time, and then lay here in this cave, weak unto death. For know you, I was callow and lacked faith even as you did. The Sword of Onothimantos saved me."

"You are soulless by virtue of its power?" Khumanos asked.

"Perhaps. I had to wield the blade myself, and so may have done a poor job. I suspect that some part of my soul has since grown back, like a chancre imperfectly excised." The hermit shrugged, face knotted in his habitual grin. "But as you can see, it did me no harm and indeed, much good! By Votantha's grace I have enjoyed a long life."

"Yes. Long enough, I think." Leaning suddenly forward, Khumanos seized the hermit by the neck and one scrawny shoulder, dragging the tough old carcass up to chest height. "You have passed along the burthen of your wisdom." Heaving his victim aside, the Exalted Priest dragged the struggling hermit onto the prong of dragon's jawbone set into the foot of the wall. Lunging at it, he bore down so hard that the upward-thrusting fang pierced deep into the base of Solon's skull. "Now your usefulness is ended."

Turning aside from the slackening body, Khumanos gathered up his tutor's meager belongings. Then, under the starry loom of night, he strode forth from the cave to prepare the way for the Implacable One. With what he had gained this day, he saw no further difficulty in carrying out his life's purpose—to serve his god Votantha, the mighty Tree of Mouths.

CHAPTER 3
The Caravansary

The barefoot dancer leaped and twisted in the sand before the fire. With a quick gesture of her red-nailed hand, one of the filmy gossamer veils that screened her loins was snatched away and flung into the flames. There it ignited; floating skyward like a spent dream, it consumed itself and vanished into the starry night.

Sharla's dance resembled the leaping flames themselves, Conan thought as he regarded her—the light, lilting steps, the quick pirouettes and prances, all performed to the droning insistence of pipes and the urgent chiming of cymbals. Now as he watched he could plainly see firelight reflecting from the pale-sheened skin of her belly and haunches; to avoid straining his neck unduly, he pivoted his chair in its place under the shelter.

About him, the caravan quarter of Qjara was a fringe of low buildings and alleys centered on the large, dusty yard just inside the Tariff Gate. It contained a water trough, stables, and ample space for the horses and camels of a half-dozen caravans—as well as the tents of the camel-drovers, who often as not preferred to dine and sleep in the sand with their mounts. The caravansaries and inns that served the quarter were built as open stalls, oriented toward the outdoor firepits, with canopies that could be lashed down tight during windstorms.

Tonight was a quiet, off-season night. Only the one caravan was in, westward bound and not richly laden—unless, like the Stygians, one valued salt highly enough to wage wars for it. The yard was dark and still except for this one fire. From where he sat, Conan could see stars glinting all the way down to the loom of the city wall on one hand and, on the other, the lower, battlemented wall that separated the caravan quarter from the rest of Qjara.

As the dance approached its climax, the talk and drunken laughter around the fire diminished. The camel-drovers' interest was heightening dangerously; yet Sharla knew her business. When a hand clutched too close or a shadowy shape rose toward her in the firelight, she would evade it deftly—otherwise, a casual scuff of her bare foot would fling sand into the offender's eyes and effectively end the distraction.

Another of her veils darted into the fire and floated heavenward, a dissolving arc of flame. That left two of the original seven. At least so

Conan judged, if his count wasn't hindered by wine—he would never have undertaken to compute how many beakers of *arrak* he had downed this evening. Counting the veils still affixed to the whirling dancer was a near-impossibility.

The performance accelerated swiftly toward a close, as more of the woman-starved nomads of the caravan began rising up and moving in on the dancer. Sharla combined fine art with finer evasion, keeping them just out of reached as she danced.

The actual moment of near-nudity, when her last veil was sacrificed to the ravening flame, passed briefly and tantalizingly. A pale flash of sleek, supple torso . . . then the skirling and chiming wound to a close, and Sharla dashed behind a screen in the sturdy stone and timber part of the lodge.

When she emerged again some time later, her supple charms coyly draped in silk, the would-be pursuers were already being staved off with more drink and with the good-natured attentions of the less athletic but more accomodating women of the caravansary. It was to Conan's side, at the long, oiled table in the head of the shelter, that Sharla went.

"Tap-keeper, a long, cool drink!" she called out. "And for this outlander, no more *arrak*!" she teased, laying an arm on his shoulders. "He must stay sober to keep me satisfied!"

Easily she settled into the chair beside Conan. She did not twist away from his large, familiar hand as it crept around her waist—rather, she glanced bright-eyed around the room so that the other patrons might notice and stay clear of this hulking northerner who laid open claim to her.

"So, Conan," she asked, turning to him, "how did you like my dance? Did it remind you of your wicked nights in far-off Shadizar?"

Conan laughed, pondering. "Such a dance in the Maul in Shadizar, by such a maid . . . nay, the fools would not appreciate it! The audience would be too intent on slitting each other's throats, or purses, or on avoiding such a fate. But here in the desert . . ." he moved his hand up the dancer's back to stroke her lithe neck ". . . why, girl, a dance like that is a wonder, a gem beyond price."

"Oh? I danced it specially for you." Seeming less than completely satisfied with his praise, Sharla twisted from beneath his touch and turned to accept her drink.

"Your dance . . . my child, it was the flight of a star streaking across the heavens!" a third voice broke in. "It was the gallop of the swiftest, costliest racing camel of Afghulistan! O Lovely One, I am Memchub." The speaker was a plump, short-bearded, silk-robed man of eastern Shem—chief merchant, Conan guessed, of the caravan currently laying over in Qjara. Approaching the dancer from behind, he laid covetous fingertips on her shoulder. "If you would but come and sit with me, I will tell you more of what I thought of your dance. Yea, I would commend your talents to Ellael's bright stars above—"

"Nay—thanks for your praise," Sharla said shortly, "but go see one of the tavern maids for companionship. I am an artist, and will someday dance in the temple of the One True Goddess, or in noble Shadizar—and tonight I have an escort." With a toss of her head she indicated Conan, who loomed up straighter in his seat to lend substance to her point.

"An escort?—I see, a fine, manly young ox! I have employed many such, and could use a few more of them just now on my caravan." The Shemite glanced dismissively past Conan, back to Sharla. "But surely, as an artist you yearn for finer things—the worldly and genteel conversation a cultured man can offer you, polite treatment for once, and rare little gifts and trinkets—" Pulling aside his embroidered silk vest from his silken shirtwaist, he jingled the beaded purse that was tied there "—pretty gold coins from faraway lands—"

"Here, now," Conan said, grasping the merchant by one shoulder and twisting it until silk tourniquetted the soft flesh, "the wench wants to be left alone—"

"He is right!" Sharla said. "But Conan, remember, Master Anax doesn't want you damaging his customers needlessly—you can let him go if he promises to behave." To Memchub she said sweetly. "If you want company, I'm sure sweet Babeth will be happy to entertain you."

The harlot Babeth came swiftly at the mention of her name, leaving a less prosperous camel-keeper abandoned on a nearby bench. "Indeed, I will be pleased to share the company of such a sophisticated aristocrat as you," she tittered, pursing her plump berry-stained lips at Memchub. "It would be a rare pleasure to spend time with a man who doesn't prefer to romance a girl while leaning on his camel!"

The merchant, massaging his crumpled shoulder, blinked at Babeth with grateful relief, no longer daring to meet Sharla's gaze. She spent some moments introducing the two and shooing them off into a corner. Then she turned to back Conan, who had returned to his drink.

"Why so pensive?" she asked, easing down beside him. "Dreaming again of your beloved Hyborian lands? They make the doings of this watering hole look paltry, I suppose." She placed her pale hands on his sun-bronzed shoulders, insinuating the carnelian gems of her fingernails underneath the embroidered seams of his short, open vest. "And yet if you took more part in the life of this town, you might find it tolerable. Tonight, Conan," she purred in his ear, "instead of taking me for a stroll though the date orchards or a dally in the oasis, why don't you spend the night inside the city wall? I hate to think of you crawling back to your barren camp in the desert after leaving my side."

"Umm," Conan murmured, "that feels good. Scratch lower down." He shifted his burly shoulders beneath the dancer's probing fingernails. "But no, girl, I will be at my best ease in my camp outside the wall. I am a Bedouin at heart, I like yon drovers . . . the sand my pillow, the stars my blanket." He nodded to indicate the huddled forms drinking and dicing around the fire.

"Besides," he added less lyrically a moment later, "if I take up residence in your quarters, idle tongues will whisper that I am kept by a woman. That would not redound well for your reputation here, or mine. Remember, Sharla, I am a drifter, a loose sword. With the next caravan north I'll be gone."

"Yes, I see. Of course you are right." She withdrew her fingers from his back and sat chastely beside him. In time she entered into idle conversation with the tapkeeper Anax, who loitered nearby. Conan, though not excluded, was left to wonder how deeply he may have insulted her—with the inner knowledge that, more than her honor, it was his own convenience that decided his actions.

But the steady flow of *arrak*, primed with his dwindling supply of drachms from his last caravan, washed most of his worries downstream. In time he even forgot Sharla, his attention turning to another female who sat talking to a succession of others in a corner of the place.

The open-sided hostelry was laid out with long trencher-tables and benches at its center, and smaller round tables and wicker chairs off to the sides. At the front it verged on the open yard and the campfire, beneath a canvas awning supported by tent poles; rugs and cushions were spread there for those outdoor types who preferred to squat, as in a desert pavilion. At the back, in the most civilized part of the room, were a booth for dispensing drinks, and the stone stairway to the higher-priced lodgings above. At a round candle-lit table next to those stairs sat the woman who caught Conan's eye.

She was dressed in the manner of a desert maiden, in a long, dark, hooded dress. Her mouth and nose were veiled, but her delicate brow was visible under the hood, over kohl-painted eyes as darkly radiant as the plumes of peacocks. She sat sipping from a tiny cup, entertaining different people at her table for short intervals; most were employees and regulars of the caravansary whom Conan recognized. When they sat opposite her by ones and twos, they seemed to engage in some good-natured, ritualized transaction involving no transfer of money or goods. At times, her voice could be heard gently lilting in laughing discourse above the skirling of the musicians' flutes.

She had an air of propriety and restraint overall; yet Conan repeatedly caught her looking his way. It was as if she couldn't keep her eyes away, and sometimes he imagined that each hasty glance was followed by a blush. It was unclear whether she meant to summon him, but at length, when the latest female visitor arose and took her leave, he found himself ambling over to sit opposite her.

"I am Conan, a traveler out of Aquilonia." Settling into the chair in an easy posture, he smiled into her mystic eyes. "You seem to know most everyone here, but I do not recall seeing you, so I thought I would make your acquaintance. Tell me—when they come to sit and talk with you, what is it you are doing?"

She was ill at ease, blinking her dark eyelashes rapidly; there was a definite blush on her veiled face as she looked him up and down. "Doing?" she stammered in slightly breathless accents. "Why, I tell their fortunes!"

"Aha, you are a seeress!" For just the fraction of an instant Conan balked—not so much from his mistrust of wizardry, as from his recollections of the vast, inexplicable things other rune-casters had professed to read in his future. But then he chided himself: how could a young woman like this, tender and gentle as she obviously was, bode him any ill?

Smiling again, he leaned forward on the table. "You do not charge for your services?"

"Take people's money, you mean?" She shook her head, still seeming caught off guard. "No, it is just a pastime for me . . . a skill I am not fully mistress of. I would not want anyone to take my poor prognostications too seriously."

" 'Tis only a lark, then," Conan nodded. "Good. Because . . . what is your name?"

"I? I am Inara."

He nodded again matter-of-factly. "Because, Inara, I would think that a long, clear look at the future would have to reveal its share of doom and sorrow."

"Oh, yes," she agreed readily, "I have seen that. Fortunately the fate of most people in Qjara, in the near future at least, seems to be . . . unremarkable." She spoke a little nervously, still avoiding looking at him directly. "I tell them my visions just for the fun of it, and for practice. I ask no payment, but occasionally . . ." she raised her veil with two fingers and sipped from her dainty cup, which was nearly empty ". . . I let someone buy me a portion of Samaran *narcinthe* to keep me alert."

"*Narcinthe*—the wine of jasmine petals?" Conan picked up her cup between thumb and forefinger and sniffed the fragrant bead of amber liquid within. "Heady stuff, this." He signalled the tapkeeper, holding up her cup and his beaker splayed between the fingers of one hand. "Anax, two more over here."

"This will be my second cup—I never take more than two," she said, her eyes gazing up shyly over her veil into his. "I have to come here for it, we do not have it in the . . . farm district." She looked away again, abashed. "It is what brings me my second sight."

"What, you mean the *narcinthe* allows you to see the future?" Conan shook his head. "I never heard of it having that effect. Wipe out the past, yes, wine can do that . . . but uncloak the future?"

At his words she stifled a giggle. "I do not read the future as from a scroll, nor see future things enacted in a magic pool or mirror. But yes, it is the *narcinthe* that brings on the impressions I do have."

"And those impressions are?"

Inara shook her head, flustered. "I just see things about people, and I get a sense of what will happen to them. It has to do with my feelings about them, too."

"What things do you see?"

"I have to take some time and look hard. For

instance, that man over there . . . the one who is watching the dice game at the long table?"

"Yes, the Turanian."

"Right, in the green turban. He wears a slave collar around his neck."

"No he doesn't," Conan said, turning in surprise from the game's spectator to Inara's unblinking eyes. "Do we speak of the same man?"

"I meant to tell you, I see the bronze collar chained about his neck. That is my vision." Shaking her head, Inara sipped from her cup. "It means he has been a slave."

"Or will be one, you mean."

She shook her head. "The collar is old and worn, so I take it to mean he was one before. If it were new and shiny, it might be in his future." Inara blinked at Conan from behind her veil. "Anyway, I asked him. He showed me the scars on his neck, from the years before he purchased his freedom."

"Humm," Conan grunted. "That proves little, then. We do not need seers to see the past—at least if it is in living memory."

"It proves much to me. And I make it a point always to speak truly."

"Yes, I don't doubt that you believe it, girl—but how can you tell your visions from what you are really seeing? The turban, say?"

"There is a certain shimmer to them. I see them clearly only when I look from certain angles—and only when I drink these eastern spirits." She saluted him daintily with her tiny vessel, tilting up her veil again with two fingers.

"And what of the man just below the turbaned one? The dice-player—the evil-looking fellow with the scar over his eye?"

"He is not there." To Conan's puzzled glance she replied, "I see the cup shake and the knucklebones go bouncing, but only the dimmest outline of the hand that makes them do it, and of the hand's owner." She shook her head somberly. "Dead or missing, he will be. And very soon, he is already fading from the spirit world."

"Humm. Eerie." Still digesting this, Conan prodded her onward. "And the woman clinging to his arm, the laughing one?"

"She is fat with child," Inara said. "The kohl about her eyes is running down her cheeks from tears."

"I see—that is, I hear! Your gift may be genuine." Conan looked challengingly at the woman. "And what is it the spirits show you when you look my way, that you find so fascinating?"

"Why, nothing." Seeing that he did not believe her, she hedged further. "Anyway, these things are not always important. Often they have no meaning at all but . . . a whim." She averted her face.

"Out with it, girl!" he said, looming over her in his seat. "I've faced the worst before this and lived to tell of it!"

"When . . . when I look at you," she stammered, "I see you in a warrior's outfit, clad only in armor. Nothing else."

"In armor?" Conan muttered. "A full suit, I hope!"

"No," she confessed, blushing furiously, her gaze locked to the table. "In a chestplate and greaves only. A gold helmet, too, crested and plumed, with a golden sword . . . your weapon is so splendid!"

"Well . . ." glancing down at his spraddle-legged posture, he found her deep blush suddenly infectious. He hauled his chair up close to the table, planted his elbows on it, and crossed his forearms. "No shame in it, I suppose," he opined after a moment. "Some Corinthian nobles fight thus, 'tis said. Mayhap it means only what I already believe . . . that I am bound northward, and to high estate."

When at last their eyes chanced to meet, there was no stopping it—both of them broke into laughter. Suddenly quaking, disintegrating with it, they upset their drinks and drew surprised stares from all over the inn. The young woman leaned back in her chair in a manner unsuited to her dignified dress; the Cimmerian tried to clutch the table for support and to preserve his modesty. In the course of it he also gripped her small, fair hand; when he released it, he did so tenderly, as one sets free a wild bird.

"So, Inara," he coughed at last, "what do they think of your occult talents at your home . . . in the farm district?"

She shook her head. "They will have none of it. My family are pious followers of the One True Goddess, and rectitude is their law. In our house no spirits are allowed . . . of either kind, liquorous or mystical." She righted her cup on the wet, aromatic table. "When I can stand it no longer, I come here to meet my friends."

"I see."

"Anyway," she added, "the folk here have more interesting fortunes."

Conan scanned the room, his gaze daring any whose attention their laughter had caught to continue staring. None did; even the dancer Sharla had taken up other company—with Babeth and Memchub, the merchant whom Conan had earlier shunted away. As if to shame her erstwhile protector, Sharla now murmured in the rich man's ear; the wench Babeth sat on his far side, looking a little neglected.

"Tell me, Inara, what do your visions show you about the caravaneer there, who dandles the dancing-girl beside him?"

"I see no man," Inara was quick to answer. "Sharla lounges against the white belly of a richly-dressed, cud-chewing camel!"

Another gust of mirth followed, as uproarious as the last but shorter—because, in the middle of it, Inara clutched Conan's hand. "Oh my!" she gasped. "Here are armed men, temple warriors—they must not find me here!"

As she spoke, Conan saw the guards in their dusty-blue tunics assembling outside—lean, fit swordsmen with long-handled blades sheathed over their shoulders. A half-dozen in line, they fanned out beyond the fire. Then they moved in among the hostel guests, pausing only to peer into a face here, or bark a curt question there. Discipline and arrogance were evident in their every movement. They wore no armor except bright silver caps, close-fitting, with short cheek-guards and shallow trailing edges at their napes.

Inara, with trepidation in her eyes, shrank back into the corner to make herself invisible. Conan muttered to her, "Don't worry, I'll make a diversion—watch for your chance, then leave."

Careful to turn his back first to the seeress, Conan arose from his chair. Then, shoving past other patrons, he swaggered across the inn to where Sharla and her companions sported.

"So, Conan," she said as he came near, "you have met the little sprig Inara! Tell me, how went your fortunes with the veiled young tease?"

Feigning wrath, Conan ignored her words. He hoisted her out of Memchub's lap, spun her aside, and seized hold of the merchant's silken sleeve. "Now, knave," he roared, "you will learn that the penalty for woman-stealing is dearer than that for filching camels!"

Yanking the unfortunate caravaneer from his bench, he twirled him by an arm, tripped up his shuffling feet, and propelled him onto the table where the dice game was in progress. Outraged shouts and blows immediately erupted, along with strident voices from the sidelines—including the sterner, more authoritative tones of the temple warriors.

"Hold and desist!" came the most imperative cry, causing Conan to turn and meet the rush of the enforcers. At first he thought they'd drawn blades—but then he saw they brandished sheathed swords whose hard metal scabbards served as cudgels for belaboring the swearing, scuffling patrons.

The first pair of guards he easily eluded. Sidestepping one, ducking beneath the man's swinging stave, he drove his shoulder up into the other's midsection. That hurled the fellow onto yet another table of tavern guests, whose collective fighting and fleeing broadened the riot.

The next temple warrior was harder to best—a slim, knot-muscled fighter whose jaw was square with righteousness and whose gold-trimmed helmet implied higher rank. His quick, aggressive moves anticipated those of the brawling Cimmerian; his scabbard-stave even grazed Conan's brow as the northerner bolted past, elbowing him deeper into the fray.

Conan's strategy then was to move along the fringe of the room. He laid hold of hapless bystanders and hurled them into the fight, interposing their unwilling bodies between himself and the most intrepid of his pursuers. This served his purpose of confusing matters even further—until the brawl ceased, halted by sudden, unmistakable sounds: the chiming of a fine steel sword-blade unsheathed, followed by a cry of "Die, thief!" a crunching stroke and a high, gargling scream.

Conan turned. Pushing his way through the suddenly slack combatants, he crossed the room to see the cause. There, facedown on the floor near the open corner of the caravansary, one of the inn patrons lay, a gaping sword wound in his side. His guilt, it seemed, was undeniable—in one hand he bore a short, curved dagger; in the other, a plush money belt whose strap had been slit some distance from its still-clasped gold buckle.

Over the body stood the ranking temple warrior, whose long, gleaming blade was still beaded with fresh blood. With a soft-booted foot he rolled the body over onto its back, making sure it did not stir. After wiping his blade clean with a silk kerchief he took from his waist, he tossed the soiled rag onto the corpse's chest. The caravaneer Memchub bent down meekly to retrieve his purse; the would-be thief, Conan saw, was the dice-player with the scar over his eye, whom Inara had singled out for death.

"Here you see the consequence of disorder and riot! Henceforth, honor the peace of the One True Goddess!" The warrior-chief scanned the crowd with a look of stern righteousness as he spoke. "There are others here who are at fault—you, outlander, are not schooled to civilized ways. But step carefully in Qjara!" His cold gray eyes honed in on Conan.

"Why, you blathering windbag, slayer of pickpockets!" Conan thundered. "Dare you to menace me with fist or steel, instead of mere words—?"

"Enough," the warrior-priest rapped out carelessly, overriding Conan's threats. "The death of one miscreant is adequate to enforce the peace for a night." Again wiping his sword with a silken kerchief, he returned it to the scabbard held out by one of his troops, then addressed the room at large. "Disperse from here—go about your business, and do not interfere with ours!"

To Conan's astonishment, the crowd's response to his words was a scattered cheer.

"Hail Zaius, greatest of the temple warriors! Hail to the goddess Saditha! All hail!"

And as the crowd parted in obedience to the officer's dictum, Conan caught enthusiastic whispers from the patrons.

"Did you see, the thief had a blade—he tried to slay Zaius!"

"That was his twentieth kill—Zaius will be the greatest temple swordsman of all time!"

Puzzling at the foreignness of it all, Conan reined in his annoyance and said no more. Scanning the room, he saw that Inara had departed, so his aim was fulfilled. He marveled at her prophecy concerning the dead man—surely it proved her skill. He turned to leave, but then his thoughts were galvanized by one last thing he caught being muttered between two of the temple warriors.

"The rumor we heard was false after all—the Princess Afriandra is not here."

CHAPTER 4
Slaves of Shartoum

Tulbar the Hyrkanian awoke from his shallow, wary sleep. He lay silent, listening to the fitful breathing of those around him, and to the canvas of the tent tugging and flapping in the night wind. He could not guess the precise hour, for the moon had not yet risen—at least not high enough to cast its glow on the fabric of the tent peak overhead. But if his instincts had not deceived him, the orb would soon dawn high over the eastern crags. Then would be the time to move.

Since boyhood, the moon's glow had been as sunlight to Tulbar; it was no accident that Ulla the Moon was patron goddess to his native clan of thieves and adventurers. Whether Tulbar foraged among country farmsteads or raided the castle keep, the moon blazoned and blessed all his undertakings. It had lit his way half around the world—and now, when things seemed at their darkest, it would signal his greatest triumph.

His friend Hekla too would heed its call. Possibly the little sneak-thief was now awake like himself and waiting, in his place near the back of the tent. No chains bound them here, no bars or even walls; and they were not like the miserable Shartoumi slaves, to be cowed by the threats of a few strutting guards. Once there was light enough to move by, they would be gone.

Tulbar could scarcely believe his good luck, his and Hekla's, in having been taken captive by the Sheikh of Shartoum. Caravan raiding, to be sure, was no great crime in the southern desert; Tulbar's offense had been to place himself in competition with Sheikh Fouaz by raiding a camel-train bound through territory the Shartoumi considered his own private hunting ground. Magnanimously, Tulbar and his confederate were spared, and merely taken captive with an eye to future use by the sheikh.

Such a use wasn't long in presenting itself, once a troop of soldiers from somewhere called Sark, escorting the eerie, dark priest Khumanos and a pair of acolytes, arrived at the sheik's outpost on its salty inland sea. To Fouaz, the prospect of selling his own people into slavery came even more naturally than thievery—and so, while the sheikh set his many wives to stitching themselves new harem-clothes from the silks, beads, and golden cloth Khumanos unloaded in great brassbound chests, a dozen score of his subjects were rounded up from onion and date orchards. Herded like cattle, they were marched off by their Sarkad guards to the hazy eastern hills.

Tulbar and Hekla were thrown in as part of the bargain. At first the Hyrkanians cursed their ruthless captors and rebelled at carrying the supplies, digging tools, and tent panels the Sarkads burdened them with. Once they were in a position to steal horses or camels, they planned to escape into the open desert. But gradually, along the arduous route of the march, a rumor spread: the slaves were to be set to work digging precious metal and gems from mines high in the hills—presumably to enrich the coffers of Anaximander, king of the distant city-state of Sark.

That news made the Hyrkanian pair heft their bundles and water jars with zest. What adventurers were ever better suited to exploit such an opportunity? They would find out the location of this treasure, load themselves down with it, and vanish—perhaps to return someday with their own crew of diggers or fighters and unearth the main hoard. The trek was difficult, with some of their companions—women, mainly, and old men—falling and dying along the way. But Tulbar and Hekla stuck zealously with it.

In time as they marched they saw a change come over the land. The hills rose high and were no longer barren, but strangely fruitful. Yellow-silted streams, rich with water-weed and pond scum, carried moisture to long, lush valleys meandering among barren desert ridges. Grasses grew there, as well as swamp-thorn, shrubs, and stunted trees. No fish or birds inhabited the district, or at least none the travelers could see, but the meadows seemed alive with scuttling rodents, toads and tortoises, and large, noisy insects. Ofttimes the slaves dined on things the soldiers killed with their bows; though the creatures were hard to name precisely as rabbit, marmot, or water rat, their meat was chewy and flavorful.

As they marched, the aspect of the desert grew increasingly strange. Some of the vegetative forms seemed unusually lush and swollen—weeds whose leaves waxed pulpy and enormous, and shrubs with twigs thick and pliant as clutching fingers. There were fantastic varieties of cactus, and occasional full-sized trees with limbs knotted and twisted into burls as large and bulbous as human heads. Before some of these, Tulbar saw the priest Khumanos kneel low in obeisance.

In all, with the plentiful water, the thick, tasteless vegetable marrows and fruits, and the peculiar wild game, travel was far easier in these valleys than in the open desert. The gorges gradually narrowed and the crags rose wilder, but still the converging streams watered the land.

Hot mineral springs were the source of the bounty, it appeared. The ancient trail that was their route crossed the wellspring of one: a low, shallow cavern festooned with sulfur deposits, gaping open like a yellow-fanged mouth in the hillside. Its green-rimed lips enclosed a steaming pool that bubbled thick with brownish foam and with clumped, floating moss. From it, down a bed of yellow-crusted pebbles, drooled a hot stream sending off wispy, curling tendrils of steam. A rotten, sulfurous smell was thick in the air, and Tulbar noticed that the bloated vegetation seemed to wave and shimmer all around the pond, even without the faintest breath of wind.

Yet the water proved drinkable, and kept them trudging toward the heights.

In a steeper, more desolate region just under the looming gray crags, they came at last upon the mine workings. Vast tailing piles extending down the hill betold a long history of excavation—though the broken ores underfoot resembled no precious metal Tulbar had experience of. The shafts themselves were sealed by great oval stones, and further protected by priestly seals of beeswax and intricately-knotted string. After being ritually unsealed by the priests, these barriers required the efforts of every slave, toiling against long, knotted ropes, to displace.

One of the great stones trundled out of control; it crushed two of the men stationed near it before grinding to a stop. The arch-priest Khumanos showed no more concern over this than he had over wayside casualties along the march, although one of the acolytes performed an all-too-familiar rite to speed the departing souls.

The mine-shafts were three in number, spaced several hundred paces apart through the hill canyons. The tunnel mouths did not require much repair or clearing out, other than the removal of cobwebs by the bushel. The webs were populated by swarms of fat, pulpy-pale spiders that fought back with a painful sting. The mine props, though of untold age, were sound, and in the less brittle bedrock of the deeper shafts none had been deemed necessary; so there was no need to send workers to fell the last few twisted trees of the valley.

Tulbar, when first entering one of the shafts, made a peculiar discovery. As he shuffled deeper into the mountain, the fading glare of daylight was slowly and gradually replaced in his eyes by a greenish glow native to the mine. It came from the rock itself—from the moss, someone said, although he soon found that the light shone brightest of all from the newly dug deposits of ore. It was an eerie sight—the greenly effulgent stones, almost shimmering and faintly warm to the touch in the depths of the cave, faded to nondescript dusty-pale rubble when hauled in baskets up to the outer air.

This natural source of light spared the miners the stink and hazard of oil lamps. That first day the slaves were set promptly to work in the greenish glare, the men chipping and raking stone, the women hauling it in baskets to the surface. The ore seemed to lie in narrow, continuous veins, so that little digging of the surrounding rock was necessary to reach it. The luminous stuff broke apart readily; there were natural cracks and fissures in its mass, and even hollow pockets. These spaces sometimes harbored, to the diggers' wonder, clusters of many-faceted, pyramid-pointed crystals; when the pockets were cut into, they sent beams of warm emerald radiance lancing across the dusty air of the mine-shaft.

Presumably, given the trouble and expense this foreign King Anaximander was undertaking to obtain it, the metal to be refined from the ore would be of rare value. That, and the relative ease of the digging, raised the question in Tulbar's mind of why these mines had not been stripped centuries ago—why, for instance, the men of Shartoum did not march here and dig out their fill of the ore. As a partial answer to this, the Hyrkanian gathered that the metal would require some elaborate method of refining, such as a desert brigand like Fouaz would scarcely be capable of.

Furthermore, the mines seemed to be some kind of royal monopoly of the kings and priests of Sark, protected by intricate curses and threats of military reprisal—a store of wealth left in the ground, no doubt, for the dynasty's heirs. Religious ritual played a hazy part in it, too; at various times, for instance, Tulbar's crew was sent to work in the three separate mine tunnels. Although the ores obtained from each were obviously identical, the priest Khumanos took pains—or rather dealt out pains—to ensure that they were never commingled. The rocks were heaped into pack-baskets stitched carefully shut with withes of different colors:

black, red, or yellow. The least negligence in the packing process or any discovery of theft was sure to draw down swift and severe lashings from the Sarkad guards.

The arch-priest Khumanos impressed Tulbar as a cold, remote leader. He commanded the two junior priests he brought with him curtly, in the terse, guttural Sarkad tongue. These acolytes, though somewhat aloof, displayed ordinary human traits and weaknesses—zeal and officiousness in the performance of their priestly duties, anger and even occasional sympathy toward the Shartoumi slaves. Khumanos, on the other hand, performed his blessings and invocations dispassionately, clearly intent on getting each prescribed detail of the ritual correct. Though he was the only one of the Sarkads who spoke the Shartoumi Bedouin dialect, he seldom spoke to the slaves, and never made a public address offering them reward, remonstrance or hope. His motives in leading this mining expedition were to Tulbar a matter of dark, uncertain speculation.

Khumanos became the focus of more attention as illnesses began to plague the workers. They were vexed at first by sores, itching rashes, and small, troublesome wounds that refused to heal—unaccountable problems, since their work was survivable, their diet near-adequate, and water was plentiful enough for washing. Tulbar and Hekla were spared most of these ills, but on several occasions the Shartoumi slaves named reluctant representatives to beg the arch-priest for help.

No aid was forthcoming, since there was little to offer. The explanation Khumanos gave was the same one he clung to later, when the more serious ills such as dropsy, palsy, and creeping ague began to disable the elder laborers and the women. Saying their afflictions were due to the venomous bite of cave spiders, he rebuked the slaves to clean their mine workings more fastidiously.

Yet all their past hardships mattered little, Tulbar told himself; very soon this murky business would be behind them. A rakish triangle of moonglow now lit the eastern panel of the tent overhead; the light it cast was certainly sufficient to move quickly and silently between the slumbering bodies in the tent. Hekla, too, would be ready with the swag the two had accumulated by their skill at sneak-thievery. Gathering his still-supple limbs beneath him, Tulbar crept silently to his feet.

He found the way clear across a dozen sleeping bodies to Hekla's. There were no sounds in the tent except the rough, stertorous breathing of the sick and the dream-hounded. He saw little to fear; the guards had grown slack in their duties, and most of these toilers were so drugged with fatigue that not even a deliberate shaking would rouse them. Tulbar stepped high over recumbent forms and came to the space near Hekla's mat.

The little thief did not appear to have heard him; his mangy camelhide was pulled all the way up over his head. That was unlike Hekla—perhaps he was ill. Careful not to alarm his friend, Tulbar laid a hand on the sleeping form to rouse him. He did not like what he felt, so he picked up a corner of the blanket and peeked under it.

The light . . . ! Suddenly afraid, the Hyrkanian jerked away the blanket and let it fall aside.

The gems, the crystals he had filched from the mine and given Hekla to conceal—they now cast their green rays in a blazing webwork across the sleeping mat. In the course of the night they must have burned through the sacks and pouches that held them—and, he saw, burned through more than that. There, at the center of the blinding green constellation, Hekla's small, slight body had been reduced to charred bone with blackened bits of ash adhering to it. The smell was charnel, the heat of the gems' rays palpable to Tulbar's upraised, sweating palms.

His gasps and the harsh emerald glare aroused others; they crept forward to gaze at the scorched skeleton, some moaning or crying out in terror. Moments later the guards arrived. They flogged the watching slaves into a cowering mass in the corner of the tent; then carefully they began to gather up the remains and the stolen, deadly gems.

Tulbar was singled out as the thief's friend and accomplice. He was taken before the archpriest Khumanos, who confronted him without wrath.

"You are restless among us," the priest told the sullen thief. "You were never of the Shartoumi, and now you are without friends. The burden of duty our god Votantha lays on your shoulders is difficult to bear. I understand." From around his neck he took an amulet or relic of some kind—an ancient, corroded knife-hilt tied on a thong. "There is a service I can render, a charm that will ease the sorrow of what has befallen you." Pointing the decrepit stub of a blade toward Tulbar, he moved closer.

Chapter 5
Challenge by Moonlight

Temple dancers pranced and leaped to chiming chords around a turquoise basin set before the alabaster statue of Saditha, the One True Goddess. Barefoot on blue-veined marble, the agile priestesses moved in a stately circle, chastely clad in flowing skirts and ribboned headdresses. Each one stepped, spun in place, kicked high and strode on as new measures unreeled from skirling flute and strummed cithern.

The day's heat was softened by the deep shadows of the temple's pillared portico. At one end presided the statue, erect and graceful: a gowned warrior-woman with the butt of a spear grounded beside her shapely, sculptured foot, her face as austere as a war-helm. In the middle of the court, the dancers circled the basin, before the intricately-carved wooden door that barred the inner temple chamber. At the other end of the portico stood a heavy table laid with fruit, cheese, and hard biscuits, free for those who had come to view the dance and do homage to the Goddess.

It was near the table that Conan lingered, close against a velvet curtain stretched along the eastern row of pillars and somewhat behind the rest of the visitors. He stood within easy reach of a bowl of spiced citron, fresh fruit hard to find in the caravan quarter. Though Saditha's holy temple professed to welcome all, he was unsure how he might be greeted here, and reluctant to begin another brawl. Temple warriors were in attendance, as were high city officials and cultured Qjarans of a class he seldom glimpsed. They were intent on the dance—and so Conan was the only one who noticed when a hand was laid on his arm. Not a firm, authoritative touch, but a soft, insinuating one.

"I see you have left behind your hero's armor today and worn decent clothing," a female voice purred.

"Yes, girl." Conan turned discreetly. "And you have been keeping off the *narcinthe* . . . well, now, Crom!" Though he easily recognized the voice, he blinked in surprise at the unfamiliar aspect of the woman close behind him, standing screened between the edge of the curtain and a broad pillar. "So it is true, then! You are not Inara, but the princess Af . . . Afri—"

"Afriandra," the young woman graciously supplied. "And what brings you here, Conan the outlander? Have you decided to swear holy fealty to the One True Goddess?"

The northerner was in no hurry to answer as he absorbed the vision of young womanhood so close to him. The face she turned up was healthily aglow, all but innocent now of makeup; far from her former veiled, black-clad style, she wore a loose cotton dress belted with dainty gold links and hemmed with gold trim at the shoulders and knees. Her hair was soft pale brown, pinned up with beaded clasps and further adorned with sprigs of blue flowerets. Her calves and forearms, shapely and slim, were circled halfway along their length with gold bracelets and the gold-threaded bindings of her sandals. Her bearing was easy, relaxed enough for princess or queen, and bold, as she rested her hand inside Conan's arm through the curtain and waited for him to speak.

"I am come to watch the first temple dance of one of the wenches from the inn," he murmured at last, nodding with deft casualness toward the circling dancers. "It is Sharla—known to you as well, I think." He glanced around, but no one else in the audience seemed to see the princess where she stood screened by curtain and pillar, so taken were they by the light, graceful steps of the ritual dance.

"I doubt I am as well-acquainted with her as you are." Viewing the dancers from behind Conan's shoulder, Afriandra smiled demurely. "Do not worry, she will be accepted as a novice . . . a lay priestess, I think the usual term is. Not of the highest rank, but secure in the bounty of Saditha." The princess looked up at him. "In past visions I saw her dressed in priestly robes, and told her so."

"Ahem, good." Conan decided to dare the question. "Priestesses of Saditha, then, are not celibate?"

"No. Purity is not a requirement of the priesthood—rather, open fraternization is encouraged for the sake of gaining and holding male worshipers." Afriandra cocked her head to view the celebrants. "Sharla dances the ritual well enough, if only she will learn to stop grinding her hips. My mother will make sure of that with her swatting-stick, when she drills the dancers."

"Your mother, the queen?" Conan asked, looking back to her.

"My mother is High Priestess of Saditha as well—she is just over there." Afriandra nodded toward a pink-gowned, matronly cleric who stood with the musicians at one side of the dance. "It is a tradition in Qjara for the king to marry the highest officer of the church, who is always a woman."

Conan frowned, regarding the full-bodied, statuesque female warily. "You have a way of placing honest foreigners in deep jeopardy, girl—by conspiring with you, I've crossed not only a king but a head priestess too. Your adventurous farm girl Inara was a perilous disguise—"

"True. But even so, I thank you for your help. If it were put abroad that the adventuress was Princess of Qjara, the scandal would have simmered in more places than the temple quarter." She looked up at him solemnly. "I know I can trust you to keep the secret . . . or is it still a secret? You did not seem overly surprised when I approached you. Is word of my identity abroad?"

"I heard it whispered by one of your temple guards. Even they were not certain." Conan's own voice was scarcely above a whisper; no one nearby appeared to be watching them yet, and he wanted to keep it that way.

"Wonderful," Afriandra sighed. "Oh well, the ploy is lost to me anyway, now that Zaius knows of it."

"The great temple warrior is a stern guardian to you, it would seem," Conan said. "To me he seems but a pompous windbag—"

"He is more than a guardian." Afriandra tossed her hair restlessly. "My parents have said they will give him my hand in marriage."

"What?—" Conan had difficulty subduing his astonishment. "You mean, King Semiarchos and Queen Regula would hand over their daughter and their city to that prating priestly buffoon?"

"It is a tradition, as I said—the bloodline of the royal dynasty is renewed each generation by the merit system of the church hierarchy. This time there is no male heir—so instead I am to wed the highest male officer of the temple."

"Will the ruling power pass to you, then, or to him?"

"He will be named King Zaius . . ." she shook her head. "But I, I must try to wield what power

I can. I have my mother's support, and Father's too, if not their true respect. In our city's history there have been few reigning females. But with Saditha's blessing, I can uphold my family's power—"

"And your view of the future?" Conan interrupted her in a whisper. "What do your prophetic visions tell you when you look at Zaius?"

"I never saw him when I was under the charm of the *narcinthe*," Afriandra replied. "The other night at the caravansary, I avoided looking toward him . . . lest he recognize me."

"Does he love you?" Conan asked.

She shrugged uncaringly. "You have seen Zaius—can he love any but himself?" Suddenly her hand, which had lingered in the crook of his elbow, began playing more insistently at the inside of his arm. "Conan, I must talk to you . . . meet me tonight! Do you know the courtyard on the west side of the palace, just outside the high wall? The one with the fountain?" Her voice was hushed and urgent. "Come at moonrise, I'll be there, I promise!"

After a furtive glance at those nearby, the northerner narrowed his eyes suspiciously at her. "What, then—do you want me to smuggle you a flask of your dream-potion? I would not be your errand boy—"

"No, silly!" Emphatically she wagged her head no. "Just bring yourself. If I want to see you in armor again, I'll provide the helmet and the greaves . . . Nay," she added at his uneasy recoil, " 'twas only a joke! If you come, I will be able to speak more freely about something that is troubling me." Moving her hand to his neck and hauling his shaggy head irresistably down toward her, she strained upward and planted a kiss on his lips. "Just come, will you?"

The moon shone down from the eastern hills, far away across the city rampart. Its fat uptilted crescent seemed to pour out liquid radiance onto the bleak slopes, and on the walls and roof-edges nearer to hand. Quicksilver light pooled in the fountain at the center of the square, outlining the lily pads and flower stems that broke its still surface.

Against the light a lone figure moved—a slim, graceful female form whose reflection flowed and melted from one lily pad to the next as she circled the fountain, searching. Her pinned-up hair and translucent gown were frosted white in the moonlight, and her pale skin gleamed; anywhere but in this thirsty desert land, she could have been judged a water nymph for her beauty and delicacy.

At length, where the arching branch of an olive tree overhung one side of the pond, she sank down onto the stone rim. She trailed one hand in the water in an attitude of waiting, glancing around from time to time with a sigh.

As she sat, a strange darkness gathered in the tree limbs above her. Silently it flowed, to congeal just over her head: a solid mass which blocked the moon and made a formless reflection among the lily pads. Then in utter silence, it dropped to a place just beside her on the curb of the pond.

"Afriandra! Nay, girl, don't cry out, I am no gloar-fiend!" With a restraining hand on her shoulder, the figure kept her from darting away.

"Conan, where . . . how did you come here?" she asked, shaking off her startlement and embracing him impulsively in greeting.

"I had to come before moonrise, to slip past the guards at the various gates," he told her, settling down on the cool stone next to her. " 'Tis not so easy to move about your town by night without arousing suspicion."

"You brought your sword, I see." She reached gingerly past him to brush the hilt of the Ilbarsi knife at his waist. "Did you fear a trap?"

"Not really." Conan shrugged. "But I don't want to fall afoul of your custom of temple justice. I would use this first, if I had to," he said, slapping the hilt.

"Is that the reason you dwell outside the city wall?" she added, looking up into his eyes. "So you won't have to surrender your sword to the temple guards?"

"Mayhap; it is only temporary, anyway," he said, his eyes scanning the square. "I am waiting for the first caravan northbound to Zamora. I had hoped to avoid trouble and entanglements in your city . . ." he glanced down at her hand on his arm ". . . but things seem to be conspiring to get me involved."

"Oh, Conan, do not fear," she said, caressing his shoulder. "I will not entangle you here or keep you from your caravan." She edged closer to him under the moon. " 'Tis only that I am allowed so little contact with travelers and foreigners. A man of your wide experience might be able to . . . ah, instruct me better, in certain matters . . . than anyone from a small, unwordly city like Qjara."

"You're not asking me to murder someone, are you?" he asked, pulling back a little from her caresses. "One of your royal relatives, perhaps, or some temple schemer? I am many things, I admit, and a handy killer at times. But I am not for hire in courtly intrigues as some have thought."

"Nay, Conan, nay!" she laughed softly, now almost sprawling against him. "I only meant to sound you out about some general aspects of city conduct and . . . religion."

"Religion?" he muttered dubiously. "If you are bent on converting me—"

"No, no," she laughingly assured him, placing the fingertips of one hand over his lips as if to silence him. "Just tell me: what think you of our worship of the One True Goddess? I know that goddesses are rare in this part of Shem. . . ." she trailed off, removing her hand from his lips so that he could answer.

"They are rare in most parts," he assured her. "In the great empires of Hyboria, goddesses rule alongside gods, sometimes with greater power. In their conquests, mayhap," he enlarged a moment later, on reflection, "those imperial lands have combined the deities of their various territories. But the Shemitish city-states generally worship only one god, and that generally a male—or a conspicuously male animal, or some hooved and hairy combination of man and beast. Why do you ask?"

Patting his lips daintly again, she shook her head at his question. "Just tell me this, Conan: how does the godly law of our Saditha compare with those other cities?"

Conan harrumphed. "To speak true, girl, I find your city's ways almost tolerable. That is one reason I tread lightly in your town, because I respect your customs. In many Shemitish lands the king also holds the office of head priest. Often as not, he wields the power of both offices with a cruel hand." Conan's voice grew harsher as he spoke. "Their laws are many, the penalties cruel—and their god itself is likely to be a senile tyrant with a bull's horny temper and an insatiable appetite for babes or young virgins." He shook his head in disgruntlement. "Not like Crom, my native god, who lets a man live out his life before he has to suffer judgment! Or Mitra of the Hyborians, who teaches earthly wisdom. Worship of the southern gods is usually enforced on all the citizenry, often with shameful rites and mutilations. . . ." Conan vented his mounting unease with a faint, shuddering sigh. "I steer clear of such when I can help it."

Afriandra nodded understandingly. "But here, then, you do not find us as cruel?"

"Here? No! In Qjara I am accepted, if not overly trusted as a foreigner. You protect your own, but the powers and privileges of your leaders are not too irksome—except for somebody like Zaius, your betrothed. You yourself, the noblest girl of the city, are friendly enough to sit with me here, thus. . . ." His arms found their way around her as he spoke.

"Ah, 'tis so, then! I feared as much." Growing suddenly slack and pensive in his embrace, she nodded to herself. "Tell me, do you know anything of Votantha, god of the city of Sark, to the southwest of here?"

"No—nothing more than what I have already told you." Resignedly, Conan let his arm settle loose around the girl. "I have never traveled there."

"My royal parents have been approached—sent a letter in a gold scrollcase, with golden ink," the princess explained. "As a gesture of friendship from city's king, the state temple of Sark wants to establish a religious mission here in Qjara. A school of priestly acolytes, it would be, with a shrine of worship near our own high temple of Saditha."

"Beware," Conan aid, "it could be a step toward conquest. The god of a foreign country is often the first trooper of their invading army."

"I fear as much," Afriandra sighed. "But my father is taken with the idea, if only as a way of strengthening his hand with my mother. Zaius of the temple warriors has heard of it, too, and seems to favor it. They have even discussed the notion of marrying Saditha and Votantha together in a godly union and worshiping the two jointly, as a bond between our two cities."

"Your mother, then, sticks up for her One

True Goddess?" Conan questioned. "She looks to be a . . . formidable woman."

"Alas . . ." Afriandra shook her head uncertainly "she dotes on Zaius, her temple champion. One thing is certain, she loves him better than I do. And his view of the matter may sway her." She looked up to Conan. "But you are saying this foreign god would be a tyrant?"

"Yes, I doubt it not. And Zaius is just the one to crave the added power, if he is to be king of Qjara." Conan looked her in the face. "You must fight it, girl, if you want to hold on to what you have."

"Aye, it is troublous," she sighed again. "I think I can face him—but how it frightens me sometimes, to think that under Saditha's law he will become my sole consort, the only man I can ever kiss! I have always craved a soft, feeling man, one who is not afraid to show emotion, yes, and passion—" in demonstration, she heaved herself up against Conan's chest and placed a warm, probing kiss on his lips. "Ah, this is good," she murmured. "How I dread the thought of Zaius's rigid embraces . . . his stiff, cold lips!"

Conan exhaled, his hands idly probing the extent of Afriandra's lithe warm back. "You will find that stiffness is not entirely a fault in a man," he ventured, adjusting her supple weight against him.

"Yes, but not in the wrong places," she chided him. "Now, a man like you . . . I have no doubt that you can be stiff where and when it is needed, and soft and pliant otherwise. . . ."

Leaning back against the olive trunk, she drew him down against her. She commenced trying her best to smother him from beneath with eager, questing kisses, an effort that went on for some minutes.

"So, Afriandra! " a harsh voice suddenly intruded. "Is this how you disport yourself at evening? First the taverns and brothels of the camel-drovers, and now a roll in the dirt with an unclean foreigner?"

The words rang out sharply and familiarly in a combination of wrath and righteous injury. They came from a tall, shadowy form who stalked around the curve of the fountain from a gate in the nearby wall. He stood gesticulating over the couple, but without drawing his sword—the very man they had been speaking of moments before, the temple warrior Zaius.

"This is how you dishonor me!" he raged on. "Me, designated High Champion of Saditha's Temple! Am I then to wed a tarnished princess? Am I to accept, under the Goddess's sacred wedding canopy, the pawed-over leavings of a filthy infidel?"

"Die, wretch!" was Conan's cry as he sprang up from Afriandra's reclining form. As his long knife flicked out of its belt loop, he was stayed only by the extreme desperation of the princess's clutch on his arm. Half-dragging her along with him, he halted some two steps from the motionless, indignant Zaius.

"Conan, you cannot slay him thus!" the princess pleaded on her knees behind him. "He is sacred to the Goddess!"

"True enough, foreigner," Zaius agreed. "This is not your quarrel, so begone! It would be a high sin to soil a ceremonial sword on your unclean pelts and innards." He thumped the heel of his hand on the ornate hilt at his waist. "And to cross my sacrosanct blade with such a black, filthy barb as yours—" he waved a hand distastefully at the Ilbarsi knife in Conan's grip "—why, it would dishonor our entire city!"

"The words of a coward," Conan said, "who hides behind a woman—or a goddess!"

"I hide behind none, but I stand before the Goddess," Zaius proclaimed. "How would you, a savage foreigner, know anything of that—or of how to comport yourself among civilized men? I have never seen a northern cretin like you made into a decent offal-slave, much less a free citizen of a pious land—"

Conan sprang at him then with a throaty, inarticulate roar. Tearing his hand free of Afriandra's grip, letting his blade clatter loose on the paving stones, he was upon Zaius, pounding and buffeting him with clenched fists. A drub, a thump, a sweeping cross-stroke—all the blows connected, but only glancingly, with a retreating target. Had Zaius dodged and sidestepped with less than the spryness of an expert swordsman, any one of the strokes might have felled or killed him.

Zaius found himself unable to do more than struggle clear of his attacker. Having never before met with such savage fury in an opponent, he was spun and staggered by each stroke that caught him even in passing. The Cimmerian smote him, bruised him, and drove him back toward the corner of the court—until the princess once again overtook her protector.

"Conan, stop! It dishonors the Goddess, even to insult him thus . . ."

Rescued ignominiously again, Zaius stood before them—crouching, panting, his gray tunic rent and disarranged, his sacred sword drawn half out of its scabbard in a white-knuckled grip. But he was quick to regain the shredded remnants of his dignity before the club-fisted Cimmerian.

"Insult me!" he exclaimed, easing his fine sword back into its sheath. "How can a temple warrior possibly be insulted by one so low? My priestly fighting skills do not include the lofty art of rough-and-tumble on a taproom floor! If I were to face such a lout in a true test of swordsmanship, why, I would show him prowess he could not begin to appreciate—" At Conan's growl of menace, he turned to the princess. "Afriandra, send away this ruffian, and come with me to do holy penance before Saditha's altar—"

"Zaius, you slack-spined coward," Conan's voice rumbled back at him low and murderous, "I will have your bleeding gizzard! I will not skewer you or bash you to pieces here in front of the girl alone, because it might unduly distress her. But I challenge you to a public fight, as is your holy custom! Single combat with swords, to the death, outside the temple of your vaunted goddess!"

"Ho," Zaius marveled aloud, "you are the arrogant one indeed! Know you not, the sacred temple duels are only for those born faithful to Saditha! A foreign infidel can never participate. It would be an impious travesty. Now leave us!"

"Yes, Conan, go, please!" Afriadra said, moving between the Cimmerian and his adversary. "I asked your help—now I ask it again, in this more than anything! For the sake of our city and our faith, leave Zaius and me to our miserable fate!"

Chapter 6
Forge of the Nether Gods

Exalted Priest Khumanos walked unshod up the slope of jagged, brittle volcanic ash. Long leagues of travel had left his feet hard and callused, their tough edges abraded white with use. Where his soles were not thick enough to stand the punishment, they bled dark crimson with each step. The stains marked his path over the rubble of the rocky waste, making it easy for his disciples to follow; but the holy man plodded onward, never looking down or even noticing.

Hard as he drove himself, he demanded even more from his flock. Some of these were barefoot already, and the shoes of the rest were gradually being shredded from their feet by the razor-edges of black glass and frothy pumice that formed these new slopes. All the toilers, male and female, bore heavy pack-baskets laden with dusty greenish stone—burdens that bent some of them near-double, soaking up the dark sweat of their hard, unremitting labor. The Sarkad troops overseeing them moved heavily as well, with the weight of their arms and the stores of food and water they carried and guarded. The two acolytes under Khumanos went unladen; but they, bringing up the rear, had the burdensome duty of urging fallen slaves to renew their efforts, or of performing the death-rite for those who failed to rise.

Their crossing of the lowlands, coming from the mines in the hills above Shartoum, had been relatively uneventful. Protected by truce, they had seen no sign of the wily sheik's raiders, nor had their party been molested by any of the renegade bands and rival tribes that frequented the region of the inland sea. Most remarkable luck, this, since every slave believed that the metal ore they carried was of great rarity and value. Some whispered that, at the end of the journey, shares of the wealth would be parcelled out to them as a reward for faithful service.

But any talk of this, of their homeland by the Sea of Shartoum, and of all other topics grew scarce as the days wore on. More and more they followed Khumanos in silent submission, as they would a holy leader. If any caviled or found fault with his cause, he had a near-miraculous way of winning them over to steadfast obedience by means of a single brief interview. The others, noting this, decided that he was holy, and tried to turn the harsh fact of their captivity into a stern virtue. They respected the example Khumanos set of privation and selflessness—and imitated it, since they were given no other choice.

Meanwhile, a new range of mountains loomed before them. Always the peaks had lain low and jagged against their Shartoumi horizon, called by their tribe the Chimneys of Shaitan because of the fires that flared redly against the night sky and, by day, the billows of evil-looking smoke they exhaled. Now their blood-trail led them steadily up toward the huddled, misshapen peak. Trudging onward, they learned dumb faith; for it took a faith of fanatic intensity to convince them they would survive.

Khumanos found the path, watching as before for signs and roadmarks he had been told of but had never seen. Not quite as before—say, in the Valley of Fire—because then he had owned a mortal soul. His determination had been clouded by hopes, fears, aspirations; where now he possessed only a purpose. His perceptions were unhindered, his judgment flawless in the service of his king and his godly master.

He spied a lone peasant far ahead, toiling in the sparse but fertile soil of the high volcano slopes. The grass-groats the man was tending flourished green and man-tall against the red shoulders of the narrow valley. Into their lushness the farmer disappeared an instant later; Khumanos knew that word of his approach would be carried ahead of him.

Later, in the burning noon, the priest led his band of toilers up over a stony hummock into a broader volcanic basin. The place was a blind cirque, ringed by fuming cinder cones and black basalt crags. Its farther reaches were a wasteland of ash mounds, cyclopean stones, and smoking fumaroles; nearer at hand could be seen a foaming mountain freshet, tilled fields, and a few trees. Around the rambling cinder huts of the dwellers, human shapes moved busily and a little furtively—Khumanos knew he was expected.

By the time the party reached the dusty, level space between the huts, and the slaves sagged to earth under their burdens, only one man was in sight. This was a bearded peasant, a wizened elder clad in a peaked cap, sheepskin coat and trousers, and high-laced buskins to keep out the loose cinders. Khumanos, leaving his followers to obtain water as they might, strode forward and addressed the man without preamble.

"You have carried out your charged duty?" he asked. "Are the implements ready?"

The fellow nodded sharply, his wrinkled old face creasing further in a smile. "Our clan has done as your lordships commanded. All has been preserved these seven centuries." The peasant made a quick, respectful bow. "The metal is greased faithfully with palm oil, the frailer parts shielded from heat and ash, and the whole guarded against thieves and profaners. The timber, too, is ready as ordered—and well-seasoned. This lot was cut seventeen years agone." Smiling again unctuously, the man held forth his hand as if for payment.

Khumanos made no move to comply. "Show me," he said. Turning, he raised three fingers on high and flicked the upraised hand toward him. Promptly three Sarkad troopers detached themselves from the huddle of slaves crowding about the water basins and came forward.

The elder had wordlessly turned and stridden from the circle of huts. The Exalted Priest followed, with the troopers hurrying to bring up the rear. The way passed over a stone path between waving grainfields, but very soon they walked on a worn trail over bare cinder mounds, angling between smoking vents and ponds of bubbling, oozing mud.

As they went forward, the earth's heat increased and deposits of standing water disappeared. The air became noisome and metallic-tasting, and the blue sky overhead took on a grayish tinge, doubtless from fumes filtering up through the cinders all around. Ahead lay the broadest source of the effluvium, a yawning gash at the foot of a dark basalt cliff. Amid shimmering heat waves, the crevasse poured forth a plume of dark, roiling smoke, its underbelly shimmering eerily in the reddish glow of the vent, before it towered on high and trailed away in the winds from the desert.

Near the rupture in the earth, signs of human industry were present. Great devices loomed there, wavering in the reddish glow—huge metal troughs and basins, giant molds carven of black basalt, bound and hinged together with red-rusted steel, and a looming, gallowslike crane. In high, slate-roofed enclosures on either hand, protected from the volcano's corroding heat by thick cinder walls, long poles and paddles were stacked along with racks of heavy iron chain. In all, though the place was desolate and dusted with ash, it had a look of recent upkeep and readiness for use.

"The timbers," Khumanos called ahead to the old farmer, who stood in the shelter of one of the sheds. He was dwarfed by the size of his surroundings, his shoulders hunched against the blast of heat. "Show me the lumber you have made ready."

"First, our payment," the elder one demanded, shuffling toward the Exalted Priest with an outstretched hand.

"First the lumber," Khumanos answered, making no move toward his purse.

"As you wish." Shrugging, the old man turned and gestured Khumanos after him, leading the way around a stony hummock that sheltered them from the worst of the volcano's heat. "The fumes that come up though these cinders are fine for seasoning wood. They harden and preserve it."

"Indeed," Khumanos said, following the old one closely and motioning his troopers up on either side. "I will require your help, of course—yours and your kinsmen's, to aid and instruct us in the use of the implements."

"Of course," the farmer said, nodding back over his shoulder. "Here is your timber."

Ushering Khumanos and the three troopers

around a jagged basalt outcrop, he showed them a cave that opened into the side of a cinder mound. Sheltered within its mouth could be seen the ends of a half-dozen stout, planed tree trunks.

"And the wheels?" Khumanos questioned. "Those are part of our agreement. I do not see them."

"They are in the cave—there in the shadows, if you come closer." Dogging the priest's footsteps, the old farmer extended his hand. "Now the gold, by our age-old contract."

Nodding distractedly, Khumanos reached under his tunic and undid a cord about his waist. He extracted a heavily clinking pouch and shoved it into the old man's hand, then followed him into the cave mouth. He paused to inspect the timber; it was solid yellow-white, resonant to the thump of a knuckle.

"The peasant! He has vanished into the cave!" one of the troopers cried.

The three guards, who had obediently ringed the mouth of the cave to prevent the old one's escape, now bolted forward and disappeared in pursuit of the farmer. Scuffs and clatterings of stone could be heard, along with clanks and impious curses as the Sarkads bruised themselves against invisible stone walls in the dimness. A pause then, with more muttered curses as a tinder light was struck.

Some moments later, one of the guards reappeared in the mouth of the cave. He found Khumanos inspecting the wheels—a dozen or more man-high disks of wooden plank, bronze-rimmed, with bronze bushings at the hub. "Exalted One, there is no sign of him—no more than some stains on the rock from a tallow candle." The ranking trooper hesitated. "It will be hard to follow him through this cavern."

"Likely it has branchings and exits downslope. Let him go." Khumanos turned and led them back toward the rest of the party. "It matters not, the caretakers always run away," he said. "Doubtless they will remain hidden until we are gone."

Over the ensuing days, vast labors were undertaken in the throat of volcano. The ore was carried near the rim of the smoking vent and placed there in three separate piles, from the three respective mines. Each mass of ore, one batch at a time, was laid into a great iron trough, a vessel broad and bargelike, with iron loopholes hammered into each corner and a raised lip at one end.

Chains were then hooked into the loopholes, and the metal trough levered by means of long metal poles to the very rim of the pit. This was slow work, especially as the trough edged near the vent, because the heat and sulfurous fumes issuing from the hellhole were well-nigh intolerable to mortals. Teams of slaves labored for short periods and then reeled back, choking, as the next shift crept forward to take their places.

Even so, what came next made the levering look easy. The corner chains were hooked to a much longer, heavier chain, which ran through the eye of the giant metal crane that loomed next to the fiery pit. To serve this tall, imperious master, the hapless slaves toiled at an iron windlass mere steps from the volcano's rim, hoisting the full weight of trough and ore off the ground. Again by means of levers, with more effort and risk, the crane and its burden were swung out over the blazing abyss.

Then, with slow, deliberate clacks of the ratchet, the windlass was slacked off. By a seemingly endless length of chain the trough was lowered, to bake in the heat of earth's inner hells. The wait was brief, necessarily, lest the iron vessel itself melt or burn away at the chain's lowest extent, where the fire was most intense. Almost as soon as it had been lowered the trough was raised again, urgently, with the rough, cursing assistance of the guards. Link by straining link, clack after agonized clack, the trough of ore and the full, ponderous weight of chain were hauled back to the surface.

Once raised and pivoted away from the furnace-blast, the ore was seen to be a mass of red, glowing embers: like coals in a fireplace, but encased in a trough of metal that was itself red-hot, even white-hot in places.

Promptly, without allowing it to cool, half-naked slaves raked and turned this bed of ore with long forks and paddles. The slaves did their best to keep back from the searing heat, though their heavy tools themselves glowed red at the ends. Then, back into hell's chimney, the trough was swung out and lowered again; then hoisted, raked, and lowered . . . thrice in all, without rest, under Khumanos's watchful eye and the long whip-lashes of the Sarkad overseers.

By the end of it, the stone and dross of the ore were burned entirely away. All that remained, roiling in the bottom of the trough—to those whose eyes had not grown too swollen and parched to see it—was a thin tide of molten metal, glowing green within the pinkish glare of the basin and its taut chains. This time the trough had to be raised to its full height overhead. Then it was swung gently aside, most cautiously indeed, since a splash of quick-metal could—and did on one occasion—burn a fist-sized hole in a luckless slave's chest, searing to the heart in a single, angry gasp of steam. Next, the glowing tray was lowered gently, carefully, onto a tall steel framework that caused it to tilt, letting the molten ore flow to one end.

The articulated framework was then levered and angled even higher, so as to pour the last of the molten metal out over the raised lip. It flowed, an emerald-bright, fuming cascade, down an iron channel to a funnel mouth in the top of a hinged stone mold, whose metal bindings had been wedged shut in readiness.

Once filled, the mold ticked and settled from the added weight and heat. Its seams emitted an eerie green light, and within a few moments the stone itself smoked with the metal's searing energy.

Shortly after that momentous step, with night thick overhead, Khumanos decreed praises to Votantha, signaling the end of their day's labor. The slaves crept off to their rest—sore with burns and fatigue, their beards and eyebrows scorched away, their very lungs singed with the volcano's fiery breath. Not a one of them was so dulled by labor as to forget that, once the product of their toil was removed, two more batches of ore remained to be raked and smelted in hell's fires.

On the second day following, when the mold had grown cool enough to be approached, the pins were knocked from its metal hinges and latches. The sections were pried apart to reveal a towering mass of silver-white metal of indeterminate form, roughly wedge-shaped. It was part of a larger statue—that was the best the slaves could guess, before Khumanos ordered that tent canvas be roped securely around it. It was then lowered onto a wooden sledge made from timbers left in the cave. Before any further work was done at the volcano mouth, the slaves were bidden to drag the sledge to the caretakers' farmstead, where it was left under guard.

Khumanos oversaw the making of two more metal statues by identical means. The same trough was used, along with distinct but similar molds found at the site. In each case the Exalted Priest dispassionately viewed the result, pronounced it satisfactory and, before the guards or prostrate workers saw it closely, shrouded it with canvas by his own hand. As the labor wore on the slaves grew more efficient and, if anything, more manageable. Accidents culled out the weak and the sick, reducing the cause for complaint.

Even so, the third casting was smelted and poured by a substantially smaller crew. Khumanos had ordered that the first statue be started on its way, hauled down the mountain by some one-third of the remaining slaves, with the second casting remaining under guard at the caretakers' hovels. For unknown reasons, the Exalted Priest decreed that the finished pieces must be kept separate. That precaution left fewer hands to turn the windlass and rake the ore.

The task was completed largely through the effort of one Tulbar, a Hyrkanian slave whom Khumanos had converted from sullen rebelliousness to sullen diligence. He worked tirelessly, trudging the harsh circuit of the hoist-track and then plying his ore paddle long after the other, less hardy slaves had been driven back by the heat.

Near the moment of pouring, when the trough of molten metal was being raised for the last time, the Hykanian exceeded his former standard of leadership. The great vessel caught on a stone outcrop near the rim and swayed out of line, threatening to strike the wall of the pit and spill its contents; it was Tulbar who reached out with his steel paddle to prevent it. An untimely accident then occurred: Tulbar, clinging tightly to the handle, was caught under the arm by the trapped implement and levered out over the abyss, to pitch sidelong into the trough of molten metal. Before the eyes of his fellow toilers, his body dissolved in a gout of steam, which soon diminished to mere bubblings and gurglings in the shallow, green-glowing vat.

In spite of the mishap—or rather, because of Tulbar's noble sacrifice—the pouring took place successfully. Khumanos, when questioned by one of his acolytes as to what special mourning ritual might be performed, was heard to answer in a cryptic way.

"It is of no importance," he said, turning to his inferior, his gaunt shape outlined by the bulk of the glowing, fuming mold. "The death of the body, the mere mortal husk, is no great misfortune. That is not when the pain is felt."

CHAPTER 7
Fury from the Desert

"Place a flat rock inside the trap to weight it to the bottom of the stream. Then a few loops of withe, thus . . ." Sitting back on his haunches, Conan of Cimmeria knotted the last twisted strands and held up the fishtrap before the watching children. "It's finished."

The contrivance was nothing more than a pair of open-mesh reed baskets. One was egg-shaped, the other formed as an open cone and laced inside the first. Yet to the eyes of Ezrel, Jabed, Felidamon and small Inos, the object might have been made of finest silk strung over gold wire.

"That's how they make them in Pictland, to fish the streams that feed the Black River. Now, let's put it in the pond overnight and see what we catch."

"Will there be more whiskerfish?" Jabed asked eagerly. "Those are my favorites."

"We'll see," Conan said, looping a twine through the rim of the basket.

"Whiskerfish are good," Felidamon contributed, "and eels too. I would teach my mother to cook them, but she would say they are unclean."

"Doubtless the townfolk would find them good enough to eat during a famine," Conan grumbled. "But then, like as not, 'twould be a drought, and the stream would be down to a mere trickle." He finished knotting the other end of the twine around an anchor stone of irregular shape. "They must be enjoyed during times of plenty."

"Someone is coming," Inos piped up, watching a movement upstream. The others turned to see a long, angled pole threading its way toward them through the underbrush. Any sound of the carrier's approach had been masked by the talking of the stream.

"What ho!" Conan called out as a man rounded the broad bush before them. He was a desert-dweller, his clean-shaven face burned a deep brown by sun and his black, curly hair cropped short. His dusty burnoose was belted and a polished saber hung at his waist, and his hood was thrown back loosely around his muscular neck. The pole he carried before him was a thin spear, twice the height of a tall man, its heavy tip trailing one long, curving barb.

Halting in surprise before them, the man

broke into a grin, revealing his strong, yellow-stained teeth.

"Welcome, stranger, hello!" Conan called out heartily in the southern desert dialect. "Come share our food and . . ." reaching beside him, he took up his Ilbarsi knife where it stuck in the dirt; with a flick of his arm he sent it whirling through the air: ". . . our hospitality!"

The blade chunked home; it lodged in the stranger's breastbone just below the throat. The man's sudden grab for his saber dissolved into formless, plucking spasms as he sank to his knees, exhaling a torrent of dark blood, and toppled over backward. The spear he carried fell forward across the cold ashes of the fireplace.

"Why . . . why did you kill him?" Inos quavered in a stricken, reedy voice. "Was he going to steal our fish?"

"Up, children!" Conan commanded, seizing hold of the long wooden hasp. "This is no fish-spear, by all the gods and goddesses! This is made for poking at your city guardsmen and fishing them off the wall! Up, now, and follow me! Stay close, all of you!"

Pausing only to retrieve his knife, Conan snatched up young Inos with one arm and set out at a brisk run. With the nomad's spear poised in his free hand, Conan trusted the others to keep up with him. He was not wrong, for in moments he heard Ezrel's voice crying close behind him.

"Conan, this is not the way to the gate!"

"There is no time to reach the Tariff Gate,"

Conan grunted back. "There will be more raiders gathering!"

"But the north postern door—"

"Is too far!" Conan barked back. "Follow me, we shan't need a gate!"

Ezrel followed, and after him the others—Jabed and Felidamon, steadying each other by clasping hands. Ahead of them the city wall loomed tall and sheer. There was only the faintest sign of activity on the top—in the form of a helmeted face downturned, watching their approach with sudden interest. To its suspicious gaze Conan bellowed, "Call out the reserves, you thick-witted lout! Your town is under attack!"

Arriving at the wall, he raised the pike before him. It was long enough, when held off the ground, to hook the outer edge of the battlement. Seizing Inos by the scruff of the shorts, he half-hurled him up the spearshaft—and then, reaching behind him, threw on Jabed as well to urge the smaller child along. "Go on, you two, clamber on up!" he told them. "I know you can, I've seen you shinny up palm trunks!"

Bracing the pike's butt with two hands, he watched the pair delivered into the arms of the guards at the top. He then boosted Felidamon up onto the spear—if a girl, she climbed nimbly as any boy—and finally laid hold of Ezrel. The elder boy, when he already had one foot braced on Conan's bent knee, hesitated. "You go first!" he cried. "It will be easier for you to steady the pike from the top, and then I'll climb."

"No, lad!" The Cimmerian shook his black

mane impatiently. "The hook will never support my weight—it may not even take yours unless I brace it from below. Now go!" He tossed his head toward the fringe of riverside brush behind them, where armed nomads were breaking into the open. "If you dawdle longer we'll be overrun!"

In a trice Ezrel was up to the top of the wall. "Protect yourself, Conan!" he shouted back to his friend. "I will go and find a rope."

Conan did not intend to wait for anything so unlikely. Trying his weight against the hanging spear, he felt the pliant bronze hood bend, then break off as he had anticipated. Without wasting his breath on a curse, he snatched the pike and ran straight away from the wall, toward the scattered line of advancing nomads.

The one directly in his path balked to see him coming, lowering his own long-hafted pike. He was a wiry young Shemite, his jellaba undone and hanging loose about his waist, his chest bare. He angled his spear to fend off Conan's, but to his surprise, the broken point did not drive in on him. Instead, the butt of the northerner's weapon struck him across the jaw, knocking him over backward as Conan reversed direction and headed back toward the city wall.

It loomed tall before him; instead of slowing, he pounded faster, straight toward the sheer brick pile. He thrust the spear out before him butt-end first, gripping it in both hands. Then, digging its haft into the dirt at the base of the wall, he vaulted, twisting his entire body side-way into the air. The slender shaft bent beneath the force of his weight and speed; yet it held, and on the upswing it gave back every ounce of his momentum.

An instant later, arching feetfirst, hair and garments trailing, he landed on his side, having vaulted more than thrice his own height.

No sooner had he thudded down on the hard, rough masonry than a city guard came running at him with spear raised, shouting curses against invaders. After kicking the fellow's legs out from under him, Conan rolled atop him and drubbed his helmeted head once or twice against the parapet, bawling at him, "Fool, I am not an invader! I am your friend, dog!" When the guard was slow to arise, Conan took up the spear the fellow had dropped and turned to face the enemy.

The guards on both sides of him were already embattled, fighting off lean, wiry nomads who swarmed up ladders, spearshafts, and hook-ended ropes. The standing guard were few, not more than one for every twenty paces of wall; now, as they fought feverishly along the edge of the parapet, some fell to arrows and jabbing spears. Additional troops could be heard mustering in the city garrison below, but it would be long minutes before they arrived. Meanwhile the swift, unexpected attack threatened to carry the wall.

Conan plied his spear viciously, darting along the parapet to smite attackers as they clawed their way to the top. He trod on the hand of one scar-faced marauder, causing him to slip back down his spear; another he jabbed in the neck as he mounted the battlement, sending him falling back with a wail. A third he toppled over backward with his spear-haft as the man hauled himself upright. Yet while the Cimmerian was thus occupied, two more beseigers gained the wall unhindered beside him.

The city guard who had first menaced Conan was on his feet now, facing the newcomers with drawn rapier. But even as he stalked forward, a grappling hook hurled from below caught him by the neck, dragging him down to his knees. He struggled, clinging to the paving stones to keep his place on the wall as the attacker started up the knotted rope. Conan dove to the side and jabbed the invader in the face with his spear, forcing him to loosen his grip; but more nomads behind him seized hold of the rope, hauling the guard over the edge with an agonized scream.

That left a clot of attackers, now a half-dozen strong, atop the wall; between them and the Tariff Gate only Conan and a pair of beleaguered guards remained. Rather than leaping down into the caravan yard, where fresh defenders raced toward the rampways, the marauders turned toward Conan. Clearly their best hope would be to secure the gate and try to throw it open for their fellows.

Fortunately, the narrowness of the way made it hard for more than two fighters to advance abreast. Snatching up the hapless guard's abandoned rapier, Conan shifted his spear to his off-hand and prepared to meet the rush. One marauder dodged afoul of Conan's whirling blade, lost his sword overside with a clang, and a moment later plummeted after it himself, trailing blood from his gashed throat.

Two more nomads darted in to take his place, while a third in the rear tried to add his say by thrusting between his fellows with a long, barbed spear. Conan dodged the point and drove in sideways against the shaft, using it as a handy lever to force one of the forward pair off the wall—swiftly and mercifully, with no more than a broken bone or two from the fall. The second attacker lunged at Conan, only to receive the point of the spear in his midsection. The hard-driven blade passed straight through him, jutting out from his back—and as the man behind tried to dodge past him, a savage twist of the shaft sent the point hooking into *his* vitals as well. The men, pinned together like two fish on the same spear, plummeted from the wall in a frenzy of struggles and agonized shrieks.

So went the carnage. Conan fought and slew, expecting at any moment to feel a hostile edge strike him from behind, or to take an arrow in the armpit; he kept moving briskly, tirelessly, to make himself a difficult target. Another raider went down before the northerner's feral swiftness, and another. Then, of a sudden, the last nomad who faced him moaned with fear and spun away in gasping flight.

The fugitive had gone no more than five steps when he was embattled again—this time by a gray-clad opponent who fought in the tight, economical style of Saditha's temple swordsmen. The nomad thrust left, only to see his blade brushed aside with a soft hiss of steel; then he slashed right, to find the force of the blow expended on empty air short of his leaning target. He hacked downward, again narrowly missing—then his soft burnoose tented out sharply in back with the impact of a blade-thrust.

He staggered backward; his still-quaking body twisted aside, then was shucked from the wall like a sack of offal. The victor strode triumphantly forward. He raised his blade to offer the same treatment to Conan, and the Cimmerian crouched, his weapons ready in defense. The adversary before him was Zaius, temple champion of the One True Goddess.

The Qjaran's lip curled in arrogant disdain, his sword poised ready; Conan, for his part, felt a shudder of anticipation at the impending fight. But was it hesitation that he sensed, a faint pallor of uncertainty in Zaius's face? Or perhaps it was only the cheering that arose from below—from down in the caravan yard, and beyond the intersecting wall of the temple quarter.

"Hail the heroes!" the voices exulted. "The wall is clear, our city is saved! All hail Zaius, and the savage foreigner too!"

With scores applauding, expecting them to share in the triumph, the two could scarcely fall to blows. They lowered their weapons and Zaius wheeled away, turning a disdainful back on his rival.

The shouts of acclaim from the citizenry were

a little premature, Conan thought; for, in places, the nomads still strafed and jabbed with spears and arrows at the wall's defenders. But he could see that the tide had turned; the rush of attackers had ceased, with the survivors now commencing to drag the bodies of their dead back into the brush along the river.

Inside the wall lay another world; the spirit was festive rather than affrighted. Bands of civil militia in bright, seldom-used helmets and breastplates were belatedly arriving to man the defenses. These beamed with relief at finding the fight already over, their drummers and trumpeters taking the opportunity to practice their rusty skills. Ordinary citizens, too, were flocking to the wall, women and children included; in their forefront Conan could see the four urchins he'd rescued, waving up at him in adulation.

Over the din a deeper trumpet call sounded—a flaring, belling note like that of a wounded bull. One of the guards beside him murmured, "The royal summons, so soon!" He began wiping thin, congealing blood from the point of his saber with a kerchief.

A moment later, Zaius formed up his line of a half-dozen temple warriors. With a brisk command he marched them back along the parapet. The two city guards nearest Conan followed in a less rigid step. One of them called to him, "You may as well come too, foreigner, since you are one of the heroes of the day."

"Where, to the palace?" Conan asked, tagging

along reluctantly. "Isn't it too soon to abandon the wall? What if the raiders attack again?"

"The new watch will take our place," the guard said. "They will call us back if we're needed. Do not fear, the desert folk are seldom good for more than one attack in a day."

"A nomad raid every year or so is fine sport," the other guard proclaimed. "It keeps us in trim—excepting the unlucky ones," he amended, leaning aside to look at the half-dozen Qjaran bodies at the base of the wall, all presumably slain by the departing raiders.

"Do they attack the city so rarely?" Conan strode briskly along after the two.

"Some years are worse than others," the talkative guard replied. "There is drought in the southern lands, with hard living for some of the tribes. These raiders were Khifars, Khadars, and Azilis mainly, by the look of their arrow-fletchings. They hurl themselves against the towns in desperation. Either they win great spoils," he laughed, "or they return home with riderless camels and fewer mouths to feed. Either way they survive."

As they paced the wall behind the temple troops, citizens in the yard below flowed alongside them, cheering and shouting all the while. The rampways they passed were blocked by reinforcements waiting to deploy, and by wounded guards being assisted down; in any event the heroes did not descend, but continued straight along the wall.

The crowds were soon diverted to pass through the gate to the temple quarter—whose inner wall was nearly as high as the outer parapet, though less massive. Beyond it, Conan was afforded a view he had never seen, of lush orchards and pleasure-gardens surrounding the stately buttresses of Saditha's temple and the royal palace.

At length, paced by Saditha's dancers and celebrants in the groves below, they turned onto a special causeway through the temple grounds. It led straight into the citadel, through an archway fortified as strongly as one of the city gates. In the broad inner court, a throng of merrymakers awaited them. At the center, on a raised reviewing stand, stood the royal family of Qjara.

All three wore bright ceremonial armor, made for withstanding the invaders in principle if not in fact. Afriandra was there, catching Conan's eye from across the courtyard. In spite of her military garb, she lounged front and center like the pampered princess she was. Behind her stood her royal parents, King Semiarchos and Queen Regula.

"Citizens, warriors, faithful followers of Saditha!" The king commenced speaking as soon as Zaius's temple warriors had deployed in a line before him. "The barbarous assault has turned aside and dissipated, like so many others before it." Semiarchos was a stately figure, tall and white-headed beneath his slender star-pointed crown. He wore a long white beard whose coiled ringlets lay across his embossed silver breastplate. "The battle reports and eulogies are already sung to the goddess. Our dead and wounded, thankfully so few, are being gathered up and blessed. The city walls remain under triple guard in case some new danger should arise.

"As is the custom at the close of battle, every citizen who stood and faced the enemy is entitled to the special boon of Qjara's king. By my command, this recognition is now being dispensed among you. For those hurt or killed in the fight, the honor will be extended to their wives and widows."

As he spoke, robed priestesses moved among the warriors gathered in the center of the court. One of them passed near Conan, taking something out of a small basket she carried under her arm. With a scowl, and before she could have second thoughts about his entitlement, he extended his hand and took it.

To his surprise, it was no mere trinket or medallion but a square gold coin, thumbnail-sized and solid, stamped on both faces with the sigil of the Qjaran crown. With a practiced gesture that simulated scratching his groin, he tucked it into the otherwise empty pouch inside the waist of his breech-wrap.

"Of the many heroes who have this day ennobled our city wall with libations of their blood and sweat," the king was saying, "one stands forth most notably. This is one who holds aloof from the common run of Qjaran life—and whose skills and singular aims distinguish him even more." King Semiarchos scanned the crowd loftily.

"I refer, of course, to the temple warrior

Zaius, High Champion of the One True Goddess Saditha. He is a ritual fighter of the Eighth Degree, whose match has not been seen in our city these past three hundred years." As he spoke, the king beckoned Zaius to step forward, to the sound of cheers. "His conduct in today's fight was especially praiseworthy. Arriving on the scene at the height of battle, in command of a detachment of temple swordsmen, he himself led the reprisal with great effect. He slew four of the enemy—thus bringing his accredited total of kills to an unprecedented twenty-four. How privileged we are to have such a hero stand in defense of our city and goddess!"

To the feverish cheering that passed all round the yard, King Semiarchos smiled and nodded. His white-bearded face wore a proprietary air, as of a prospective father-in-law. Zaius, the object, of the adulation, stood stiff and unresponsive, as if his foremost manly virtue were being stone-deaf. Amid the fervor, Conan saw Princess Afriandra look up to her father and murmur something to him. He nodded back with an indulgent air.

"A further boon of Saditha," the king resumed as the applause began to fade, "is the aid our city received this day from a foreign visitor—Conan, I believe his name is." Semiarchos extended a regal finger, all eyes but Zaius's following it and regarding the object. "He was the first to bring tidings of the attack, and he went on to take a toll of the enemy alongside our defenders."

Again the cheers, less hearty this time. They were punctuated by murmurs and stares of dismay at Conan's scanty, uncouth dress and the spatters of blood that still crusted his nether limbs. A large part of Zaius's sword-discipline, Conan thought, must lie in keeping the blood and spew of warfare from his neat gray uniform.

As the fleeting applause faded, it was Queen Regula's turn to address the crowd. She stepped forward, a splendid figure of womanhood, though past her youthful bloom. The helm and breastplate she affected made her look not unlike the statue of Saditha herself, although she bore no spear.

"As you know," she intoned in a firm, full-chested pulpit voice, "it is customary for Qjaran heroes to be granted Saditha's special blessing, in the form of a sacred kiss bestowed by the reigning Queen and High Priestess on behalf of the One True Goddess." The prospect she described was contemplated by Conan with mild interest and a little resignation; but then he attended her further words. "Today, however, since the sole heir to Qjara's throne is a female, and one of exceeding honor and virtue, it has been deemed suitable by the king and the temple to have her confer Saditha's benison—the lovely Afriandra, Princess of Qjara!"

At this announcement, to his surprise, Conan felt slightly shaken, his face flushing warm and cold simultaneously. He hardly knew whether to turn away and flee this fiendish entrapment, or whether to press forward swiftly and lay first claim to Afriandra's pouting, berry-stained lips.

She arose and, stepping down from her seat, strode several bold paces to Zaius where he stood before his line of temple warriors. Straining up to this unmoving face, she placed her lips on his and plied them there a moment—leaning and squirming a bit extra to get some response from his rigid form, all in vain. Applause rose and swelled around them, then subsided as she pulled back with a dissatisfied glint in her eye. She glanced impatiently around; Conan swore that her gaze shot straight at him.

He was not, indeed, certain that he was meant to receive the boon of the Goddess from the princess's lips. It could be that, as an unclean foreigner, such a blessing was forbidden him. But if killing a mere four men was the sole qualification—why, then he was ready to earn a whole evening and night of kisses.

It mattered little; now as ever he asserted himself, striding past the temple warriors and seizing Afriandra up in his arms. His mouth met hers in a bruising contest; the pavement beneath him surged as red tides swirled through his brain. His limbs flexed convulsively, clinging to her as to the sole piece of shipwrack in an angry, tossing sea. Around them he heard surprised murmurs, followed by ribald hoots . . . yet they remained clasped together a considerable time, Afriandra returning his embrace with intense and obvious eagerness.

After a small eternity, hands pried anxiously

at Conan's shoulders; amid the crowd's buzz of pleasantly raucous scandal, the two were drawn apart. Had there been applause, Conan wondered, or was it just the hiss of hot blood seething and dissipating in his ears? Afriandra, stumbling slightly as she was helped away, plainly had similar difficulty returning to the earthly realm.

" 'Tis done as decreed; two bold kisses for two bold heroes," Queen Regula was saying—though the blush that suffused her features suggested that the outcome was far from what she had decreed or expected. "True, the one called Conan is an outlander, and not a communicant of the temple—" as Regula glanced down at him with eyes that hinted disdain and a little fear, Conan gathered that her priestess's mind was racing for explanations. "But clearly he has been singled out for special favor by the Goddess, acting through her sacred delegate, Princess Afriandra."

Indeed the princess, returning to her elevated seat, looked pale and breathless enough to have been recently possessed by a goddess. Now she avoided Conan's eyes along with everyone else's.

"So, in view of this highly beneficent omen, it is my duty to welcome the stranger Conan into the bosom of Saditha's temple, and confer on him all privileges thereto, as an honorary Qjaran."

The queen's glossings and explanations could themselves have been divinely inspired, Conan thought. Her words seemed to meet acceptance and satisfy the crowd—except for one sharp, strident voice: Zaius's, as he strode before the dais and appealed to the king.

"How can a ragged infidel be honored before the realm as I am—nay, more even than I! This outlander is unclean—a blight, a smudge on the honor of battle and the purity of the temple! Reward him for his unsought help, by all means, your Majesty, but do not exalt him! Cast him out quickly, before his rank savagery takes root in our city, among our youth!"

"Zaius!" Conan rasped angrily as he tried to push past the temple warriors who now protected their leader.

"Nay, look at him," the champion raged on. "He is an animal, worse than the nomads he slew, lacking the first rudiment of how to behave in a civilized land! He might make a manageable servant someday, like a wild mountain ape—if some wise master were to pluck out his teeth, his nails and his private parts, and school him to obedience with a whip! Short of that, he can be nothing but a threat to order and decency—"

"Zaius!" Conan, hurling temple warriors to either side, confronted his nemesis. "I respect the ways of your city enough not to gut you here and now!" His hand clutched reflexively toward his knife, though he did not grasp it. "But I challenge you, Zaius, as before! Listen, all," he said, looking around.

"If I am now favored of the temple, with all

the sacred privileges of your countrymen—why, the only privilege I claim is to slit this vile buffoon's slandering gullet! *For life and honor, before the Goddess,* I call on you!" At Conan's use of the ritual words, gasps and exclamations issued from the crowd nearby. There was no longer any doubt that the challenge had been heard.

Sneering back at the target of his contempt, Zaius gave his answer. "Very well, then, before the Goddess—for your life, and for Qjara's honor!" He looked out at the crowd with a supercilious smile. "If it enables me to end your noxious life, without making my sword and the arm that wields it unclean . . . why then, gladly I welcome you to the temple! One stipulation, though . . ." Turning back to Conan, he spoke with feigned, exaggerated politeness. ". . . One thing for which I must ask your very gracious indulgence.

"In days to come there is a meeting at the highest level of leadership—" he glanced to King Semiarchos for approval before he went on "—the planned visit to our city by a foreign ruler, King Anaximander of Sark. I have been asked to take part in these high deliberations—a matter which rivals even your urgent demand on my time, outlander! If you will allow me some few days' dispensation to meet this obligation first, before I am constrained to soil my hands with the removal of foreign rubbish—" he smiled archly around at the crowd "—why then, I am at your service!"

Lacking suitable words, Conan spat onto the

pavement at Zaius' feet—an answer which was evidently taken as affirmative."

" 'Tis set, then." Queen Regula's voice wavered slightly as she once more addressed the crowd. "A duel of heroes—*for life and honor, before the Goddess*!"

Chapter 8
Mission to Qjara

King Anaximander of Sark made his entry to Qjara from the south. Eldest and grandest of the city's three portals, the Old Gate was little used since the caravan quarter and its adjoining entries were built along the river. King Semiarchos and Queen Regula, in an extraordinary gesture of welcome, rode to the city's south wall to meet their guest, driven in a bronze war-chariot by Zaius, the temple champion.

Because they faced no danger, they took only a handful of holy warriors with them. Anaximander, for his part, had offered to enter Qjara without bodyguards. The hundred-and-a-half troopers and the camel-train that had escorted him across the desert, he ordered to camp outside in the dry grainfields. He declined his hosts' offer of the caravan quarter or a riverside camp—to avoid, as he told the Qjaran king, any lapse of discipline. Even when apprised of the recent nomad attack, Anaximander declined graciously on his men's behalf, explaining that they were inured to vigilance and hardship.

The only Sarkads who accompanied Anaximander into the city were his troupe of temple dancers. This half-score of fit, comely young men and maids bore up his royal litter lightly—the more so once he alighted from it to join his hosts in their splendid conveyance.

"Greetings from the city of Sark, its humble priest-king, and its high god Votantha," he told his Qjaran hosts, bowing stiffly from the neck.

"Welcome, O Brother King," Semiarchos proclaimed. Extending a hand, he guided Anaximander down from his sedan chair into the chariot. "Blessings upon you from our city and goddess. You will ride back with us, then?—good. Here, Zaius, hand me the reins. You dismount and follow close behind. Then our honored guest can ride in comfort with my noble wife and myself."

"This, then, must be the fabled queen and high priestess Regula." Anaximander's look was keenly evaluating. "A partner well-suited to a king as prosperous and well-loved as yourself."

"Many thanks," Semiarchos said, pleased.

"Yes, thank you, O King," the queen said, coloring only faintly. "Both in my royal office and my priestly one I exalt this historic day, and welcome you!"

"Rightly so, for I am leader of the civil and the religious administration of Sark rolled into one." The chariot wheeled round and got underway, jolting and jostling in the cobbled gateyard. Anaximander, obviously unused to standing in a wheeled conveyance, steadied himself with one hand on the bronze rail. "You receive me very familiarly, Semiarchos! Some kings would be insulted by such an airy, informal reception. But I am not one to let a grudge fester for long. On the contrary, I find your foreign ways most instructive. And your city—it is more prosperous than ever!"

"You have seen Qjara before?" Queen Regula asked with interest.

"Only in gracious dreams and visions," the Sarkad king assured her. "I have never traveled this far north."

The Old Gate led into the merchants' quarter, along a boulevard lined with the stately villas of Qjara's wealthiest families. Anaximander, standing with his royal hosts in the rumbling chariot, nodded approvingly at their grandeur and at the smiling, well-dressed citizens who waved from doorways and balconies. "Your nobles do not cower or abase themselves before you," he said in an appraising tone. "They are open-minded, and most willing to trust a foreigner."

"Yes, most certainly," Semiarchos said. "Their wish for good relations between our two cities is as fervent as Queen Regula's and my own."

The way proceeded through the old marketplace—a raucous, odiferous alley, now scrubbed and flower-decked for the momentous occasion. Near its center, the chariot rolled past a low-curbed public fountain, in whose basin naked children splashed and frolicked while their parents waved and greeted the kings.

"You are plentifully blessed with water," Anaximander observed. "A watchful god looks down on you."

"Yes, our Goddess is generous," Queen Regula affirmed.

"This," Semiarchos explained, "is one of four municipal fountains charged by an aqueduct my father, King Demiarchos, built along the wall of the caravan quarter."

"Ah yes, the caravans," Anaximander said, "they follow the water. You are enriched by a good many of them too, I trust."

"Yes, as a rule. This year's season may be late in starting, though. The same copious snows that fill our river bottoms still block the passes to the north."

"Indeed." Anaximander smiled. "But when those caravans do wend their way southward and westward, they will find a city that is eager to welcome them, I do not doubt."

"Yes." Semiarchos nodded, beaming from his guest to his wife. "That is a certainty."

The Qjaran king, plying the reins at the center of the chariot, was the older and more broad-chested of the two regents. His silver-gray hair and beard hinted at a lineage harking more from Corinthia in the north than from the opulent Shemitish states nearby. At his side stood Queen Regula—chestnut-haired, if one discounted the gray streaks at her temples, yet statuesque and full-featured, and fairer by far than the tall, lean Sarkad King with his oiled black curls and square-cut beard. The joining of these three royal personages seemed somehow pregnant with history, likely to generate forces that would cause vast changes in the lives of those around them.

The street took them briefly between thronged tenements, then across a broad intersecting boulevard and through the lightly guarded and seldom-closed Trellis Gate to the Qjaran temple quarter. Just beyond the flower-draped gate spread the Agora, an open stone-paved meeting place for civil and religious gatherings, enclosed by the high, colonnaded facades of Saditha's temple and the royal palace.

"What a fine, spacious, royal enclave you enjoy," Anaximander exclaimed. "How free it is of defenses and unsightly military trappings." He gazed around admiringly as the chariot rolled forth into the plaza, which was fringed with enthusiastic onlookers. "We are now at the heart of Qjara, are we not?" the foreign king asked. "Here, just across from the splendid temple of your goddess Saditha, would be the perfect spot for our holy mission, and the shrine I would like to erect in honor of our two cities' newfound brotherhood.

"Shrine?" Semiarchos asked. "You mean an altar, or an idol?"

"More of a monument, actually, to serve as a

focus of our rituals." Anaximander spoke lightly, reassuringly. "There would be no real need to erect any new buildings. The acolytes we send to you could lodge in the town—assuming, of course, that you would permit it."

"This monument would be comely to look on, I hope," Queen Regula ventured. "Not too austere or menacing, I mean to say . . . ?"

"No, no, good Queen, I assure you! In point of fact I had in mind an ornamental statue in the form of a tree. Of course, the shape has religious significance to us." Anaximander smiled graciously at Regula, laying a hand on the shoulder of King Semiarchos as the latter guided the team past the crowds in the Agora. "One such is even now being cast by my temple artisans, from a rare and precious metal found in the southern hills. I will be happy to have it sent here, a gift from my city to yours. It would convey the true regard I have for you."

"Anaximander, you are too generous!" Semiarchos cried. "If it is of surpassing value, then let me offer to share the cost—"

"No, not at all, my good friend! Say no more. Whatever the cost, it will be less dear to me than the harmony between our two lands." Anaximander clapped his host familiarly on the shoulder. "The main thing is to raise a monument to our alliance—here, in the heart of your city—to provide a locus for the followers of Votantha to worship and make sacrifice. Know you, it is the custom of our god's devotees to offer up lavish sacrifices."

"Well, then," Queen Regula declared, "be

sure that we shall bestow on your city an equally gracious shrine, and fine sacrifices too! Let us see to it that the cultural exchange you have so kindly proposed enriches both our realms, and not only Qjara."

"Gracious Queen, I am sure the benefits to my city of Sark will be great indeed."

As Anaximander spoke, the chariot wheeled up before the steps of the royal palace. Behind it trotted the temple warriors, followed by the brightly robed dancers who bore Anaximander's litter. These groups halted, then proceeded after their royal masters into the palace. The colonnaded front entry of the place opened into a vestibule, where the highest dignitaries of Qjara waited to greet the visiting potentate. The very loftiest of this group, including the swordmaster Zaius, were then led by servants into a broader gallery. Plush divans, pillows, and tables spread with all manner of sumptuous food and drink awaited the guests' pleasure.

There, the two kings and the swordmaster were entertained by Saditha's temple dancers, under the stern direction of Queen Regula. The young women darted and whirled about the hall to the lilting of musicians, in a manner somewhat more artistic and daring than would have been thought proper in the holy premises of the temple. The featured dancer, one Sharla, gave a surprising solo performance before the King of Sark that made his features darken in a blush, leaving the other regents laughing good-naturedly at his discomfiture.

When the dance ended he told the company, "Truly, you Qjarans are a frank and pleasant-natured people. You are not overly afraid of giving a foreigner offense with some petty trifle. Our future dealings will be a source of great pleasure to me, I can tell, if they will allow me to repay you for this little entertainment. But now, friends—having learned from my viziers that ritual dance is an honored form of expression in your city, as in Sark—my own dancers will perform a dance of sacred prophecy, the Marriage of Votantha!"

The dancers had filed into place at either side of the hall. Now, at a sharp clap of their king's hands, they sprang silently into motion, their dance paced only by the scuffing of their sandaled feet. Two of them, the fittest-looking young male and female, had borrowed swords from the guards; this was done over Zaius's protests, but with the approval of King Semiarchos himself. These two pranced and leaped in an intricate series of moves among the other dancers, simulating a fierce battle.

In all it was a dashing, exhilarating spectacle. It ended with a triumphant wedding march and tableau; the handsome young male and female swordbearers were united upon an altar formed of dancers' recumbent bodies, and were worshipped in the midst of their nuptial embrace by the remaining dancers. The performance left the royal watchers in a fervor of enthusiasm.

Queen Regula, who was openly in tears, sobbed "Beautiful . . . just beautiful! But tell me, O King, in a dance of such precision—how do you induce your performers to train so perfectly, to execute such fine moves without doubt or hesitation, even when they risk a wound, as they did with those whirling blades? Surely there is much I could learn from you. I could never make my dancers honor their goddess with such rigid control . . . pray, how do you do it?"

Anaximander shrugged airily in reply. "It must be, fair Queen, that they know their king has a sharp eye for detail—that I am watching, and that I care deeply about the result. After all, this ritual dance has tremendous significance in the worship of our lord Votantha."

"Just what does it mean, Your Majesty?" Regula asked. "The young hero is your god Votantha, I take it—but who are his enemies, and who is the swordwoman he takes to wife?"

"I cannot tell you certainly," Anaximander replied. "As I said, it is a dance of prophecy. And it foretells events among the gods, not necessarily on this earth. But if you asked me to venture a guess as to its meaning—"

"Saditha, our goddess, is a warrior-woman," King Semiarchos put in. "She has no male consort in our tradition—yet she is also a goddess of family life and fertility. That would imply a husband somewhere along the line—a god, I would think. Surely no mere man!"

"That is precisely my thought," Anaximander said, smiting the gold-leafed arm of his chair. "Perhaps the prophecy is destined to come true in our lifetime."

"You mean," Queen Regula breathed, "that

Saditha might marry Votantha, and in so doing, cement the alliance of our two cities in the realm of the gods! What an inspired thought!" She cast an appreciative eye on the muscular, olive-skinned young dancer who had portrayed the sword-wielding god. Costumed for the dance in the sheepskin so favored of wandering Shemitish prophets, he wore his fleece cap at a jaunty angle as he waited beside the slender girl who had danced the part of his bride. His beaded sword-girdle was empty now, his sandals bound high on his lithe young calves. "It would seem that your Votantha is a handsome, manly god, well-fitted to tarry with our Saditha."

Anaximander laughed. "Yes, 'tis so. To myself and to my temple priests Votantha is a stern law-giver, but to the common folk of the land he is beloved too as hero and fire-bringer, and even a merry trickster! I find these common themes in the traditions of many of the Shemitish gods, by the way." He scanned the others with an ingenuous look. "Without doubt such common ground exists between our cities."

"It certainly sounds like an interesting notion to me," King Semiarchos mused "—providing, of course, that the One True Goddess were to send us her consent through favorable signs, as interpreted by my queen, the high priestess." He nodded respectfully at Regula. "And you, Zaius, what think you of it? Would our goddess be well-advised to take a husband from our neighbor city?"

"I, Your Majesty?" The temple champion,

who had seemed somewhat preoccupied of late, bestirred himself from his sullen thoughts. "Thank you for seeking my opinion, Sire—yes, I was thinking there is much we could learn from this foreign faith. The introduction of a firm, masculine side to our worship could strengthen our city, and rectify certain moral problems . . . that is to say, it could have a freshening, invigorating effect on us all!" He turned respectfully to Queen Regula. "Not to imply, of course, that our worship of the Goddess lacks vigor."

"No, Zaius, do not apologize." The queen smiled tolerantly back at him. "I think it is safe to say it would freshen and invigorate our temple dances." She cast another glance at the Sarkad troupe, who now knelt respectfully along one side of the hall. "And it might tie in splendidly with the festivities that lie ahead regarding the royal succession." She turned engagingly to Anaximander. "You know, O King, that a wedding already is in our city's future."

"A duel as well," Semiarchos added, "but that is nothing. Zaius will dispose of his challenger effortlessly. What the queen alludes to," he explained to his guest, "is the marriage of our daughter Afriandra to this fine young champion. Since Regula and I have only a female heir, we have chosen this as the best means of carrying forward our city's traditional alliance between palace and temple. But—" the king paused reflectively, stroking the silver curls of his beard "—now, perhaps, their union could symbolize the joining of Saditha and Votantha! That is something to think on—"

"Afriandra, your daughter?" King Anaximander interrupted him. "To be sure, I have heard much praise of her wit and beauty. Why is she not with us?"

Queen Regula sighed. "Ah, a young girl's moods and indispositions! She was unwell at breakfast—but now, I think, she should join us." Beckoning to a maidservant, she ordered softly, "Aella, go and fetch the princess, if you please!"

"Aha," Anaximander crowed, "I can see that you are indulgent rulers! You tolerate your daughter's girlish whims, and even entreat your servants by name! Nay, do not apologize . . . fine, gentle folk such as yourselves are prized by Votantha! You are just the sort that I and my city seek to . . . befriend."

Semiarchos, seeming a little ruffled, shot back, "And you, Anaximander? Do you keep a queen and heirs in your home palace?" He smiled more tolerantly. "Or are you one of those self-indulgent rulers who favor a harem of fine noblewomen?"

"Neither," his guest answered shortly. "To beget offspring so early in my reign might cause . . . complications later, when the child came of age. In time I will choose a few suitable slave-girls and make provisions for the continuation of my dynasty in the male line, with myself in firm control. Such has been the custom of my fathers these many centuries."

"Yes, I see, an understandable concern." Semiarchos spoke quickly to cover his wife's disapproving frown. "We shall face the same inevitable difficulties, once young Zaius here becomes nominal king while I am still in my prime." He thumped his silver-haired chest with the heel of one hand, then leaned forward to clap the stiff, pensive swordmaster on one shoulder. "But no doubt we can take some years to school the fellow in kingship, and work out a gradual transition of power—"

"Afriandra, my child!" Queen Regula exclaimed. "Come, you have kept our exalted guest waiting long enough! Meet King Anaximander, my dear. He is about to undertake a glorious alliance with our city and our temple." As she spoke, the princess glided in from the inner doorway, bowed before the Sarkad king, and bestowed perfunctory kisses on the foreheads of her seated father and mother. The even more measured, deliberate, kiss that she offered the scowling Zaius was returned stiffly and unresponsively.

"This, dear King," Queen Regula continued, "is our daughter Afriandra, sole heir to the throne and royal line of Qjara."

"Welcome, Princess," Anaximander declared, "I can see that you are as bright and well-favored as your royal parents. Come sit with us, and enjoy the rare drinks and viands that are set forth for our pleasure. We have Zamboulan date wine, as you can see, the finest Turanian *arrak*, and a special treat I myself brought in tribute, aromatic *narcinthe* of Samara. Your parents allow you strong drink, do they not? Come, sit and talk, I want to learn much more about all of you!"

While the new round of refreshments was poured, the five sat conversing. The princess remained demurely silent, except for monosyllabic answers to King Anaximander's queries. She did seem to take an active interest in the plan of marrying the two cities' gods; indeed, she began to inveigh against it, but was quickly silenced by her mother.

"Now, now, my dear child," the queen said, "do not trouble yourself! The matter is far from decided, in any event. Here, drink up your good Samaran wine."

"Yes, 'tis true," King Semiarchos chimed in. "After all, our lords Votantha and Saditha themselves must first be consulted to see if they will give their consent to this betrothal." To Anaximander the king explained, "My wife rose to the rank of high priestess in large part because she has a fine sensitivity to the will of the goddess through her dreams and visions, as well as through the usual bone-casting and entrail-reading. It is a well-developed faculty of hers, so it should not be long before . . . Afriandra, my dear, what is the matter?"

Semiarchos's speech was broken off as his daughter sagged from her seat toward the floor, barely caught by the maidservant Aella, who stood nearby. With the queen's help she was eased back up into the chair, but then lay unconscious. On being brought to awareness by vigorous chafing of her hands and cheeks, she would not open her eyes, but said in subdued tones that she was unwell and wished to return to her room. In moments, barely able to stand with assistance, she was helped out of the gallery by a pair of servants.

"What do you suppose it was?" King Anaximander asked solicitously. "She kept peering at me across her cup—then her eyes rolled up and she collapsed!"

"Ah, young girls and their nervous ills!" Queen Regula apologized. "Do not take offense. I remember I was the same at her age! It may have been the strong drink—we never allow it, you know—this was her first. She will be well by evening, I'm sure."

"In any case," Anaximander said, "you are greatly blessed in having such a fine, sensitive daughter. You must love her deeply and look forward to the joys she will bring you in years to come. I shall pray that great Votantha grants you everything you richly deserve!"

Princess Afriandra, after receiving a healing draught of tonic, lay asleep in her chamber all the afternoon. When finally she stirred and awoke, it was to see a tall figure outlined in the dusk through her balcony window.

"Conan," she gasped, raising her head from the sleeping-pad and blinking dazedly at him, "how did you come here?"

"Ever since the raid, when I learned how easy it is to pass over the city wall, I've had trouble keeping myself away." He hovered in the half-light near the window, ready to make his escape on short notice. "I sensed that all was not well with you . . . and here I find you asleep before nightfall, most likely drugged. What is it, girl, what is the matter?"

"Oh, nothing, Conan . . . only the stress of high birth, and of entertaining foreign kings—"

"You've been at the *narcinthe* again, haven't you? I can tell by the way your eyes rove and gape." Moving up behind a bedside chair to shield his modesty, he asked her, "What about that door—does it lock? I ask it only to preserve our safety—"

"Do not worry, none will enter without knocking. I can keep them out." Easing back on the rail of her sleeping couch, she beckoned to Conan. "Come and sit nearer, if you are here to comfort me—though it is always strange to be comforted by a hulking warrior clad only in helmet and greaves. What of that golden sword across your middle? Is it real, or only part of my vision?"

"I would not be so foolish as to creep into a royal palace without my Ilbarsi knife, though it is no polished trinket." Conan knelt beside the bed, close against it for modesty's sake. "What then, child, have your visions of the future been troubling you?

"Oh Conan, it was terrible!" she said, as if with a rush of memory. "I looked at my parents' foreign guest—Axander or something, he is called. There was a strangeness about his face . . . and then suddenly it crinkled up into a burned skull with horrid, charred lumps of flesh clinging to it—I fear that something dreadful is in the offing," she sighed.

"Well, that's an easy enough prophecy to explain," Conan reassured her, stroking her hair. "Mayhap his tent will catch fire on his journey home. What of Zaius, I want to know? He is the one to watch, with our duel impending. Did you get a look at him? And what of your parents . . . ?"

"Stop it, Conan, please! I could only see the visiting king, everything else was hazy and . . . and I was afraid to look! I fainted dead away." Covering her face with her hands, she sobbed softly.

"There, there, girl." Awkwardly, Conan edged onto the bed and placed a protective arm around the princess. She snuggled close against him, still weeping, and lay her head on his chest.

He took pains to comfort her properly; the job turned out to be time-consuming, lasting until late in the evening. Once or twice timid knocks sounded at the door; Afriandra showed remarkable presence of mind, calling out brusque commands that sent the intruders away. She returned then to the breathy business of consolation as if nothing had happened.

At length she rolled over and struck a light. She touched the tinder to an oil lamp on her bed-table, laving the room in faint, wavering gold. The light made their tousled sleeping-pad an isle in a murky sea, on which the two of them reclined like weary swimmers resting on a sandbar.

Touching Conan's sun-bronzed flank, Afriandra announced, "Here is the best proof I have yet had of my gift for prophecy. My visions did not lie."

Conan stretched on the firm, cool bed, propping himself on one elbow. "You mean I . . . look the same?" he prompted.

"Every scar, every thew, is exactly as foretold." Assuring him soberly of this, she traced certain conclusive features with her forefinger.

"Glad I am that you are not seeing me headless, or lacking other vital parts," Conan said. "That gives me at least an even chance in my forthcoming temple bout."

"Conan, I meant to speak to you about that—I would have made another rendezvous with you, if you had not come here." Her voice, issuing from her nymphlike form, was surprisingly firm and even. "Surely you can imagine that it is not easy for me to have the two men whom I most . . . revere . . . ready to slaughter one another mere days hence! And not even in a fight over me, strictly speaking—since I am already promised in marriage and have no intention of undoing the betrothal."

Searching his eyes for any sign of hurt, she almost pleaded with him, "Can you not see that you have made things very difficult between Zaius and me?"

"I?" Conan bridled. "I made no difficulty! I aided you, if you recall, at your earnest plea—then, if I am not mistaken, you used me as a foil to warm up your half-baked temple hero! He, Zaius, is the fly in the ointment! He made the difficulties, not I!"

"I, used you?" Afriandra marveled. "I merely

asked your advice as a traveler, a man of the world! Granted, I should have known it would end here in my bedchamber—me, the prophetess with the infallible vision . . ." she shook her head in exasperation.

"But even so, Conan, that is no reason for you to fight Zaius," she went on chiding him. "Try to be adult about it! His tongue is as sharp as his sword, I know . . . but then, must you be so touchy about your barbarian pride? Especially here in Qjara, where we know nothing of your homeland, and whence you plan to be gone in a month's time! Zaius is difficult, to be sure, but can you not see that beneath it all he has feelings like any man—that he can be hurt like you, and has been hurt?"

"Not as hurt as he will be, by Crom's cudgel! That slandering hound—"

"Hush, now," Afriandra insisted, laying a hand on her lover's taut shoulder. "Conan, listen, Zaius has heavy burdens to bear! As temple champion he must be unbeatable. He must shrug off dangers that would make other men dissolve in sweat and tears . . . or at any rate he must seem to. And now my parents have decreed that he will go from commoner to king—being king of Qjara is no lark, Conan, it is a life laden with cares and responsibilities! On top of it all, he must deal with me and my independent ways—"

"And I can think of none worse for the job than that self-important prig!" Conan spat. "No man is more likely to turn your fairly tolerable city into a soulless prison, another Shemitish horror! I will be doing you and your town a precious favor to lay him out in shanks and cutlets—"

"Conan, he is noble and sensitive at heart." The princess was pleading now, almost in tears. "He may be limited, true, but he is what we have to work with! For my sake, and for the sake of my royal line—"

She was interrupted by a faint knock at the door. "Afriandra—Princess, are you well?" a muffled voice asked.

"Yes, I am better now." As before, she spoke up firmly and distinctly. "Go away, I do not wish to be disturbed."

"Forgive me, Princess." The door pushed smoothly open. "I cannot help it, I needed to . . ." At the sight of the two lying in the lamplight, the face in the dark doorway paled. It was Zaius.

The lips took time to form words. When they came, they were hard and cold: "Oh, I see."

"Zaius, I . . ." Afriandra began. But it was too late; the door pulled smoothly shut. In utter silence he was gone.

"Well, now, the fellow has some good sense after all." Conan eased his grip on the Ilbarsi knife he clutched below the level of the bed. "Mayhap when you are his queen, he will afford you decent freedom—"

"No, Conan, this is worse than ever!" Intently she clutched his arm. "Listen to me, you must leave Qjara at once! What does it matter to you, anyway . . . ? I can give you money for provisions! Camp in the hills, or just out of reach of the city, until the first caravans come. You must not face Zaius in this duel—if you were to slay him, it would be the worst thing for our city! And after tonight I could never dissuade him from slaying you—"

"Impossible," Conan said, sitting up and drawing on his garments. "I challenged him openly, to remedy his vile insults! Afriandra, by your own temple laws, the challenge is sacred—as it is by my law!" He slid the thick-bladed knife into its belt-loop. "I could never slink away from this fight, though all the princesses in Shem were to beg and bribe me to." Arising, he turned to stroke her hair a last time.

"Very well then, if you cannot back down . . . there is still one thing you can do to show your love for me." She looked up at him defiantly with tears streaming down her face. "You can let Zaius kill you!"

CHAPTER 9
Sea of Sand

King Anaximander of Sark rode across the desert in stately comfort. Reclining in his sedan chair, he enjoyed the irregular motion of the slave-borne journey. It resembled what had been described to him of travel over the great ocean in a small boat—the gradual crawl up the face of a dune, slowing as the bearers wearied with the steepening slope and the sand sliding away under their feet—then the delicious forward tilt; the swift, giddy descent as the slaves fought to restrain the rush of the litter down the back of the mountain of sand. And finally the slow, weary recovery, as his human steeds panted from their labor and prepared themselves for the next climb.

In an innocent, childlike way, Anaximander found it delightful. He appreciated the unparalleled softness of the ride, the lazy stirring of the gauze curtains in the breeze created by forward motion and, above all, the view ahead from his shaded seat, of rank upon rank of graceful, undulating dunes. He had been wise, he told himself, in selecting this route for the return trip to Sark, instead of the level, boring expanses of the dead sea bottoms.

He would have to discipline his bearers for it later, of course—this irregularity of pace constituted poor training and might, along with the preposterous temple dance he had made them perform during the state visit to Qjara, spoil this lot of slaves entirely. But for now the experience was a unique one, and he savored it.

If the troop of military guards had any opinion of the route he had chosen, they wisely kept it to themselves. They covered the dunes in a loose formation, spread out on all sides of the royal sedan. But now their commander, a scarred, hound-faced officer in polished bronze, spurred his horse up beside Anaximander's moving throne.

"Your Supremacy," he reported with careful tonelessness, "a procession has been sighted afar, skirting the alkali barrens to westward. It is thought to be the priest Khumanos's party, conducting the holy idol south toward Qjara."

Anaximander considered a moment. "Good, then," he declared. "It means that he adheres diligently to the schedule I set for him." After more silent reflection, the king said, "Even so, it has been long since I had knowledge of his progress, and that only by way of couriers.

Have him brought here forthwith; a private interview is called for." Thoughtfully he stroked the oiled curls of his beard. "And send along a pair of officers to keep his slaves marching in his absence, so the progress of the idol will not be unduly delayed."

"It will be done at once, Your Supremacy." The commander, lashing his mount smartly away, could soon be heard barking instructions to a subordinate. That officer rode some way further before relaying the order to his troops. Moments later, on seeing the thin dust-plumes raised by galloping steeds, Anaximander was satisfied that a squad of cavalry had been dispatched ahead. Borne forward on his own swaying voyage, he caught occasional sight of the riders as they topped distant dunes, dwindling with each further crest.

In little more than an hour they returned. This time they approached the royal conveyance from behind; the king only noticed them as they crested the last dune. With a sharp clap of his hands, he signalled his slaves to halt the sedan chair at the bottom of the dune. In the squad's midst, as he could plainly see, rode Khumanos.

From the awkward, jolting way the priest clung to the back of the horse, it was evident that the saddle was a new experience for him. He must be suffering some novel and excruciating bruises and chafes, Anaximander judged, not to mention the deep bone and muscle soreness that would come later.

Even so, when the cavalry detachment reined

up alongside, the black-skinned priest let himself down stiffly from his mount and stood there on his own unsteady legs. He did not sag or topple into the sand, as Anaximander half expected. In his gaunt, weathered form there was a firmness and resolution the king had not previously seen.

"Your Supremacy," he acknowledged with a scant bow and the merest downward flicker of his eyes.

"Well, well, young priest," the king hailed him in almost jeering solicitude, "time and harsh duty have changed you . . . for the better, I think! Certainly they have aged you. But come, ride with me in the security of my royal litter. The slaves will be able to manage your added weight, I have no doubt. 'Tis great fun swooping across these desert dunes—come and sit!"

Moving forward on stiff, unsteady legs, Khumanos paused before the vehicle. He let the king's personal attendants pull his soiled, sand-dusted garment off over his head, to be replaced with a dressing gown of soft, luxuriant silk from a cedar chest attached to the royal conveyance. The dusty-brown, breech-clouted body they briefly exposed to the light was sparse and skeletal, it seemed to Anaximander—a dark, bony map of hardship and self-denial. Aside from the coarse clout, the only adornment Khumanos wore was the stub of a broken, rusted knife on a thong about his neck—an emblem of religious faith that the king vaguely recognized. Once gowned, Khumanos ducked beneath the gauze curtain and climbed into the sedan, which the bearers had set down onto the sand.

The priest sat opposite the king, facing rearward under the high, capacious awning. When at Anaximander's signal the slaves hoisted the litter to their shoulders, the priest wobbled and almost rolled out; he was stopped from falling only by the king's swift, firm grip on his slender wrist. By then they were underway, sweeping up the slope of the next sand dune with a motion that was both giddy and smooth.

"So, Exalted Priest," Anaximander began, "you have been able to carry out our great lord Votantha's commands without fault? What of the idol? Has it been made according to the ancient formulae?

"Yes, Your Supremacy." Khumanos regarded the king emotionlessly as he spoke, his voice husky with long exertion and desert dust. "The sacred metal was obtained in the ancient site above Shartoum, from the three consecrated mines, according to our prescription of old. The seals on the shafts were unbroken, and the ore was true according to the standards the elder Solon gave me. It was carried to the Chasm of Fire to be smelted—the caretakers of the place discharged their duties adequately, as before."

"And that wily devil, the sheikh, did he cooperate?"

"Yes, sire. Slaves were furnished to me for the prescribed payment, and we were not troubled by raiders in Shartoum. We were able to complete the manufacture and set forth with the segments of the idol in a reasonable time."

"Good, then! The old Shartoumi must fear me enough not to try any tricks. I am glad your work has been completed so effortlessly." Anaximander solemnly considered a moment, combing a finger through the curls of his beard. "What of the other parties? Do you have any word of their progress?"

"According to the last dispatches I received, both processions were passing near Sark. The three parts of the idol are of identical weight and bulk, but the easternmost party has the longest route. The central one faces steep terrain, because it must cross the hills to skirt our city and lands.

"Indeed," the king concurred. "It would never do to have the idol pass through Sark. That would be a most ill omen!"

"Naturally, Sire. In consequence, the other parties may lag behind. I recently sent runners to determine their current whereabouts."

"They are in the charge of your senior acolytes, are they not? Dependable young men, I should hope."

"Yes, Your Supremacy. I have taken special pains to ensure that they regard their mission in a solemn, uncompromising way." As he spoke, Khumanos fingered the rusted sword-hilt that hung around his neck. "However, Sire, my own work crew has been depleted by hardship and accident encountered during our journey. I have had to convert nearly all my military guards to laborers. I would think the same is true of the other parties. If you could spare additional troops or bearers for our cause—"

"To be sure, priest. My full kingly will goes with your mission. You may take with you a dozen of the troopers from my personal guard if you wish. Upon my return to Sark, I will put forth a royal summons—not for conscripts, I think, but for volunteers. With conditions as they have been in our city, scores of peasants should be eager to bind themselves into slavery for the promise of as much food and water as they can carry. I will dispatch them to overtake the other two parties. That should meet your needs, I think."

At Khumanos's wordless nod, Anaximander resumed. "Good. Here, priest, take food and drink, for I am tired of your dry, croaking voice." He gestured to a hamper that sat open to one side, nested with fruit, cheese, biscuits, and stoppered flasks of wine. "Meanwhile, I shall tell you that which should make your heart rejoice and give thanks to your gracious lord.

"I am fresh from Qjara. Know you, I have prepared the way for your ministry. 'Tis a certainty, the sacred tree of Votantha's power will swiftly take root and flourish there."

Khumanos, eating and drinking without apparent zest, said nothing in reply to his king. He merely watched with alert dark eyes.

"In all," Anaximander continued, "my visit can be regarded as highly successful in both a religious and a diplomatic sense. Know you, I was welcomed into the very halls and palaces of mine enemies." Showing unprecedented frankness toward one of inferior station, the king laughed aloud. "I saw firsthand their pathetic weaknesses, those same traits that make them odious to our lord Votantha. The open-handedness, the moral laxity and ease . . . and their hateful arrogance, assuming that others' vices are identical to theirs!" The ruler smirked in genuine distaste. "Fortunately, such faults as those invite their own extinction. Be assured, priest, in every religious, political, and spiritual sense I have paved the way for the coming of our great god."

"I take it, Sire, you find them fitting sacrifices to our holy master?" Setting aside gnawed fruit rinds and a drained flask of date wine, Khumanos finished his repast.

"Yes, in every way! Their wealth and ease, the richness of their lands and adornments, and above all their pathetic innocence make them perfect victims to be sent heavenward in a fiery offering! Every detail is as I first understood it to be, from the rare vision our gracious lord sent me." Anaximander sat nodding, seized by a kind of holy rapture in the gently swaying litter.

"I taunted them, you know! But in their complacency they heard nothing of it." The king shook his head in patient, infinite contempt. "It may be that my words will be remembered later, and bitterly—if only for a mere agonized instant as our sacrifice comes to fruition. Do you think, Khumanos, that you can arrange that, in the way you speak the final words? I cannot command it, I know—for the sacrifice you yourself will make places you beyond even my reach. But will you grant me this one small satisfaction, this brief moment of revenge?" Anaximander sighed. "I hope so, priest—for our lord Votantha, in his way, is a bountiful god."

The priest blinked noncommittally. "It is not my place to seek personal vindication, Sire. My concern is that the steps and rituals be carried out to open the way successfully."

Shaking off his reverie, the king looked at his guest with new interest. "Truly, Khumanos, you are changed. Aforetimes you struck me as squeamish and infatuated with the weak, pallid image of our god the temple has promoted as a sop to peasants. Now I find you firm and unswerving in your purpose, a true administrator at last! You are not balked by mere physical discomfort, be it yours or lesser men's. You owe much, I think, to Votantha's harsh mastery, and to my own leadership in his service."

"Yes, Sire. I also credit my present enlightened state to the late prophet Solon. He played a crucial part, by . . . showing me the folly of mortal hopes and passions, and the transience of life itself. This amulet is a keepsake of his guidance." As Khumanos spoke he unlooped the broken, corroded dagger-hilt from around his neck and held it poised before him.

"Old Solon, yes," the king mused. "Older than the hills themselves. And then abruptly his life ended—just at the time of your devout pilgrimage, as I recall. It is well that his arcane knowledge passed into able hands."

"In truth, Sire, I was there when he died . . . of a tragic misstep in his treacherous cave. His exit from this world was his most valuable lesson to me, a proof how frail and cheap even the most honored mortal life can be."

"And with his wisdom he passed on to you the phantom sword of Onothimantos." Anaximander shifted in his cushioned place against the litter's backrest. "I caution you, priest, do not think to try its edge against either my ethereal soul or my physical body." As he spoke, he raised one hand to the neck of his robe, exposing the collar of a shirt of silver link mail worn beneath his fine silk. "If you do, you may learn a lesson regarding the cheapness of an even more exalted life . . . your own."

"Nay, Sire. Of course not." Khumanos's tone was amazingly devoid of fear or apology at his ruler's threat. "I would use this charm only against one whose spirit or passions stood to impede our lord Votantha's will. Thus far Your Supremacy's harsh, vengeful spirit is the motive force of this mission for our god's greater glory—indeed, its source. As long as it remains so, Sire, yours is the last soul I would excise."

"Then you are wise, priest—and fitted to go on serving me and our godly master." Anaximander clapped his palms sharply to gain the attention of the horsemen outside the chariot. "Go now, and drive your caravans north to their target. I shall await the news of your success, and of your own glorious sacrifice."

Chapter 10
Before the Goddess

To Conan it seemed that all of Qjara must have shouldered into the Agora this bright morning to witness the temple duel between himself and Zaius. He knew there were exceptions—the guards atop the city's outer walls, and the farmers who toiled at their shadoofs and screw pumps to flood the fields, lest their crops be scorched by the day's harsh sun. Yet likely their thoughts roved here before the colonnades of Saditha's temple, to the fight between their city's champion and his foreign challenger.

Most likely some of their money was here, too, nestled in the pouches of shifty odds-takers who hovered in conspicuous places in the crowd. Blandly, these bearded Shemites muttered and transacted as the sun climbed toward its zenith. Their complacent air suggested to

Conan that the stakes were firmly fixed, and that no serious danger to the reigning champion was foreseen.

Here among the spectators presided both Qjara's king and queen, seated beneath a brightly woven canopy stretched on poles before the palace gate. Between them, silent amid the officious crowd of their retainers, sat Princess Afriandra. Though lovelier than ever, fetchingly gowned and coiffed, to Conan she looked pale and hollow-eyed, as from lack of sleep.

Around the sides of the Agora, a little back from the staked-off site of the duel, scaffold-benches had been erected to afford a clearer view to the great mass of Qjarans who could not crowd up to the central area. These stair-stepped racks were precarious at best; since those in front would not sit or kneel, those behind were forced to stand upright on the narrow planks and poles, leaning on the shoulders of their fellow citizens to steady themselves. The best vantage of all appeared to be the top of the narrow, ivied wall of the Temple Quarter; perched there, amidst a ragged fringe of youths who had dared the climb, Conan spied Ezrel and the other three urchins who frequented his camp outside the wall, though less so since the nomad attack.

In spite of his recent notoriety, there were few watchers whom Conan could truly call his friends. He stood now at the core of these, forming a small, alert group at the edge of the staked arena: the tapkeeper Anax, Babeth and some of her sister tavern-girls, and a handful of servants and entertainers from the caravan quarter.

Their numbers did not include the dancer Sharla. She, instead, occupied a featured place among the filmy-robed priestesses who now began to turn and circle in ritual steps before the high, noble facade of Saditha's temple. As their dance quickened and elaborated, the murmur of the crowd faded in pious expectation. The hush allowed the faint throb of flute, drum, and cithern from the temple steps to be heard.

When it ended, the Agora lay hushed under the noon sun—ready for a ringing summons by Queen Regula in the full-bodied voice that served her well as high priestess of the One True Goddess.

"A challenge has been issued and a duelling assembly decreed! In Saditha's name, let the ritual begin!"

The stir that followed her words was not excitement or acclaim, as might have preceded a Kothian or Zingaran arena game. It was a clearing of throats, a readying for solemn business. In another moment Regula was speaking again.

"The recipient of this day's challenge is great Saditha's champion, a ritual fighter of the Eighth Degree, Chief Temple Warrior and Defender of the Goddess! It is none other than the brave and well-beloved Zaius, native to our own sacred city of Qjara. Zaius, step forward!"

Zaius, tall and rigid as ever, strode forth from among the royal favorites under the canopy. The murmur that issued from the watchers at his appearance was hardly that of applause, which would have been out of place in such a holy ceremony. Rather it was a sigh of relief and welcome, a pure exhalation of love held by this gathering for their city's vaunted savior. Queen Regula embraced him first, as a mother would; she then presented him to the adoring onlookers, keeping one serene arm across his shoulders as she spoke again.

"Zaius, do you wish to make a special dedication of this day's fight, and of the valiant blood that will be rendered up as an offering to Saditha in her immortal realm?"

Zaius scanned the crowd with evident calm; to the watching king and princess, he shot only a swift glance and a curt, unbending nod. The rest of the citizenry he regarded loftily, with no special glance at Conan where he stood along the rim of spectators directly opposite. In a voice hardened by preaching and command, he spoke.

"Indeed, I have a special dedication. This temple duel, among all those in our city's history, will long be remembered among you. I mean to honor you, citizens and faithful, with the highest display of swordsmanly skill that is possible to attain." The pause which followed this news was punctuated by excited glances and whispers. "To this end, I have practiced diligently. I fasted and meditated under the strictest regimen, and spent many hours in deep and sincere prayer to the One True Goddess." He gazed around the crowd with an air of calm virtue. "The sacrifice which I offer this day to Saditha, I dispatch to her in a noble name: that of Afriandra, princess and future queen of Qjara!"

Again, the murmur which greeted his words was not applause but worship—an irrepressible gust of admiration and excitement. Conan, listening for the faintest buzz of scandal in it all, failed to detect any. Certainly he himself had breathed no word of his personal accommodation with the princess; neither, presumably, had the other two parties involved in the triangle. So the spectators, Conan guessed, would miss the undercurrent of spite and jealousy in their temple champion's boasts. They would hear only his pious, self-righteous pronouncements.

Conan's own reaction to Zaius's speech was a more urgent and impatient craving for battle. For days, ever since Afriandra's plea to him, he had turned over in his mind the more bizarre possible outcomes of the duel—such as how much of a wound he might himself bear to acquit him honorably of the battle for the princess's sake—or, on the other hand, how severely he could maim Zaius without killing him or permanently incapacitating him as this city's stuffed hero.

Consulting the youth Ezrel, he had learned that the One True Goddess was not so bloodthirsty as to demand the death of one or both duellists. A severe wound, by tradition, was enough to terminate one of these ritual combats. For Afriandra's sake and that of her dynasty, he knew he should leave certain vital parts of Zaius intact; this annoyingly limited his options. Most recently, his thoughts had turned toward the notion of a double wounding—the stab to Zaius more serious than his own, of course, yet neither wound overly humiliating. The two together should be sufficiently bloody to satisfy all the interested parties, mortal and immortal alike.

But in this line of thought, he was perhaps being the pretentious one. Having seen Zaius fight, he knew it could swiftly come down to a choice of slaying or being slain. He, personally, inclined toward the former option—did he really, after all, have the courage to die for Afriandra's royal whims? A part of him hoped not.

"How inspiring, how selfless!" Queen Regula was royally declaiming. "In Zaius we see the purity and nobility that come from a life of service to our Goddess. Citizens, offer up a prayer—a silent meditation for our temple champion and his lofty aspirations!"

When a moment of buzzing silence had passed, the queen resumed, "The challenge to Zaius was issued, for personal grievance, by one named . . ." she glanced down to a small wax tablet she held in one hand ". . . named Conan, a commoner, not sworn to our Goddess and not of Qjara. Conan, step forward."

Moving from the scatter of his acquaintances, passing between the brightly painted wooden stakes that marked the field of honor, he strode forward onto the open pavement of the Agora. A murmur came from the crowd, fainter and more dubious than Zaius had received—whether it was awe at his impressive physique, or disapproval of his scanty, shabby clothing, he could not tell. He knew not whether he would be asked to make a pious speech for the crowd—in any event, as the queen gestured for him to halt several paces from herself and Zaius, the temple champion raised a protest.

"His sword—" Zaius waved at the tarnished Ilbarsi knife dangling from the belt of Conan's kirtle "—such a wretched object is unsuitable for this sacred duel! It is no sword, but a mere knife—and a foul, unclean thing into the bargain!" He turned back to one of the temple fighters ranked behind him. "By the grace of Saditha, make him a gift of an honorable weapon."

Handing over his knife, Conan took the gold-hilted piece the warrior offered him in return and tried its weight. "Be warned, Zaius, I swung more of a broadsword than this when I was still a babe." He stripped off the scabbard and tossed it after the retreating donor. "Do not think for a moment it is any less likely to find your gizzard than my accustomed blade."

"If you believe this day's outcome depends on what sword you use . . ." Zaius's face did not unbend even enough to form a sneer; his eyes scarcely rested on Conan. "I merely wanted to see that the proper forms were observed. You and the weapon you possess are as nothing to our city and our temple. You have no self-discipline, no honor, and no power in this contest."

"Insults from your purse are cheap coin, Zaius," Conan spat back. "Do not attempt to awe me with them—it will not save your tawdry hide!"

The temple champion almost deigned to shrug, meanwhile keeping his gaze aloof. "It matters not, barbarian—do you not see, you are already defeated! By the end of this match, you and everything you stand for will be utterly obliterated, washed away in a welter of purifying blood . . . but enough now, on with the combat!"

Queen Regula, during the exchange of threats, had already begun drawing back; now the temple warriors moved protectively with her. The field was left to the combatants.

As they retreated, Conan had an odd feeling about his rival's assurances. The temple warrior had seen Conan fight—was Zaius then a madman to face this duel so confidently?—a true zealot, perhaps, or a sorcerer? Was his mistress Saditha, perhaps, that rare sort of goddess who enjoyed taking a direct, unambiguous hand in mortal struggles? Glancing up uneasily at the portico of the temple, Conan saw her graven face stare down on him, masklike and inscrutable.

The arrogant temple champion saluted, his gleaming sword held vertical in one hand before him; Conan made a similar gesture, understanding it to be part of the tradition. The distance between the fighters was still laughably wide, a half-dozen paces or more. Conan leveled his sword and began stalking forward on the balls of his feet.

Zaius, meanwhile, made his opening moves.

Raising his saber high, he flexed both wrists agilely so that the sword described a flashing, difficult arc in the air above him. Then he lowered his stance and braced his square, rangy shoulders.

Swinging the blade mightily, he sheared off his own head.

The stroke was tightly and rigidly controlled, unlike anything Conan had ever seen. The slender sword, miraculously, retained enough force to slice cleanly through the taut column of flesh, sinew, and bone that was the warrior's neck. Swordmaster Zaius's head whirled high, borne up on a spraying, gushing fountain of copper-bright blood. Even as it tumbled to earth and rebounded, Zaius's nerveless body crumpled with it, spasming with a few random twitches. The ghastly vacancy of his neck still spouted redly, and his saber clattered loose on the stones of the Agora.

This astounding sight was greeted with breathless silence from the onlookers—not with cries of horror, barely even a gasp of surprise. One moment, then two, the stillness lasted; it was finally broken when Conan barked a short, incredulous laugh.

"Crom, what can this mean?" He turned for explanation to the nearest spectators. "What sort of low, clownish farce . . . ?"

"Silence!" Queen Regula's voice issued sharply from the front of the royal pavilion. "Foreigner, defile not this sacred moment! Enough of blasphemy and invoking your heathen gods!

"Faithful of Saditha," she now proclaimed, stepping forth into blazing sunlight, "I did not foresee this event. Our Goddess, all-knowing as she is, chooses to keep certain matters secret from mere mortals. But be assured, you are greatly privileged to stand here this day. You have experienced an act of supreme will, an expression of faith's highest power! Citizens of Qjara, you have witnessed a miracle!"

At her heartfelt words, a murmur of acclaim began to build from the dumbstruck watchers. Conan, clutching his sword in mute uncertainty, watched the crowd warily. Heads around him began to wag and mutter, considering the fate of the one detached head lying forlorn in its red puddle on the paves.

"Not in three hundred years has a feat like this graced our temple ceremonies," Regula went on. "And never in Qjara's history has a sacrifice been made with such masterful skill. No living man could have achieved it, other than the great Zaius—none else possessed his skill, his discipline, and his singleminded devotion to temple doctrine. Saditha has seen her champion's merit, and has favored him for it. He has been allowed to offer himself in sacrifice. In so doing, he takes his place among the immortals!"

The buzzing, murmuring ferment continued to spread through the Agora, with the high priestess continuing to build and embellish on it. "Doubt not, faithful ones, the lesson of this feat is nothing less than a proof of immortality! You have seen it; the evidence is plain to your eyes. How else could mighty Zaius, having first cut himself to the core and slain his mortal husk, gone on to complete the sacrifice and finish dividing his lifeless body in twain? Only by a miraculous effort of will, such as pure faith in the One True Goddess can inspire—only by triumphing over death itself!

"That, Qjarans, was his final lesson for us, the power of faith! That is what makes this a glorious, epochal hour! Hear and remember it, as you and your children worship Zaius down the centuries to come. Our city may have lost a future king, but we have gained an immortal hero!"

Queen Regula had moved forward into the Agora, coming as near to Zaius's body as she could without setting her richly sandaled foot in the darkening puddle of his blood. As she spoke, she beckoned forth attendants with one gracious hand; these knelt and began wrapping his gory remains in fresh white linen, one large bundle and one small, working quickly to keep the blood from soaking through. As they labored, Conan took the opportunity to pose a question.

"What of me, O Queen?" he demanded. "Zaius has cheated me of my chance to even things—"

"Cheated!" Queen Regula flared at him. "Foreigner, in point of fact you were bested! Defeated, more surely than if it were your own head lying severed on the cobbles!" She pulled herself erect, a statue of granite dignity. "The ritual sacrifice was made, blood was shed for the Goddess . . . and Zaius's was the hand that shed it! He is victor, and his victory shall live down the ages."

Standing apart from the Cimmerian across the fast-caking pool of blood, flanked now by temple warriors who moved forward to protect her, she turned the full, theatric effect of her voice and scathing finger against him. "As for your part in this . . . it was nothing, nay, worse than nothing! For it was you, a foreigner, hopelessly ignorant of our ways, who gaped at our hero's demise! You it was who mocked him, and who defiled his most sacred moment with a rude guffaw and vile heathen curses!"

Regula, with unerring priestly instinct, seemed to recognize that Zaius's exaltation required somebody else's damnation. Now she kindled the crowd's resentment against Conan, fanning it mercilessly with high-flown rhetoric. He could feel it in their sullen looks and low murmurs, and he tightened his grip on the saber-hilt, half convinced that he would be seized and rent apart in a religious frenzy.

"The penalty for such boorishness—well, it is no more than the penalty for anyone who disgraces himself in a temple duel. From this hour you are as nothing to us, Conan of the Hinterlands. You have no longer any place in Qjara, nor in the sight of the One True Goddess."

"Wait, O Queen," Conan protested, "whatever that means, it is unfair! I did nothing to deserve it, I harmed no one unjustly . . . I helped to save your city!" Turning from the stern faces of Regula and the crowd to the bearded visage of the king himself, Conan called out, "Semiarchos! You recognized my service to Qjara and placed me under the protection of the temple—"

"From which you are expelled," the king answered gruffly, "no differently than any Qjaran whose conduct breaches our code." His gaze was turned sternly aside from the Cimmerian; Afriandra's face, too, was averted with a fixed, tear-stained frown, where she sat beside her father under the royal canopy.

"Come now, this is madness—Zaius was a fool, don't you see . . . ? He threw away his own life . . ." Impatiently, Conan turned back toward those who had come with him to the duel. The taverner Anax and his employees, Babeth and the rest, spoke no word of reassurance. These folk were themselves the pariahs of respectable Qjaran society; but now, wearing looks of righteous, tragical piety, they kept their faces sullenly averted from Conan's.

"Before Crom, you are all hypocrites! How can this be . . ." Conan's gaze at last sought out the four ragged children, who dangled their spindly legs atop the nearby wall. They, too, failed to look his way, though Conan thought he caught the briefest, mournful glance from tiny Inos.

"Very well, then," the northerner grumbled at last, "I have no love for Qjara! I planned to leave soon, in any case. If this fine sword . . ." he held high the saber the temple warrior had given him ". . . will pay the cost of a camel, and water bags and provisions, then I will be gone from this place and vex you no more."

"It may be so," Queen Regula proclaimed, keeping her gaze fixed loftily above his head. "I charge you, foreigner, conduct any business you must, but quit our city by nightfall on pain of death. From that hour forward, by Saditha's holy law, you are outcast!"

Chapter 11
The Outcast

Along one side of the desert basin loomed the Mountains of Desperation. Opposite them, nearer the lone rider, reared the crimson flanks of the Blood of Attalos range, while farther ahead and to westward the bone-pale Fangs of Zhafur took a jagged bite out of the hot blue sky. Jagged, fanciful shapes they bore, as sketched to Conan by desert-wise Shemites in the dust of campfires; the names and the ill legends associated with them probably varied from tribe to tribe among the local nomads. 'Twas a near certainty that no reliable map of these barren scarps existed, except the ones seared into the brains of seasoned raiders and caravan scouts by years of scorching desert sun.

Between the fantastic peaks, a dusty reddish plain shimmered like the bottom of a vast copper kettle. Travelers passing this way, on top of the hardships and dangers they already faced, were vexed further with a thankless choice: whether to skirt the desolate basin's edge and keep to the less scorching, less blinding parts of it, often in the misguided hope of finding water; or whether to cut straight across its center and save time. Conan, alone atop his two-humped Turanian mount, had chosen the more direct course.

Knowing well the harsh, carelessly lethal disposition of the deserts of eastern Shem and their inhabitants, he had not intended to come this far west—rather to swing northward toward Shadizar, via the lower passes of the Desperation chain and the border kingdoms of eastern Koth. But fate had paid him in false coin, decreeing that the first watering place along his route—an oasis well spoken of by camel-drovers and judged especially trustworthy this year in view of the water-wealth of nearby Qjara—lay bone-dry. Its palm trees browned and curled in the bleak sun, and its salt-rimmed bottom lay pitted with holes dug in vain quest for the vanished water.

Conan, for his part, had not been so dangerously short of the precious essence as some recent travelers to the oasis. Their plight was evidenced by the mummies left parching in the sand nearby: camels there were, slain for the few last drams of cloying fluid left in their wilting humps, and human carcasses as well with throats laid open in fights over water, and half their stringy flesh gnawed away by starving jackals.

So far, the Cimmerian had been fortunate enough not to meet any survivors. Thus he was spared the difficult choice between depleting his own reserve of water and putting the maddened supplicants out of their misery. He dreaded such encounters as a cruel, unmanly sort of battle—just one more of the many reasons he had intended to wait in Qjara for a plush northward caravan. One with plenty of extra stock, basket-covered carboys of wine, and possibly even a share of pay or cargo due him at the end of the trek.

So much for his plans. The events that had expelled him from Qjara in defeat and disgust continued to vex his mind. For the warrior-priest Zaius to perform such a bizarre act of self-annihilation . . . why, even allowing for the peculiar beliefs of priestly fanatics in isolated desert lands, the deed hardly seemed to square with the man's arrogant, opportunistic nature. Reflecting further on it, Conan decided it must have hinged on Princess Afriandra.

But not on Zaius's love of her—for the stiff-necked temple fighter seemed incapable of love as another man would experience it. Rather, it must have stemmed from his entitlement and possession of her, and the promise that had been made by her parents of marriage into the royal family and eventual kingship.

Intensely ambitious, Zaius had nerved and honed himself to assume that highly public office, and practically laid claim to the role already. But on seeing that Afriandra would never submit to him—in particular on finding her in Conan's arms, and realizing that she would cling to and even flaunt the freedoms granted by her long lineage of kings and independent-minded priestesses—he had come to dread the union. He foresaw and feared the public humiliation that would inevitably follow, when word of her sexual and political independence became the meat of gossip.

In spite of his lifelong submission to a female god, Conan guessed—or perhaps because of it—Zaius could never force himself to bow to a woman as his superior, or even his equal in everyday life. Nor would his stubborn pride allow him to back down from the high destiny ordained for him. This put the templar in an impossible trap.

Fortunately—from Zaius's desperate standpoint—his priesthood and the obscure traditions of Saditha's warrior caste showed him the way out. Evidently, ritual suicide was respected and even exalted among temple warriors of old. By trading kingship for the even prouder and more public roles of martyrdom and godhood—by steeling his mind and body further, and resorting to a peculiarly apt form of physical discipline—the temple champion had salvaged his pride, which was after all more sacred to him than life itself.

These things Conan had vaguely sensed about Zaius; his fate was not, in hindsight, so unaccountable. What rankled the northerner more was the fatuous, sheeplike reaction of the people of Qjara. It was a city he had loved—at least well enough to hold himself back from it—and had ultimately fought and bled for. He had risked greatly for the sake of its royal family; he had even considered biding there—fleetingly considered it, anyway, while entwined in the supple limbs of its fair young princess. There lay the rub: Afriandra's reaction, above all, struck Conan as supremely unfair.

The folk of Qjara having been gulled by Zaius for years, with the formidable help of his high priestess, it was no surprise that they should fall for his final, outrageous imposture—carried out as it was under the guise of a just and solemn rite—nor that they should exalt him to heaven at the expense of a foreigner. Conan accepted all this, knowing the blinkered dullness of tame civilized folk.

But Afriandra had seen through Zaius, or claimed to; she even viewed the high priestess Regula with a daughter's skepticism. She first drew Conan into palace intrigues as a tool to shape her own future and her dynasty's; then, when faced with the bloody consequences of her scheming, she joined the hue and cry of denunciation against him. That, to Conan, seemed at best thoughtless and at worst cynical, when a word or sign from her, even in secret, might have made him more inclined to linger and defend his reputation. She could at least have sent him on his way more tranquilly.

Of course there was nothing new about it. Here he was for what seemed the hundredth time, embarked on a grueling and dangerous journey because of a female. Whether trudging toward a woman, or off on a quest decreed by one, or fleeing one's jealous wrath, the way was always hard.

And now, because of the blighted oasis, his camel lacked the reserves of moisture and stamina needed to face the steeps of the Desperation range. He knew the animal must first be allowed to rest and replenish itself at a well-watered camp.

Rather than turning back to Qjara, where he was unwanted, Conan chose to seek out a more westerly watering place he had heard whispers of—called by the nomads Tal'ib, or the City in the Waste. The site, though said to be a reliable source of water, was shunned as a topic of gossip by the desert riders he had diced with in Qjara's caravan quarter. Either they wished to give the place an ill repute to keep others away, or else they genuinely feared it.

The latter motive seemed more likely. If they wanted to keep strangers away, they need not mention it at all—yet rumors of water in the desert were hard to kill. On the other hand, what menace could possibly hover about the place to keep a man from the fluid he needed to survive? Wild animals, forbidding terrain, hostile tribes, all tended to be taken in stride and dealt with summarily if they came between the tough, clannish desert riders and the free use of an oasis.

These hardy Bedouins feared only one thing: the supernatural. Reflecting on it, Conan realized that nothing else would account for their tone of dull avoidance and their mute resistance to further questioning about the City in the Waste.

Even so, he found himself guiding his camel westward across the valley's desolation. Ofttimes ill spirits guarded a charm or treasure, after all. The taste of his stock of dates and figs had not yet grown cloying to his dusty mouth; his waterskins, though lighter now, sloshed reassuringly from his saddlebows; and the unknown threat of Tal'ib was still offset in his imagination by the faint lure of some unguessed prize.

Late that afternoon a hot wind arose, rushing toward the slopes of the mountains to northward. Conan had spied what looked like the end of the valley ahead, lying under the glare of the declining sun; but now the wind raised clouds of fine dust and stinging alkali, making further travel impossible. He prepared for a gusty night. But around sunset the wind abruptly ceased, leaving the desert cool and tranquil under a canopy of black velvet spangled with countless stars.

Such nights as this would have been perfect for travel; but then it would have been too hot to rest during the day, and in either case the sun would take its merciless toll. So he lay himself down to savor the night's chill.

Next morning, toward dawn, the wind returned. This time it roared southward, brisk and icy from the mountain canyons. With it came an odd impression. It may have been just a half-delirious dream; in any case, once Conan had unrolled from his blankets, the roiling dust and darkness were too thick to permit vision. But amid the soughing of the gale, he thought he heard heavy wheels trundling and creaking, like the wagons of an army rolling past in the night.

Although the low rocky mounds marking the end of the valley looked near to hand, it took Conan the remainder of the day to reach them. Such was the way of the desert . . . where mirages, real and illusory, appeared over vast distances without warning, sending shimmering lakes and phantom cities to tempt more wayfarers to their deaths than any siren's song on the shoaling sea.

Once Conan's mount breasted the earthen slope formed by the last clotted hillocks of the Blood of Attalos range, a new prospect greeted him—one that was, if anything, more barren and desolate than the landscape he had just traversed. While the valley behind him appeared to be the bed of an ancient dead sea—which, in the sunset, swirled with the chaos of another dust-storm like the one that had started the day—the terrain ahead mirrored nothing more than the pale barrenness of a gaunt crescent moon which now leered down on it from a sky purpling to cobalt.

The plain stretched dead flat in the dimness, from the near-vertical base of the northern mountains to the scarified jaws that sustained Zhafur's Fangs in the distance. Across the waste, shards and monoliths were scattered like fragments of stone idols crushed and hurled down by a giant's hand. In the near distance, along the base of the Desolation chain, lay what looked like the ruin of a city long toppled and abandoned. And nearer yet, in the lower pediment of the mountains, spread a dark fringe of vegetation. There, where jumbled boulders choked the entry of a narrow gorge, might be water.

From the scant description he had been offered, Conan knew it must be the oasis of Tal'ib, the City in the Waste. Urging his camel toward it, he sensed that the beast approved of his choice, as it lumbered forward with a quickened gait.

Even so, as rider and mount drew up under the massive dark haunch of mountains, night overtook them. No gale blew here, mercifully. There were only a last few eerie patches of radiance as the sun lit the bellies of clouds high in the heavens.

Conan headed straight for the canyon mouth, and was not long in finding promising signs—blackish-green palm fronds glinting from crevices of jumbled stones, and soon afterward a pebbled stream splashing through the open. Finding a flat space in the mouth of the gorge, a spot safe from the overhanging cliffs and hedged in with plentiful forage for his camel, Conan gathered up dry twigs and kindled a campfire.

The city ruins—faint as they appeared, with scarcely one stone standing atop another—lay some distance downstream on the spreading plain. Conan resolved that any exploration of them could wait for daylight. This steam had obviously been the source of water for the former city; it ran down from a mountain gorge choked with rubble from landslides. There was no sign of current habitation—not even marks of visitation by caravans or herders. Yet the water ran plentiful, cool from its passage through the depths of the boulder-choked chasm. The reason for its disuse, Conan speculated, must be some dark taint of fear associated with the ancient city. By making camp so far upstream of the ruins, Conan hoped to avoid it.

A hot porridge of groats and stewed figs tasted better, or at least different, than the same ingredients eaten dry—especially when chased down with plentiful gulps of water. Thus sated, Conan lay himself down between the fire and his camel. Doubling his blankets against the chill draft that poured from the canyon, he went to sleep.

It was late, well after the fire had died and the thin shard of moon had followed the sun down in the west, that the sleeper was disturbed by furtive noises. Scratchings, these were—scuffings, and an odd, rasping whisper that stood out briefly against the mumbling of the stream.

Awake instantly, Conan made no sudden move. Grasping the hilt of his long knife beside him, he flexed first his neck and then his whole body where he lay, trying to gain a glimpse of the intruders.

Judging by the smell, they could have been sheep. He could make them out, low forms ambling toward him under furry, rumpled backs that reflected only the thinnest fringes of starlight. Conan half expected to hear baa-ing at any moment, or the scrape of cloven hooves on pebbles . . . but he did not, and there was something strangely purposeful in the way these shapes flowed into and around his camp.

Suddenly his camel was roused from its huddled sleep. Hissing and spraying angrily, it unfolded its long legs and commenced heaving itself upright. Two or three of the hunched beings were already around the beast, harrying it in a most unsheeplike way; as they strove to pull it back down to earth, the creatures straightened up into near-erect, two-legged postures.

Conan rolled from his bed, swung his heavy knife overhead and slashed the knotted halter rope, allowing the camel to lunge free of its attackers. He sprang up to face the marauders, who responded with slavering, jabbering snarls and swiftly fanned out around him.

Hunched, apelike beings they were, robed in filthy hides bound about their middles. Their musty stink wafted to Conan more sickeningly, now that it contained the scent of fear. Human they might be—in some degree, judging by their cooperation and half-verbal sputterings. It appeared, too, that under their stolen hides they were at least partly hairless. They stood armed, bearing sticks or stones and, in a few cases, the two lashed together in the form of a crude ax.

The dim outlines of the faces, where visible under their ragged, hooded robes, looked vaguely monkeyish. But in the faint starlight, the lower parts of their faces were rendered shapeless by a hideous length and profusion of teeth. These glinted at unnatural angles, protruding from their slack mouths and even from ill-healed ruptures in the skin of their cheeks and jaws.

The camel had stilted away, fending off its pursuers with savage kicks and bites; the rest of the ape-things now turned their feral attention toward Conan. In defense, he snatched up his woolen blanket, whipping it over his forearm as a makeshift shield. When several of the marauders rushed at him, he raised his muffled arm to fend off the blow of a club, kicked one in the vitals, and jabbed his blade into another, sending it reeling back clutching its side. He drove in close to the wily ax-wielder, striking the creature a stunning blow on the skull with the hilt of his knife.

The other ape-things, undeterred by his show of force, surged about him in a clutching, snarling mob. Some hurled stones with savage recklessness, striking their own fellows more than their dodging, elusive quarry. Jagged nails tore at Conan's hair and clothing, raking his skin with a clutch that felt strangely heavy and tenacious. Hideous fanged visages leered and gibbered in the starlight, blowing foul carrion breath in his face.

An ax was raised in a pale hand to strike at his head; in the dimness he sensed that the fingers wrapped around its haft were many, far too many. He struck at it with his blade, shearing through the handle and some of the fingers—but those remaining, jerked away in pain, were still more than a normal hand possessed.

Desperate blows, kicks, and slashes of his long knife bought Conan a momentary respite; yet dozens of the creatures still stalked him, the females surging in to the attack as viciously as the males.

He realized he couldn't hold them off much longer, and for once he was weary of killing. Darting low, he snatched up his waterskins and saddlebags from beside the dead fire. He took off at a run, heading downstream in the direction his camel had gone. An ape-thing loomed up to head him off in the dim light, then another; each in turn was felled by a glancing stroke of his knife. He ran clumsily, his pouches and near-empty flasks jolting and sloshing against his knees; but in a while he sensed that his attackers were far behind him.

Stopping to listen, he heard no sounds of pursuit. Occasional snarls and chitterings echoed from the camp; but around him the brushy desert and high slopes were peaceful, outlined in faint starlight.

Conan guessed that the hunched, deformed things would have difficulty overtaking him. Likely they lived in the fallen rocks up-canyon and shunned the open desert. Even so, he walked some distance in the stream, hoping to confuse them in case they were capable of tracking him by scent.

As he emerged from the looming canyon walls there was more starlight. By its glow he easily found his camel, browsing in the rich forage alongside the stream. Managing to catch the skittish beast's halter rope, he led it further away from the danger.

Having abandoned most of his food in a meal sack at camp, he scarcely felt like killing a dozen more of the ape-things to win it back. It might hold them off, in any event, for food had surely been the object of their attack. And if they were ready to devour him, humanlike as they were, then quite likely they now feasted on the remains of their own fellows whom he had slain or wounded. That, and battling over the spoils, would account for the faint shrieks and sputterings that still echoed down from the canyon.

These were no apes of any breed Conan had seen before. And if indeed their forebears had been human, they must have fallen a long way. They might be the age-old inhabitants of this ruined city, or of the savage race that destroyed it—but in his heart Conan knew that no such abject creatures could raze a city, much less raise one.

He wondered what force had laid them so low—deprived them of human wisdom and arrogance, stricken them to a shambling crouch like baboons, and rendered hideous their faces, their hands, and Crom knew what more of their anatomy. An evil sorcery, or mayhap the same power that had leveled the city?

Its ruins now spread not far ahead, glowing

palely radiant under the broad dome of starlight. Not wanting to venture too close lest he awaken some other nocturnal horror, Conan settled himself and his camel in an open space away from the stream. He used his Ilbarsi knife to hack off dry shrubs near the ground, ringing the camp with them so that it would be difficult to approach noiselessly. Then he lay down beside his camel, pillowing his head on his few remaining possessions, and sank into a fitful, wary sleep.

Chapter 12
The City in the Waste

Conan was abroad before dawn. After scouting the nearby desert, he crept upstream and paid a visit to his former camp. Circling it cautiously, he found no ape-things, living or dead; just a few chewed, bloodied pieces of his lost clothing and gear.

Now that he looked closer in the dusky light, he could see signs of the creatures' habitual presence—a trodden path here, a dried spoor or gnawed camel bone there. Turning his attention to the jumbled rocks of the upper gorge, he decided it must be the beasts' lair. The tumbled monoliths and the crawlspaces between them would make a wretched dwelling place, but at the same time a formidable one. There was no telling what might already be watching him from the weedy crevices of the pile; the thought deterred him from exploring further.

Returning downstream, he filled his water bags and fastened the scant but adequate remainder of his belongings to the back of his camel. Morning sandstorms in the eastward valley shrouded the low sun, washing the barren plain and the high slopes around it in a smoldering copper-pink light. In this eerie ambience, before the heat could rise, Conan set out to examine the ruined city.

From the brush-dotted knolls overlooking the ruin, it did not resemble any dead city Conan had ever seen. Most of these started with straggling mounds of rubble at the outskirts and rose gradually through more massive, enduring ruins toward some natural height or man-made fortress near the center. But here stood no such prominence. The ancient wall was visible, a low ridge of masonry girdling the tract in a roughly circular shape; the only sizeable mounds of rubble lay just inside it. At its center, instead of the massive walls of palace, temple, and granary one would look for in a city of any size, there stretched a level space, so flat and featureless it almost looked glazed over.

Of course, Conan reminded himself, the nearby city of Qjara had a paved open plaza at its heart, and a spacious caravan quarter within its compass. This place might reflect a similar tendency of the residents to wall in open spaces—where perhaps they dwelt in tents, nomad-fashion, or raised cattle in open kraals. Such was possible for a people as remote and time-lost as the builders of this ancient pile—yet it seemed unlikely.

The very existence and site of the place suggested a thriving agriculture. It stood at the edge of the flat, spreading valley bottom, with the ancient course of the mountain river passing through its outskirts. Around and below the city, the stream must surely have been diverted through canals to water a large expanse of orchards, pastures and grainfields outside the wall.

Now in the yellow-lit distance, only a few faint ditches remained as vestiges of cultivation. The stream, displaced by the rubble of the wall, trickled through a shallow rocky wash it had dug along one side of the ruin. Thereafter it spread in branching channels to dissipate and die in the barren, thirsty desert.

Urging his beast forward, Conan kept a watchful eye for ape-things, or worse haunters of the forsaken place. But there was little cover here, only scrubby grass and ankle-high shrubs clinging to the meagre shade of roughly squared stones. The footings and rubble mounds themselves were so low they afforded no concealment.

Along the ring of wall, Conan vaguely hoped to find an arch or a gatepost. Such a monument might identify the city; it might even display carvings or graffiti that told its history—such as, whether its former occupants were human.

But in this he was disappointed. The wall at its loftiest was less than Conan's height sitting atop his camel—and by some circumstance, its rubble all seemed to have toppled outward. The low, trailing piles were choked with dust and sand of centuries, leaving no visible sample of the stonemasonry that must, judging by its massiveness, have been skilled.

Regarding the name of the place, Conan could make a rough guess. The nomads called it Tal'ib, after all; and from his experience of eastern Shem, a tal or tel was a mound or ruin. So it could simply mean the ruins of Ib, or some such cognomen—come to think on it, in tales murmured around campfires, had he not heard whispers of an ancient city named Ib? Or more properly, Yb, pronounced with the sneering southern inflection. An accursed place, according to legend, stricken by the hand of an angry god for its sinful, faithless ways. If any place fit that description, this was it. On seeing a path of clotted rubble over the hummock of city wall, Conan dismounted and led his camel across.

He was surprised to find the inner face of the wall in a somewhat less ruined state. Here, vertical surfaces of finished stone stood to the height of a man. Here, too, were the intact remnants of stone carving Conan sought, though not resembling any frieze or relief he had ever seen.

The surviving decorations were human figures carved in a graceful, natural-looking style—so natural, indeed, that they gave Conan a shiver of surprise. They were human, undeniably: ordinary townfolk engaged in dance or stylized ritual. There was a young woman clad in a loose chiton; her arms were raised, her hands poised before her face in an attitude of frolic or worship. From a short distance away a robed man leaned toward her, reaching to embrace her in play or dance. At her feet, a small dog leaped with two of its paws in the air. A few paces further a child paused at play, seated on the ground, hands likewise raised to its face.

The shapes, even as eroded by centuries on the worn, square-jointed stonework, were vivid and natural. Obviously they were carved by the hand of a highly skilled artisan. What seemed strange was that they were mere outlines, flat silhouettes lacking any fuller embellishment of faces, costumes, or even the completion of limbs where they overlapped the bodies. To Conan it almost seemed that shadows of living people might have been traced on the wall with chalk, then immortalized there with hammer and chisel; but this idea was disproved, on further reflection, by the leaping positions of man and dog, whose fluid motions could never have been traced so quickly and unerringly by human hands.

No, undeniably it was the work of a master craftsman, transcribing from keen memory, then engraving his sketch with finely-honed skill. As for the details, such as faces—likely these had once been painted onto the carved outlines, or sculpted into soft mortar that had since worn away without a trace.

The only further peculiarity was that, rather than chiseling his design into the stone wall, the sculptor had let his figures stand out in deep, uniform relief, cutting away instead all the surrounding space representing open air.

This was unaccountable to Conan, because it involved so much more work—that of chipping away the broad and, to his eye, wasted stone surface around the figures. In any reliefs he had seen before, there would have been more objects: suns and moons, dragons, or graven mottos to fill in the space and save the workers' thews and chisel-points.

In all, this was a form of expression Conan was unused to . . . and like any great art, it bordered uncomfortably on sorcery. Turning from it in the smoldering light, he led his camel away. Try to shrug it off as he might, some part of his primitive soul was secretly convinced that he had viewed mortal spirits frozen forever by a magic spell, their living shadows burned eternally into dead stone.

Moving on past the wall, it was easy to believe in such curses; for here the city itself seemed to have been burned away to nothingness. No vegetation grew within its ragged perimeter, and what foundations remained were little more than knee-high, giving the impression of having been scorched or blasted by some tremendous force; the fire that accompanied the fall of the city must have been intense. A few remnants standing toward the city's center were fused, hanging down in crusts of ashy-dark slag, or frothed with brittle glass bubbles like the waste of a kiln. Where intact, the stoutest thresholds and cornerstones yet flaked away their substance at Conan's touch, or at the idle scuff of his sandaled foot.

A little further, and even these frail remnants

were passed; the site stretched away in a hard, stony-smooth depression that seemed to merge with the featureless desert beyond. There was but one exception: near what seemed to be the center of the devastation a lone monument stood, a jagged monolith. Toward it, across the almost-slippery black glass, Conan led his camel. His shadow and the beast's were long and spectral in the eerie pinkish light, and the stone's stretched an equal length, pointing westward like the finger of a sundial.

Arriving at its base, he saw that it rested atop the slaty ground. It must have been hewn roughly to shape, dragged here and set upright some time after the city's fall; otherwise it could hardly have survived the comprehensive destruction that leveled all else.

The obelisk bore a single inscription: not words, but a figure. It was that of a tree, or something resembling one, with twisted roots and a thick, straight trunk. Its wavy branches bore not foliage, but a number of round, bulbous fruits. These were seamed and gnarled, possibly meant to have human faces or mouths, it was hard to tell. The symbol was deeply etched, and whitened to stand out against the black stone of the monolith.

Was it done by taloned, apelike hands, Conan wondered—hands gifted with an unnatural surplus of fingers? It hardly seemed possible, in view of the fineness of the task, not to mention the cutting, hauling, and raising of the stone.

The petroglyph was evidently some kind of religious symbol, possibly that of the ancient city's god. As such it made Conan uneasy, and he turned away from it. Commanding his camel to kneel, he climbed onto the brute's back and urged it westward, in search of an unchoked pass through the Mountains of Desperation.

The ruins of Yb, it such they were, soon lay well behind. As the sun rose hot on Conan's back and the cryptic dark flank of mountains unfolded before him, the mystery of the city's doom faded in his mind. This first canyon looked too shallow to pierce through the mountain chain, he decided; that one ahead could prove more promising, once the view opened out a little more. . . .

And yet, before he had found a route that looked passable for himself and his plodding beast, a new distraction arose. Away across the desert, vanishing and reappearing from moment to moment in the shimmering heat, he spied a procession. Afoot, they appeared to be, but grouped around a central object or vehicle that served as the focus of their efforts. Conan hoped at first that they were a northbound caravan; but their route, it soon became clear, bore eastward through the valley, opposite to his own. In any case, their slow pace and the size of their burden made it unlikely that they meant to tackle the northern mountains.

Whoever they were, they did not look dangerous. He approached them openly with the eager, involuntary elation any lone traveler feels at the chance to meet and talk with his fellow humans. If nothing else, he told himself, they might let him expend the small remainder of his money to replace some of his missing food and gear. And yet, as he drew nearer, he began to see that they were in far worse shape than he was.

They were bent and starved, for one thing, burnt scarlet or scabbed black where their ragged, filthy clothing furnished incomplete protection against the fierce sun. Some toiled barefoot over the hot, glaring alkali; others were bareheaded, their scalps so badly scorched that only a few straggling wisps of hair remained to shade them. The bulk of the unfortunates, twoscore or more, toiled at ropes and levers to trundle forward a heavy six-wheeled conveyance.

The wheels were of thick rounded planks, paired in caissons made fast to a long, unwieldy, shrouded bundle. A scant dozen guards walked free, though themselves heavily burdened with food sacks and dry, stiff waterskins. Among the whole party there were no pack or saddle animals; camels, in any case, would never have let themselves be harnessed together as draft animals, and horses would not have survived. The ferrying of such a massive burden across the desert required human drays, nothing less.

As Conan's camel bore him into earshot, the piteous pleas of the toilers could be heard, rasping forth from parched throats via lips split and husked thickly with thirst. "Water, fine sir! In the name of the Almighty One, a sip of water, please Milord, or a rind of fruit! We thirst, O

Master, we die! Show mercy on us, we beg you!" As he halted his camel some dozen paces from the procession, the pilgrims let their wheeled burden rumble to a halt, sinking to their knees with exhaustion and raising their arms in feeble supplication.

Here, then, was the situation he had feared—and yet by Crom's grace he had a full stock of water, enough to soothe the thirst of each and every sufferer, if only temporarily. Untying his water bags—all but a half-empty one for himself—he lowered them to the ground beside his camel.

One of the party, a tall, thin black man who had walked ahead of the others, came forward to meet him. He did not cringe or beg, but walked with the air of a leader—a priest, Conan guessed to himself. Two of the armed guards, moving as fast as their obvious fatigue would allow, came forward to flank him.

"Greetings, wayfarers," Conan called down to them. "You can share out my water, since you are in such dire need of it." He waited in vain for some expression of thanks. "A goodly source of water lies but a day's walk from here," he essayed again. "With luck, all of your party can make it."

The priest looked from the water bags to Conan. He spoke in the desert trade dialect, southern-accented. "The water will help," he said with an odd flatness of intonation. "You say there are springs between here and Qjara?"

Something about the man's question vexed Conan—as if he did not know the distance involved, or the number of oases, and did not care to. He must indeed by a priest, trusting his own life and those of his hapless followers to the whims of a fickle god. He was barefoot and hatless, his clothing just as scant and ragged as that of his flock—a zealot, no doubt. Conan had never before seen a black man whose skin was sun-scorched and peeling. The only token of rank he wore was the old, corroded hilt of a knife, dangling from a thong around his neck. A useless weapon, its blade a mere rusted stub; it must be a holy relic, Conan decided.

Impressively, the southerner made not the slightest move toward the water. Now, at a nod of his head, the guards took up the water bags and bore them back toward the waiting sufferers.

"No, stranger," Conan finally rasped to him, "there are not nearly enough springs to water you to Qjara. The Stork Wadi is dry, strewn with the bones of fools who staked their lives on it. Yon dead city—" he jerked his head back toward the simmering east—"is abrim with water, but haunted by demon-apes who devour wayfarers. I must needs return there now, to replenish myself—I would suggest that you do the same. Rest and fill yourselves there, but keep careful watch—and then head back to wherever you came from."

The black priest did not shake his head, did not even blink. "We shall continue to Qjara."

Conan shrugged impatiently. "Very well, then, if you think your people can bear the hardship. Rest up first, travel late and early, and lie under canopies at highest noon. Of course, you will not be able to drag this ... whatever it is." He waved at the shrouded, wheeled behemoth in the toilers' midst. "You may as well abandon it right here."

"It is a sacred object; we shall bring it along with us," the priest declared flatly. "Tell me ... you seem to know the desert, and the road to eastward. What is your name?"

"Conan, of Cimmeria. And yours?"

"I am Khumanos, Exalted Priest of the Temple of Votantha, from the city of Sark in the southern desert. I find myself in need of a scout. Do you know Qjara?"

Conan sat cagily atop his camel. "Indeed, Khumanos, I am fresh from there. I know the place and know aught of your mission, as well. But now I am bound for Shadizar." He shook his head in grave dubiety. "Impoverished as you are, I hardly think you can make it worth my while to guide you back the long, weary way I have already come—"

"Why did you leave Qjara, Conan of Cimmeria?"

"I told you, I am headed north." Swallowing the obvious question of why he was so far west of the city instead, he continued, "I was unable to wait and join a caravan because of some peculiar business involving a priest of their local goddess. Sheer nonsense, I trow! By a fluke of their temple law I was bidden to leave, and my pride would not let me do otherwise—"

"Enough. Sergeant Astrak ..." Without taking his eyes from Conan, Khumanos snapped two fingers back over his shoulder toward his followers. A stout, helmeted man, carrying dusty canvas bags counterbalanced across both shoulders, detached himself from the mob near the water bottles and jogged forward. "The gems," the priest specified as he arrived.

Fumbling in one of his sacks, the sergeant produced a wooden casket. After turning the latch he cracked it open—to reveal its bright silver-lined interior, heaped with roughly formed jewels that blazed greenly in the piercing daylight.

"Ahem," Conan hedged, trying not to seem overly impressed, "I never saw such stones before. I suppose you mean to tell me they are of some value—"

"All the jewels you can grasp in one hand," Khumanos interrupted him. "That will be your reward, once you see this idol safely into Qjara." At a nod of the exalted priest's shaven head, the soldier snapped the casket shut and returned it to the sack.

"Well, now," Conan reasoned aloud. "If I come as your guide, the pedants of the One True Goddess can hardly turn me away."

Khumanos regarded him evenly. "You will be an envoy in the pay of King Anaximander of Sark, a servant of the Temple of Votantha. Your place is assured by a solemn compact made between the kings of Sark and Qjara."

"I see." Serene in his place atop the camel, Conan felt in no hurry to accept. Certainly this was no shining opportunity, helping yet another arrogant priest and his miserable herd manhandle their holy fetish across this infernal waste, with gems of unproven value as the prize. Yet, on the other hand, he could hardly relish the prospect of a lone trek over these barren mountains with inadequate food, clothing, and bedding. However wretched this band might be, they would certainly fare better with his help than under this Khumanos's heedless captaincy. From their standpoint it would be a kindness, an act of mercy—at the end of which, if he still chose to, he could refit, find a proper caravan, and travel north to Shadizar in style.

At the root of it all, he sensed, was a strange hankering to return to Qjara. Something told him he was not through with that proud city yet. "All right, then," he answered Khumanos at last, "we head eastward."

Chapter 13
The Stone Ship

It would have been hard for Conan to foresee how slowly the bearers of the great idol moved. They toiled doggedly, patiently, as if numb to their labor from long hardship. It was unclear to him whether these were willing pilgrims or slaves, and he was not sure he wanted to know. Many had perished along the way, certainly; their places had been filled in by helmeted Sarkad troopers who now, instead of wielding the rod, sweated under it.

Those men, the troopers, were by far the strongest physical specimens, setting a hard pace for the frailer ones to sustain. The band toiled silently, without ribald banter or the hymns and chanties Conan would have expected to hear. Even when idle they kept silent, glowering as if the very souls within them had been killed by pain and hardship.

All bore grisly burns and sores, even the guards who wore adequate uniforms and carried only shoulder-burdens—indeed, Conan was beginning to doubt whether these blemishes were truly from the sun. He had never seen such deformities or experienced them himself, even from the severest exposure; now he misdoubted whether the rashes, weals and other plagues the worker suffered, such as the widespread loss of teeth and hair, might not be from some other cause—from starvation, or bad water imbibed in the southern desert, mayhap even from poison soils they had wrestled their massive burden through. At worst it might stem from some ill sorcery, possibly relating to their harsh lord Votantha or his godly enemies.

In any event, their path was grueling. On that first day Conan met the party, they did not reach Tal'ib. They halted in barren desert, sinking to earth under the wheels of their juggernaut, barely stirring from where they lay. To alleviate their suffering, Conan carried empty water bags ahead on his camel, filled them from the stream, and rode back to furnish the party with water for the next day.

When at last they reached the City in the Waste, they camped well down the stream's course, near its junction with the ruined wall. Conan was careful to have Khumanos assign sentries, though he ended up standing most of the watches himself. Once or twice he thought he heard stealthy sounds or saw a flicker of movement in the brush. But he hoped the ape-things would never learn of the camp, or at least not venture downstream in force to attack it.

He was affected by the eeriness of the scene—the frail moon listing like a sinking coracle in the west, its light gleaming across the wan desolation as over a dead-calm sea. Mountains loomed vast and formless on the one hand, fanglike and remote on the other; around the fireless camp, the litter of slack bodies might have been asleep or dead in the haunted dark. The shrouded, supine idol in their midst resembled the twisted, ill-preserved corpse of a giant on its funeral caisson. Now, in the wan glow of stars and moon, it seemed to give off a light of its own—the greenish luminosity of decay creeping beneath its matted, filthy winding-cloth.

Behind them, across the listless, dying stream and blasted wall, lay the shallow depression that had once been mighty Yb—the hard, glassy cauldron that had brewed the death of a city.

Conan heard a rustle of motion—distinct this time, and close at hand. Turning, he stuck out his blade—and almost hewed into the tall, silent form of Khumanos, looming black against deeper blackness.

Muttering an oath, Conan returned the weapon to his belt and eased back down onto his haunches. "By Crom, priest, did you mean to test my wakefulness? You almost tested the keenness of my knife as well! Do you never sleep?"

Khumanos squatted down opposite Conan. "You are a swift fighter, wary and vigilant."

"Yes. I should hope to be, when two nights agone I was set on by fanged, slavering cannibals not far from where we sit!" A moment later, the Cimmerian shrugged off his unease. "Even so, I think we are safe here from the monsters. I urge you to have your followers remain a day or two—rest, bathe in the stream, and restore your strength."

"We will continue onward tomorrow at first light." Khumanos said, not shaking his head or refuting Conan in any direct way. He eased down on to the ground where the fire would have been, if there had been a fire.

"That would be unduly hard on your people, Khumanos," Conan argued. "They will go faster in the long run if they rest now, and will have a better chance of surviving to the journey's end."

"With great Votantha's help we shall endure," the priest said with finality. "In the southern wastes we became lost in a sandstorm and wandered far from our path. There we were set on by nomads, who slew many of our guards before we drove them back. Other guards have had to take the place of our fallen bearers. Even so, we have found our way this far."

"A hellish bad journey," Conan observed. "It sounds as if your almighty lord were testing your mettle."

Gravely Khumanos nodded his shaven head. "For some, the hardship is too extreme. They cannot bear it." He held the rusted dagger-stub away from his chest, examining it in the moonlight. Then he unlooped it from his neck, clutching it before him in one hand as if it were a divining rod or holy wand. "They would rather perish inside, feel nothing at all, than face the the degradation of their bodies and the failure of their hopes—or even witness it in others." He looked questioningly to Conan.

"I, for one, would never seek to die—I cannot understand a man who would." His eyes and lips narrowed as his thoughts ran back to Zaius. "For me, while there is breath left in my body and blood in my veins, there is always hope." He exhaled the moment's melancholy. "What is that rusty relic you are playing with, anyway, Khumanos?" he asked the priest. "A remnant of the blade that killed your hoary god's grandfather?"

"This, the Sword of Onothimantos?" the priest asked, holding up the object. "It is a powerful talisman, bequeathed to me by a wise elder. It has changed my life."

"A symbol of your faith, no doubt. But as for this holy quest you are on, to glorify your god—" Conan's keen eyes fixed the watchful Khumanos—"I say it is a fool's errand, a bout of needless suffering you foist on your brainless followers. So do not bother to try and convert me to your beliefs. I would never take a hand in such folly—"

"—Were it not for the pay I promised you," Khumanos supplied for him.

"Nay. Not even for pay, if I did not have my

own private reasons to come along." Conan finished with a shake of his head.

"You have a strong, independent soul that resists suasion and control." The priest was weighing the stump of his amulet-knife in one hand.

"Aye, 'tis so. That is why you find me alone in the middle of this infernal waste."

"Indeed." Khumanos nodded thoughtfully. "Your stubborn, wary spirit makes you a fierce fighter and a cunning desert hand."

"Yes—which is why I am of use to you." Conan gazed quizzically and a little dangerously at the priest. "Why—did you expect a spineless, simpering toady instead? Just what are you worrying at?"

"Nay, nothing. It is Votantha's will." Looping his amulet around his neck, the Exalted Priest tucked it out of sight in his burnoose. Then he arose to make his way back toward his sleeping place.

"Well, then . . . good night to you, too," Conan said to Khumanos's back, wondering just what the interview had been about.

Later that night there was one further alarm, when Conan spied a figure roving the barrens across the stream, in the leveled city. A tall, lean figure, dark-clad against the chalky-pale waste—surely it was Khumanos again! Striding over to the priest's bed, Conan found that, surely enough, the tattered blanket was empty.

But what was he doing so far from safety, recklessly alone? Conan started after him, then stopped. He gathered breath to shout, but thought better of it. The robed priest went at a brisk walk, going steadily toward the monolith in the middle of the barren zone.

Khumanos reached the pillar, slowed, and circled it, halting at the side where Conan remembered seeing the carving of the many-headed tree. Likely the rune was visible in the pale starlight reflecting off the hard, glassy ground. The priest bent before the pillar, as if to look closer. Then—Conan swore he was not mistaken—Khumanos knelt before the monolith, bowing his head to the ground as if in abject worship.

A shiver plucked at Conan's shoulder blades while he watched. An ill thing, this seemed—but then, what did it really mean? Was the sarsen-stone still regarded by pilgrims as a holy place? Perhaps he could learn more from Khumanos concerning the fate of this ancient city. He vowed to corner the priest and ask him at the first opportunity—but not tonight.

Early next morning, true to Khumanos's word, the procession was under way again, toiling over the low, blood-caked hills that separated the valley barrens from the dead sea floor. The band made the crossing under the day's most intense sun; during the worst of it, Conan dismounted from his camel and lent a reluctant shoulder first to the rigorous uphill push, then to restraining the triple caisson from rolling too precipitously down the farther slope.

The idol was even heavier and more unwieldy

than he could have anticipated; its dusty, shrouded bulk had a way of collecting and radiating back the desert heat; and on top of it all, it steered badly. Even so, the descent was managed successfully, with only one man's back crushed under the groaning wheels. Once they descended to the hard alkali floor of the ancient sea, the way was clear; with no detour for water necessary or possible, the track lay straight ahead, toward the notch between the red mountain range and the black one.

Travel continued until sunset, when a blinding alkali storm blew up. Then the laborers crawled beneath their idol to gnaw a sparse dinner and sip their meager ration of water. Conan, feeling less than gregarious, huddled in the lee of his camel. Covering his face against the rolling curtains of stinging grit, he dozed and dreamt once again of racing chariot wheels.

Several times during the night he arose to gaze out on the desert, windless now, stretching white beneath a velvet canopy pricked by clear, cold stars. It was peaceful, deathly still. But by dawn's faint light the demon-winds lashed up again, predictably, shrouding the world in a fuming pall of alkali dust. With their fury came yet again the eerie creak of wooden wheels.

This time the wheels rattled closer at hand. Conan flinched and his camel snorted in outrage as a huge, rumbling shape hurtled past in the gale. The northerner's first thought was that one of the caissons had broken loose—but that was impossible; in any case, the wheel that nearly grazed him had been finely crafted, spoked, with metal rims.

Was his wretched party under attack in the storm? If so, by what manner of inhuman warriors? As he squinted through tear-streaming eyes, another dim shape loomed up in the swirling dust.

Snatching up his knife and, through long habit, a water bottle, Conan rolled to his feet. He crouched and leaped, hurling himself over the rail of the chariot as it bounded past. He would learn the mystery of these phantom raiders or die trying.

The driver at the reins needed no killing. He was already dead—a leathern, grinning mummy in pitted armor, bound to the rail of the teamless car by his tangled rawhide traces. Overhead, a tattered sheepskin canopy caught the gale; it filled like a lateen sail, lashing the vehicle onward. The remains of the horses, and possibly of one or two passengers, rattled below in the dust; a tangle of harness, frayed hide, and worn old bones were all that depended from the chariot-tongue.

The long pole, meant to be yoked to the horses' necks, curved down smoothly under the fighting-platform and emerged at the chariot's rear in the form of a bronze-sheathed runner to keep the car from tipping over backward. Teamless now, the platform teetered between the tongue and the rear skid, which acted as a rudder. It was the wind and no other earthly force that propelled the car on its driverless course.

Here, then, was the phantom chariot told of in local legend. Conan only half-remembered the story; he had thought it a prank to be foisted on raw hands in the caravan trade, a lurid myth intended to widen eyes and vex dreams around dying campfires. . . . But the next moment, brittle planks gave way underfoot; Conan, with his legs tangled in the harness trailing under the car, was forced to cling and struggle to regain his footing and keep from being dragged with the desiccated remains behind the hurtling car.

The story of the phantom chariot was an obscure one; but now Conan remembered that young Jabed had recited a version of it in the camp outside Qjara. Some twoscore years previously, so the boy had prattled, in the reign of King Semiarchos's father Demiarchos, the old king's younger brother Pronathos had set out on an expedition to enhance his family's wealth and his city's glory. With a hundred men-at-arms, assorted camels, horses, chariots and supply wagons, brave Pronathos rode off in search of the legendary Stone Ship, an unimaginably ancient vessel that was fabled to lie in a remote reach of desert, laden to its stone gunwales with golden coins, weapons and armor.

An apocryphal story this, even less plausible than the phantom chariot tale itself, and only half-believed by the cultured citizens of Qjara. But in a desert outpost lacking near neighbors and foreign wars to occupy them, the hardy youth of the town were ever prey to such boisterous escapades, as they were to the violent lure of becoming temple warriors.

So Pronathos and his hundred explorers rode off into legend. A fortnight after their departure a fierce dust storm blew up, blanketing the eastern desert for days and wiping out any trace of their passage. The expedition was never heard from again; nor was any evidence of their fate brought back with the searching parties dispatched by the grieving king.

But in later years, it began to be whispered in Bedouin tents that the souls of the treasure-seekers had been captured by the storm, and now sought to lure other adventurers to share their doom. It was murmured that, during the fierce, flukish winds that so often raged through certain desert valleys at dusk and dawn, the faint creaking of chariot wheels could be heard. These, it was said, were the riders and wagons of Pronathos's lost troop; hounded by gold-lust and the curse of the desert gods, they still combed the waste for the fabled treasure of the Stone Ship, all in vain.

But here, as Conan could intimately tell from the splintered wood he so desperately clutched, and the racing wheels that rumbled and slewed on either side of him—here was the true source of the legend. The chariots and wagons of Pronathos's band, driven like leaves before a gale and still carrying the grisly remains of their passengers, roamed the desert yet. By some strange whim of the gods the wagons regularly traversed the flat, dead sea—rolling forth at dusk, back at dawn with the freakish but predictable winds, shuttling to and fro on a cosmic errand no human mind could hope to understand.

And the wilted skeleton on this fine old chariot—whom Conan clutched next to him with brotherly closeness as he clung to the vehicle's sparse, rattling frame—was it the lich of old Pronathos himself? The remaining crusts of silver inlay on the corpse's split, flaking armor seemed to suggest so. Seeing this, Conan mumbled a respectful greeting and tried to afford the venerable commander more room at the chariot rail.

Knowing all this—or rather, surmising it as he strove to keep his balance on the wildly veering car—Conan was faced with a decision: whether to cling to his perch, or whether to fling himself off onto the desert floor, to find his way back to the camp in the blinding storm. He could jump clear, he judged, without great risk of bodily harm—providing that another vehicle in the ghostly caravan did not loom out of the haze to trundle him flat. Quite likely, once the wind abated, he could walk back to find his camel and him employer's band. The water bottle that dangled beside him, pinned to a crevice of the chariot with his Ilbarsi knife, promised him a day or two's survival.

Even so, holding tight to the rail, he experienced a sense of velocity and surging adventure. Here was the key to a riddle that had vexed the desert folk for generations. He felt compelled to see the mystery through to its source. If at the end of it lay a reward from King Semiarchos—or, as the legends hinted, a fabulous treasure—why, so much the better! For this one mad moment, it was the lure of adventure that drew him.

Actually, as he had learned at sea, flying before the wind was easier than facing its fury with one's feet solidly rooted on land. Its force seemed gentler and less parching, and it did not tug so fiercely at the cowl and skirts of his cloak. Overhead the chariot's ragged canopy belled and shivered occasionally, but did not flutter in the gale; and around him the dust, which ground like a harsh torrent over desert wanderers, ghosted forward with him in tall, graceful curtains shot through with fleeting sunbeams. Only rarely did these vapors part enough to show him the dim outline of other vehicles in the train—such as, straight ahead, the high, swaying wagon that had first rolled so near him. But as he listened from moment to moment, catching on different sides the creak of wheels in varying notes, he sensed he was part of a swift and numerous host.

The mad race thundered on for the better part of an hour—southward, to Conan's judgment—before the wind showed any sign of abating. Then, abruptly, it ended. The wheels beneath him slowed and creaked to a halt; dust clouds melted and settled to earth like dying ghosts, leaving him in the midst of an eerie landscape.

It was a remote, untraveled canyon of the Blood of Attalos mountains. On all sides the hills ran down red, their color sanguine above the bony white of the dead sea floor. To the rear, the hills merged anonymously together, their slopes artfully overlapping to conceal the entry to this blind inlet; ahead, the tallest peaks of the range heaped up gorily to the sky. Around him, a fleet of derelict wagons and chariots stood bleaching in the sun. And a little beyond them, embayed in the broad inlet formed by the blood-red hills, rose a jagged stone outcrop in the rough form of a ship.

Here, then, was the ghost caravan of Pronathos—a half-score sturdily built vehicles, decrepit now and rubbed bare of paint and gilt by desert winds, with pennants and awnings dangling in gray tatters and festoons, yet still capable of thundering through the desert on the wings of a gale and striking fear into the hearts of camel-drovers. Stepping down from his own chariot—which had stopped a hundred paces short of the others, probably because of the extra burden of his own weight—and taking up his knife and waterskin, he trudged to the others and looked into them one by one.

Some few of them contained mortal remains—armored skeletons still huddled where they had died, trying, presumably, to ride out the ferocity of that first great dust storm. Little else they contained; the wagon-bottoms were stove in with age, and all the sacking and harnesses trailed loose, dragged behind along with the bones of oxen and asses. The vehicles were reduced to mere trundling skeletons of their former selves—made light and bare as if by supernatural design, to fly before the demon-winds.

And yet here, if only in death, they seemed to have found their goal—for the rock outcrop ahead, from its odd, fortuitous shape, could scarcely be anything but the Stone Ship of fable. Its prow reared high and sharp, a jutting wedge formed by layered sheaves of frothy, porous rock. Its gunwales sloped back about the length of a Turanian trireme, falling away at last to merge with the white-rimed soil near the stern. Even the stub of a mast was visible, along with herringbone ridges down the side that could have been oars—in all, a most astonishing mimicry in natural stone of a seagoing vessel founded in quaint, antique style.

And yet, Conan decided, it could hardly have been a deliberate sculpture by the hand of man—for the adornments were too wild, with stone ridges and spires too wavy and fanciful to imitate any true vessel. It was as if the rough form of a ship had been laid down first, then frosted and embellished by a whimsical titan working in liquid stone, to create a shape that rose elfin and ornate even before the assault of countless years of gritty desert winds.

Picking his way toward it, Conan was bemused by certain debris he saw jutting from the soil—bones, scraps of armor, the frame and wheel of a broken chariot. These proved to him that the expedition had, after all, found its way to this spot before meeting with extinction. A cruel irony it was indeed, if before dying they had found their goal, perhaps even seen the treasure it was said to contain. . . . Fired by these thoughts, Conan hastened his steps. He bounded up the final slope toward the stone monument, vaulted to the rail and cast his eyes within.

He trod the stern of a true ship, of this he was sure. Stony and ancient as it was, and frosted and filigreed as well, the layout of the deck was unmistakable. Transom and tiller, windlass and oar-bench, all were disposed efficiently enough to set to sea on the first tide. A desert-bred man might have been uncertain about such things, but not Conan, with his experience on far-flung oceans. As he climbed the shallowly listing angle of the deck, an explanation came to him which, if bizarre, was at least possible.

This desert basin was most certainly an ancient sea; from where he stood, gazing out over the crumbling rail, he could see faint lines and shelves high up on the slopes of the red hills. These, to his mind, represented the sea's former waterlines and beaches, in times far past living memory. Since the valley had been a sea, he had to assume it had sailors, too—whether of the human breed or of an older race it scarcely mattered, for in any case the demands of shipbuilding would have been much the same. Judging from the look of the craft, its sailors must have been man-sized and fairly skilled in the ways of the sea.

But even the most skillful sailors occasionally lose a ship—and that was where he now stood, on the deck of a ship sunk in some prehistoric gale or battle—an oared ship, by the look of it, possibly a man of war, with a complement of some two hundred men, or pre-men. Gazing closely at the oar-benches, he almost imagined he could see ancient bones protruding from the yellowish stone—was that a claw-curled hand there, and the bowl of a skull, brown and gnarled like an old bread crust . . . ? If such they were, they were half-embedded and half worn away, the stone encroaching mercifully to obscure their shapes. . . .

The stone, the growing, enfolding stone, that was the key. Gazing about him, he knew now that the jagged, frothy stuff was coral. For, in the warm, shallow reaches of the Vilayet, had he not seen even objects shaped by man in recent years—anchor-stones, amphorae and the keels of scuttled vessels—encrusted and cemented firmly to the bottom by hungry, swift-growing coral?

Such was the case here, most obviously. This ancient ship had foundered, to become the crown of a coral reef that grew up around it. In time the living stone filled in the hollows of the rotting timbers, until nothing remained but a ship's living statue. Then, when the sea melted away, the hard, obdurate coral outlived it, enduring over centuries or eons to the present day. A prank of the gods, indeed, Conan thought—one to make the legend of the phantom chariots seem like the most fleeting, transient jest!

Coming to the midships part of the vessel, Conan drew a further conclusion: whatever cargo the stone ship may have contained, Pronathos's men had found and rifled. For here, in the broadest, deepest part of the hull, an excavation had been made in recent years. Coral timbers had been cut and hacked away, opening an oblong cavity whose size was not explained by the small amount of stony debris that lay about. Vacancy now yawned down to the bed of hard, round pebbles that Conan easily recognized as ballast-stones.

As to the fate of the treasure, a glance around the derelict provided no clue. It might have been buried elsewhere for safekeeping; or again, it might have been carted any distance on the finders' ill-fated journey into the desert. There stood the great wagons, four surviving ones standing tall and sturdy, their rent sheepskin canopies hanging slack in the scorching stillness. The staved-in boards of their beds seemed to imply that their loads could have been dropped anywhere in the waste—and if it was heavy gold, why, belike it still remained there in the dust, waiting to be found by some half-mad desert rider . . . who would think it a mirage, most likely, or go the rest of the way mad with excitement.

Jape upon jape, irony piled on irony—the gods were in a droll mood today! Conan strode onward and upward, meaning to take in the view from the ship's bow. It rose high above the desert, ending in a jagged, coral-webbed fragment of jib.

Stepping onto the broad expanse of the foredeck, he imagined that the rough, crusted planking resounded hollowly under his weight. Breathing the parched air, he scanned the vast, desolate canyon around him for any glint of yellow metal. Then came a sharp, grating crack; the hoary planks yielded underfoot, and the lone explorer plunged into darkness.

Late the following day, at a point not much further along their route, the solemn procession of Exalted Priest Khumanos was joined by a cloaked, hooded wanderer. It was their scout Conan, returning from his unexplained foray in the desert. Having traveled all night and day, and the last dozen hours of his trek without water, he moved heavily to their eyes, swaying as he walked and evidently near to collapse.

Khumanos did not question him, and he volunteered nothing of his adventure; but he drank greedily and seemed happy to regain his camel, food, and blankets. One night's rest, even with the howling windstorms, seemed enough to restore him. By early next morning he had set out again to the oasis of Tal'ib to draw more water for their party's trek to Qjara.

CHAPTER 14
Convocation

In the shimmering heat of desert noon a lone rider approached the walls of Qjara. His mount was in good trim, but heavily laden; the rider himself was a tall, massive man. The muscles of his broad shoulders rippled under sun-bronzed, sweat-sheened skin as he hauled the beast out of its smooth, loping run. He reined it to a halt before the caravan gate.

"It is the outcast heretic Conan!" the guard before the gate called immediately to his fellows atop the wall. His announcement brought down their derisive laughter.

"Well," he then demanded of the traveler, "what do you want here, northling? Was our eastern desert too harsh for you?" The gatekeeper's courage was evidently pricked to the fore by the lances and barbed arrows of the city guards on the wall above him. "If it's drink you want, now," he ventured, "there is water aplenty in yon river! And if you need a place to rest . . . why, lay your head in the weeds of its bank, as you formerly did! Ungrounding his pike-butt as he spoke, the guard laid its shaft diagonally across the gate to bar the way. "For, once proscribed by the temple of the One True Goddess, you may nevermore enter these walls!"

"Save your bluster, little man," Conan drawled, sitting easy with one leg cocked over the hump of his camel. "If I wanted to be inside that gate now, I would be; and your head would be a split ripe calabash for crows to sup from." He rested his palm on the grimy hilt of the Il-barsi knife at his waist. "But such a deed would be unseemly for a high emissary of Anaximander, Priest-King of Sark, and an envoy of the Sacred Temple of Votantha! Therefore I politely ask your permission to enter."

"What," a voice rattled down from the wall, "you are saying you represent our king's ally? You claim to come here on church business?"

"If you do not believe me, then ask the guardians of yon idol." Half-turning in his saddle, Conan gestured back toward a draped, wheeled conveyance that was being dragged by shuffling bearers from the patchy side of a date orchard across the river. The party came not by the main caravan road, but down a desolate valley that angled toward the trackless western wastes.

"By the Goddess," the voice atop the wall exclaimed, " 'tis the holy procession bound here from the South. Notify the temple! And muster a cavalry squadron to guide them to the palace!"

After some minutes of trumpet blasts, drum rolls and warrant officers' shouts, a troop of horsemen trotted forth from the caravan gate; Conan turned his camel to accompany them. By that time the idol-bearers had almost reached the river, so that riding forth to meet them was a matter of mere protocol. Dismounted, however, the soldiers were able to furnish some help manhandling the heavily burdened caissons through the wet sand of the river ford.

Even so, grave Khumanos vetoed any suggestion that horses be roped to the juggernaut to haul it into the city, or that the Qjaran soldiers take over the labor. The pilgrims finished their journey as they had long endured it, matted and filthy, ragged and unshod. Their sore, chafed limbs strained against the massive wheels and worn, creaking levers to inch their burden forward.

Soon the idol, followed closely by the cavalry, trundled through the caravan gate. Leading the way alongside Khumanos, Conan walked his camel past the chastened guards who had formerly barred his entry. As they came inside, priests and civil officers of middle rank were just beginning to arrive to greet them.

At Khumanos's insistence, the idol was not dragged further into town. It remained in the caravan yard, still shrouded, to be protected from defilement by squads of Qjaran and Sarkad guards. Its bearers, by the priest's decree, were to remain with it, lodged in the caravan quarter until certain essential details of the consecration ritual were complete.

This decision was not disputed by the Qjaran officials—perhaps because of the weak, stricken, and even repulsive appearance of the pilgrims. In spite of Conan's efforts to ease their way, their state had not improved over the last few days of the trip. Rather the opposite; it almost seemed they might be carrying some plague into the town, with their sun-reddened, ulcerated skins, their patchily bald heads and bleeding, gap-toothed mouths.

However, no public mention was made of such fears. Instead, in the welcoming speeches made before the crowd gathered at the gate, the guests' sorry physical shape was hailed as a pious mortification of the flesh, a proof of the sufferers' steadfast endurance and religious faith.

Conan, as the party's scout, was hardly praised as a hero or saint; yet at least he was acknowledged as alive. The petty officials obviously remembered his recent expulsion from their city; now they seemed obliged to accept him as one of the holy missionaries from Sark. Their tolerance was in large part shared by the citizens; in any case, in view of the northerner's size and obvious fighting-fitness, it would have been hard for ordinary townfolk to mutter curses or spit at his passing. In only one instance did a temple guard clutch his sword and seem ready to have at him; that young hothead was dutifully restrained by his fellows. So

Conan was received back into Qjaran society—most particularly into the company of his former associates at the caravansary.

For his part, Conan felt content to tread the streets of the town that had exiled him—to stare down passersby, and enjoy comforts he formerly had denied himself, of food, lodging, and camel-tending within the city walls. In the long view, he had greater plans to call himself to the attention of the city elders; but for the moment he did not press them. He resolved to keep silent about the discoveries he had made in the desert, at least until his work under the Sarkad mission was complete and his pay from the priest Khumanos was safely in hand.

Upon news of the delegation's arrival, a reception was decreed by King Semiarchos for the following day. In keeping with Khumanos's strictures, and because of the weakness of the wayfarers, it was ordained to be held in the caravan quarter rather than the palace. During the night, a lavish pavilion was set up in the broad, sandy yard—to accommodate the throngs, and doubtless to spare the royal family the necessity of entering the rustic caravan inns.

By dawn's light provisions were brought in by donkey carts; cookfires were lit and lambs ritually slaughtered for the feast. Sometime later, as the fragrance of roasting meat spread over the town, celebrants began arriving, along with priests and servants, musicians and temple dancers.

Then, at midmorning, King Semiarchos lashed his clattering golden chariot into the yard, flanked proudly on its broad platform by his queen and high priestess Regula and their sultry daughter Afriandra. The dappled four-horse team scuffed to a halt before the pavilion, and the riders alighted to greet Khumanos, with Conan watching over the heads of the throng.

"Exalted Priest, your king told me to await your coming!" Semiarchos advanced on Khumanos as if to gather him up in an embrace—but on viewing the black priest's slender, wasted form, and his air of solemn, watchful reserve, the husky ruler thought better of it; he merely clamped the southerner's bony shoulder briefly in one hand. "As the days and weeks rolled by, we feared we would not be seeing you at all! We sent envoys, but we knew not what route you would be taking. They reported no sign of your party."

Khumanos bowed gravely. "Our way was a slow and difficult one," he affirmed, disdaining to use any respectful form of address. "By temple law our holy fetish could pass through no city or abode of men, except the one where it is to be consecrated. Hence our route led through the remotest wastes."

"Ah—that explains it, I suppose." Semiarchos gazed past Khumanos to his band, who sat or reclined around the central fire-circle. "Your followers have paid a dear price in hardship, by the look of them. I can see it by their toil-worn limbs and raw, sun-blistered skin—"

"Yes, 'tis so," Khumanos agreed again. "Many were the days they spent wandering in the desert, scorched and half-blind. Sandstorms scourged them by day and thirst near-strangled them at night. Shartoumi peasants and Sarkad warriors, these were at the start, and not all godly folk. But on this march they learned to toil together without thought of self, and along the way every one of them, every survivor, has pledged eternal service to great Votantha—"

"It is a miracle," Queen Regula exclaimed. "What courage, what sacrifice . . . and what a test of faith! Qjarans, we can learn much from this splendid example: the power of devotion, and how frail mortals can triumph over well-nigh impossible odds!" The matriarch seized Khumanos's hand; clasping it warmly in hers, she pressed a fervent kiss against its parched knuckles. "The holy union that is to commence, the wedding of our two cities' gods and temples, will infuse great strength into our spirits, I can see that. Welcome, Khumanos, and welcome to your followers and your noble god!"

The queen's gesture encompassed the still-horizontal idol, whose grubby canvas windings had lately been hidden under a comelier shroud of tasseled linen. "I, Regula, as Queen of Qjara and High Priestess of the One True Goddess, proclaim our hearts, our temple, and our city at your command!"

While these preliminaries were underway, Conan moved through the throng to catch a glimpse of Afriandra. Amid the festive disarray he pressed close and was rewarded; there waited the princess, just behind her royal parents.

She was clad in a decidedly daring saffron

gown that left bare one brown shoulder and one entire thigh. Sandals with thickly-sculptured soles and a high-piled hairdo made her even harder to ignore. Her features and general bearing looked healthy, if a bit wan and nervous. She seemed to be regarding the priest Khumanos closely—though he, while exchanging pieties with the king and queen, did not visibly acknowledge her presence. Suddenly bored, she scanned the crowd; at last her eyes found the Cimmerian where he towered over the watching citizens.

In a trice she had abandoned her family. Wending her way through the unready temple warriors and startled onlookers, she passed into the shade of the pavilion. "Why, Conan!" she cried, affecting a courtesan's languid, breathy voice. "The rumors are true, then—this strange, lumpy foreign god has brought you back to us! He cannot be all bad, I suppose."

Coming before him she paused, striking an insolent posture that surely made more hearts than his thump out of control. Then wantonly she threw her arms about his neck, straining her lithe body upward to plant a full, lingering kiss on his lips.

Conan, with arms suddenly burdened and brain reeling with the scent of jasmine perfume, nevertheless remained dimly aware of his surroundings. The nearby crowd, doubtless awed by Afriandra's aristocratic beauty—as against his own rustic, shirtless splendor—had drawn back sharply from the spectacle of their embrace. Meanwhile, the temple guards posted near the king were visibly restless, showing signs of marching after their royal ward.

Accordingly, with a few hard kisses, Conan fought the girl's painted mouth into momentary submission. He swung sharply away, drawing her with him into the crowd under a protecting arm. "Afriandra, child," he grunted, slowly regaining his breath. " 'Tis good to be back to visit you, if not this camel-trough you call a town! Come, let us go and see the festival."

He led her off into new reaches of crowd that had not yet had time to be scandalized, and the threat of pursuit diminished. To divert attention from themselves, they found an attraction that already held scores of Qjarans rapt—a temple dance involving a half-dozen priestesses, conducted informally and in a folkish style.

Conan was amused to see that the lead dancer was Sharla; but of the steps that held the watchers so enthralled he saw little, because of the way Afriandra clung to him, whispering questions and jests into his ear and demanding frequent kisses.

In time she begged that he buy her a salted dough-ring, from a stick of them a hawker was vending. The irony of this was something he decided not to comment on, even as he dispensed two of the few remaining coins from his dwindling stock. Thirst from the salted breads led them into the familiar inn, where they took seats at the same table where they had first met. This time, however, they shared a single narrow bench in the corner. Afriandra crowded Conan, caressing him both above and beneath the table.

"Strange to recall," he told her, "that when I met you I knew not who you were, or even how pretty you really look."

"Yes, it was so long ago!" She shook her head, leaning it against his shoulder at risk of disarranging her hair. "Zaius was alive then. He sought me here."

"Yes," Conan reminisced. "He almost ran afoul of my blade that first night. Do you miss him?"

"That is hard to say—Zaius cared for me deeply, in his way." She clung to Conan's burly bicep. "With him, there was so little for me—but without him there seems to be nothing at all."

"Your parents haven't yet found you another husband and heir to the throne, then?"

"No," she sighed. "They are so wrapped up in this mission from King Anaximander . . . for a time I feared they would try to wed me to him, with his horrible oily beard! But there has been no more talk of it, thank the Goddess! They ignore me . . . almost as if they wanted to punish me. I think my mother secretly blames me for Zaius's death. Although she put a good face on it, it pained her." Afriandra shook her head, disconsolate. "And perhaps she is right."

"There now, child," Conan said, comforting her with a brotherly hug, "it would not do to shed overmany tears for a suicide. Doubtless when one near to you dies, especially by his own hand, there is some feeling of guilt, but . . . ho there, tap-keeper!" Conan's shout was directed at Anax, who had finally emerged from the cellar. "Bring us a flagon of good ale! But if you have not sent to far-off Belverus for it—why, then the tepid camel piss you call *arrak* hereabouts will do!"

"And a tot of *narcinthe* for me, Anax," the princess added. Her familiar tone made the innkeeper pause and squint at her in surprise before he turned to comply.

"And what of the holy mission . . . this joining of the churches of Qjara and Sark?" Conan asked. "Are you reconciled to it now?"

"No. To be sure, I like it even less—not that my parents will heed my views." She exhaled impatiently, her fragrant breath wafting against his shoulder. "In truth, Conan, after what you told me of the autocratic ways of our neighboring priest-kings, I am surprised that you make yourself a party to this expedition."

Conan waited until Anax had deposited their drinks before them. "And tell me, girl, would any less have served to get me back into this city? Or to your side?" He sipped deeply from his beaker of *arrak*.

"True—on that account I am happy." She stroked his arm. "But even so, I like not the look of it . . . these wretched toilers, cruelly burdened and driven here by armed guards, hailed by my mother as harbingers of our city's future—it is a disgrace."

"In sooth it is," Conan agreed. "I would have helped them win freedom and slay their taskmaster, if they showed any desire of it." He shook his head grimly. "I half-suspect that Khumanos brought them here by such remote, desolate ways only to keep them from deserting him at the first chance. But they would never do it now; they are meek as kittens."

"The poor wretches . . . from what I saw of them, they are weak and ill, expended in an unworthy task."

" 'Tis true." Conan nodded agreement over his *arrak*. "After galloping all ways across the desert to draw water and steal fruit for them, I can attest to it. What ails them is rooted deep in their miserable bodies and souls . . . if souls they yet have! Certainly they lack the will to fight."

Afriandra tilted her cup and drank in commiseration. "And the proposed wedding, set between the goddess Saditha and this Sarkad deity, whatever he is . . . it has taken the place in my mother's heart of my own nuptials. But to me it smacks of heresy to Saditha's faith. I like it little, and there are others in Qjara who feel the same."

"Aye, well enough—" Conan lowered his voice. "But be careful about spreading mutiny among your citizens, in case you are found out." He regarded her evenly as she sipped her demitasse. "You as a cherished princess might not suffer, but your followers could lose their heads if they make their move at the wrong time."

"Ah, well, there is little chance of opposing it," Afriandra said. "To back out now would be an affront that might lead to war with Anaximander. I would not want that, for he seems a ruthless sort of adversary." Conan watched her finish her *narcinthe*. "Come," she said, "my parents will be worrying about me—I hope they are, anyway, for there is ample cause! Let us return to the royal party."

Less prone to cling to him now, she nevertheless followed obediently in his encircling arm. The inn had filled with people as the morning grew hotter; yet the caravan yard outside seemed more crowded too, and more festive, full of musicians, dancers and mountebanks entertaining those who could not fit at the center of things.

"You seemed dazed," Conan said to the princess as they waited for a troupe of acrobats to finish using the main path. "Are you feeling the effects of the *narcinthe* yet, seeing the future of these revelers?"

"Not exactly . . . it is different this time. The people and things are mere shadows, uncertain, hazy—sometimes I feel as if I were walking out in the open desert."

"And I am not in some scandalous state of undress to your eyes . . . ?" She shook her head. "A pity," he said, though he felt relieved. His own modesty aside, if Afriandra was seeing fewer visions, there was less chance of some stray phantom upsetting her.

At length, the princess led Conan up to a cordon of temple warriors. There she took leave of him, not wishing to provoke her royal parents. Conan watched her safely into their presence and then proceeded on business of his own.

On his return sometime later, Conan sought out his priestly employer in the crowd and addressed him. "What of my pay, Khumanos? The way things are going here, I had better have it in hand as soon as possible." To the priest's blank stare he added, "You told me that once the idol was carried to Qjara, the jewels would be mine. Well, that time is here." Conan glanced over his shoulder to where Khumanos's followers rested in the sun outside the pavilion. "I saw your paymaster Astrak yonder some minutes ago—though he does not look well of late, with the pox on his face and arms—"

"It is not time for your payment yet." Coolly, Khumanos returned Conan's indignant stare. "For, did you not know . . . the holy idol of Votantha is to be assembled from three equal parts, of which only the first is here in Qjara. The labor is not fulfilled."

"What, you mean I have to go back and fetch two more?" Angrily, yet inconspicously, Conan knotted a fist in the fabric of the priestly robe. "Why, priest, that is robbery!"

"The other sections of the idol are already in transit here." Khumanos sounded unperturbed, merely fingering the talisman on his breast. "They should arrive within days. But it is best that we go forth to meet them and escort them to the city gate. Otherwise they may never find their way here, and the terms of our bargain will never be met."

"Scoundrel! Rogue! You mean there are more weary wretches suffering out in the desert? Tell the Qjaran guards to go find them, they will be happy to do your dirty work!"

Khumanos shook his head. "We can accept limited help, but I must remain in authority over this holy mission. I need you as my guide."

"Scalawag! How do I know those gems are worth anything? You have already deceived me once—"

"Two handfuls," Khumanos interrupted him. "Discharge your duty to me, and you may take all the gems you can grasp in two bare hands, held separately."

"Three pieces of idol, three handfuls," Conan declared. "I will do your bidding for that much, no less."

"All right, it is a bargain. You will receive payment after the idol is assembled, not before."

Conan grunted his assent. Impulsively, to close the deal, he seized Khumanos's hand and pumped it. After a moment he let it drop with a shiver of distaste; it felt lifeless—not cold or clammy, but rigid and dry, as devoid of feeling as the man's whole aspect. As Conan wheeled away, the priest's voice came after him: "We depart the city at dawn tomorrow to search the deserts to southward. Have your camel ready."

Afriandra was nowhere to be seen. Conan found King Semiarchos and Queen Regula conducting royal business in different parts of the pavilion, but neither had the princess in tow. Rather than confronting them, he accosted an elderly man; he appeared to be Lord High Mayor or somesuch. "Can you tell me," he asked, gripping the man's shoulder with courteous restraint, "where has Princess Afriandra gone? I have news for her . . . have they packed her off somewhere—?"

"Did you not see?" The graybeard glared at him with a mixture of fear and indignation. "She collapsed just now in a seizure of some sort, and was taken back to the palace!"

To Conan's mute stare he elaborated, "She had gone to meet the bearers of the idol from Sark, yonder in the caravan yard, when of a sudden she shrieked and fell to earth." The old man shook his head in real, fatherly concern. "Perhaps it was only the sun, or mere girlish vapors; she has been high-strung since the death of her betrothed, but who would have expected this?"

As Conan turned away the man's voice trailed off, yet the last few words came faintly to his ears. "Her eyes were wide open, but she just would not stop screaming. . . ."

Conan could not wait till nightfall to see Afriandra. His concern was not so much that her parents had sequestered her, as that they would lack any sympathetic ear for the new and devastating vision she had suffered through her gift of prophecy. A dubious "gift" at best, Conan reflected . . . especially when brought on by the heady, insidious *narcinthe* liquor.

He should have warned her against dabbling in wizardry, however harmless it might seem. Particularly during this time of religious fervor in Qjara, with two quirkish desert gods preparing either to clash or couple on the grand scale. His own customary avoidance of things supernatural had been set aside temporarily by his involvement with the Sarkad holy mission. It had seemed a convenient chance for him at the time, in the desert—but he was no longer sure of its merit, nor even that he needed or wanted the gems Khumanos offered. There was definitely something sinister about this cult of Votantha. He wasn't proud of helping to foist a new southern god on the Qjarans, in spite of the shabby way they had treated him.

Thumping at the gate of the royal palace to visit Afriandra, he was turned gruffly away by more guards than he cared to wade through. His inquiries after the princess's health were rebuffed as well; there was no privileged ambassadorial treatment for him here. Disgruntled, he returned to the caravan quarter to see to his camel and supplies.

He spent part of the afternoon arranging details regarding certain valued personal belongings. In this he enlisted the help of Anax, whom he knew he could trust a middling distance, and also an artisan of the innkeeper's acquaintance, who was known to be discreet about working with objects that might have been brought into the city without the benefit of scrutiny by the tariff officers.

Later, near the hour of sunset, Conan sat sipping *arrak* and renewing distant acquaintances. He watched impatiently as the day's religious festivities gave way to the more determined revelry of evening.

As the last pallor faded in the sky above the western wall, he took leave of the caravansary. He passed with weary celebrants through the Temple Gate and ducked down a neglected alley in the temple quarter. Here was a point along the wall of the palace where trees within the compound obscured the view from the sentry walks. The crevices in the weathered stone, though shallow, were more than adequate for his northern cliff-climbing skills. In moments, he crept insectlike to the top of the wall and rolled across it, barely making a ripple in its knife-edged silhouette against the dimming sky.

His drop down the far side was a familiar, noiseless one, into a bower of trees and flowers watered from hand-served wells. This night, with festivities occupying the courtiers elsewhere in town, the garden lay abandoned. Conan slipped across it, keeping to the thickening shadows.

At the far end of the garden was another wall, this one polished to a glassy smoothness, with joints that would have defied entry by a knife-blade or even a fingernail. But the palace's corner was embellished with slender ornamental pillars, standing out sharply from the stone; by wedging his body between these projections, alternating pressure between his shoulders and his bare knees, he was able to wedge his way up to the top of the vertical face. Then, gripping the sculptured cornice overhead with powerful fingers, he hauled himself up to the rim—and, after checking for guards, across into the deeper shadows along the parapet.

Once there, he waited motionless for a pair of sentries to pass. Then, flitting like the shadow of a hunting owl, he crossed to the palace's inner bastion. The climbs here were far easier, due to ornamental balustrade and trellises; in moments he crouched on the balcony of Princess Afriandra's chamber.

No light shone within, but he saw a riffling of the curtains . . . and a face, oval in the night. Conan's startlement eased as he saw that it was Afriandra, slow to discern him there in the shadows. Her eyes at last settled on him; then she parted the curtains, lithe in her pale silk sleeping gown, and stepped through into his arms.

"I was resting," she murmured to him, "but I dreamt of you and sensed your coming."

"You must indeed by a prophetess," he replied, "for I made no sound." Putting his hand to her chin, he turned her face up to his. "Is the mystic sight still upon you?"

"It is hard to tell . . . the odd sensation comes and goes, yet I see nothing out of the ordinary."

"You are better, then, since your collapse this morning." He felt her brow for coolness. "What was it that upset you so? Do you remember?"

"It was the same as before, when King Anaximander visited here . . . only worse. Some horrible doom is upon the idol-bearers from Sark. Even as I saw them, they were consumed by fire—their skin scorched and blistered, their bodies blackened to smoking, twisted hulks." Her voice quavered as she trembled in Conan's arms. "And worse, as I looked around, I began to see the same fiery plague gnawing at other faces—native Qjarans, even ones well-known to me! Then the city walls retreated with a rush . . . I felt all alone in a desolate, windswept place. There was a huge shadow overhead, looming and spreading from somewhere behind me. I was afraid to look around. The fear was too much, it was growing . . . then I must have fainted." Shivering, she clung tightly to Conan.

The Cimmerian held and comforted her, pondering as he did so. "Those Sarkad bearers are an ill sight to behold, with their sores and weals and rashes. Their ordinary looks are enough to make many a young noblewoman scream . . . mayhap it was only the liquor this time, acting on your uneasy mind—"

"No, Conan. It is a warning from the gods, I am sure of it!" She pulled back from him, gazing into his face for effect. "To my secret eye, the harbingers and omens gather thick as ravens around a dying ass in the desert. Some grim destiny awaits the city of Sark and all those connected with it . . . or is it my own city of Qjara? I cannot tell which!"

"There, there, child!" Conan comforted her . . . though while in her clutch, he himself felt a touch of formless fear, a shiver of that same dire futurity whose hot breath already scorched her heels. Meanwhile, Afriandra's embraces drew him back into her chamber. She clung to him first desperately, then more longingly—as if, quite literally, there were no tomorrow.

* * *

Departing by a different route, he availed himself of a low, sheer section of palace wall that provided a straight drop onto cushioning turf. This brought him to a postern gate, locked but unguarded, lying near Saditha's temple. Scaling it, he found himself in a familiar courtyard with a lily pond at its center—the place Afriandra had set for her first assignation with him, not moonlit this time, but puddled in gloom. It was here that his pursuers finally caught him.

"Ho, fellows, to me!" a voice cried out, echoing sharply across the pond. "The foreigner comes!"

Even as Conan started forward at a run, swift footsteps scuffed from the shadows to intercept him. The pursuer was a tall, agile figure, dressed in the sandals and flimsy, unarmored tunic of a temple warrior.

"Halt and await judgment!" The stranger barred Conan's way around the pond. His voice was strident but youthful, with a hint of the same drill-yard arrogance Conan had so despised in Zaius.

"Do you fear the Goddess's justice?" The interloper challenged. He brandished a drawn sword, long and polished as any temple blade; Conan's Ilbarsi knife now leaped into his hand to counter it.

"I fear only to die unavenged," Conan spat back. He feinted with his weapon, then darted aside to veer past his assailant. "Still, if your justice calls for a host of blades against one, I would as soon postpone it till morning."

He was already beyond his foe, with a healthy lead toward the walled court's nearest gate; but even as he bore down on it, two more temple warriors pelted through, racing toward him with drawn swords. From the right, where another gate lay, more footsteps came slapping with cries of "Halt!" and "Seize him!"

With a snarl, Conan turned and charged back toward his first pursuer. He struck out low with his knife to disable the lone man before the others closed in.

It was here that the temple warrior's training proved its worth. Even as the templar came on at full speed, his blade was agile enough to strike low against Conan's, deflecting the Cimmerians's vicious cut. The two runners collided, with Conan's greater size and momentum carrying through; the slighter man toppled back over the curb of the fountain, to splash and flounder in the waist-deep water.

Conan did not press after his adversary into the weedy depths; instead he barked a feral laugh and stepped clear of the curb. He turned to face the other pursuers, backing slowly away toward the square corner formed by the outer walls of palace and temple. When he reached it he waited, crouching like a panther at bay. He was now hemmed by five men with drawn swords. All were dressed in the garb of temple warriors, one of them still dripping and wringing out the skirt of his tunic.

"Have at me, then," Conan snarled, "whoever yearns to meet the One True Goddess first! You are her servants, are you not?"

"Aye, we are," the wringing-wet one declared. "I am Ismir, head novice, and woe to any who profane great Saditha's name!"

"So! Queen Regula sends a fistful of novices to do what the late and overblown Zaius would not do, or could not! Come, then, and test your swords!"

"Queen Regula—nay, we come not at her bidding!" A short, contentious-looking warrior spoke these words. "We are disciples of Zaius, as all good defenders of Saditha must be! But the queen is misled, seduced into error by cunning blasphemers like yourself! We are here to remedy that!"

"Enough, Hassad," the dripping Ismir said, "we do not have to explain ourselves to this foreign trash! Enough that we slay him—I claim the honor, if you others will but guard this corner of wall—"

"Wait!" Conan forestalled them. "You say you are not pawns of the queen—you act on your own, then?"

The leader impatiently shook his wet thatch of hair. "Aye we are a cabal—mutineers, if you will. But not heretics, and ever faithful to the goddess's truth! We are sworn to save her from being polluted by unclean foreign gods and fetishes, such as the one you have dragged into our city!"

"The god Votantha, you mean . . ." Conan's knife still hovered ready, yet plainly it was less greedy for blood than it had been moments earlier. "You are rebels, purists in your faith, and you blame me! Yet I am no devotee of Votantha—I was only Khumanos's scout."

"You brought them here, did you not?" Hassad accused, waving his sword. "And you ingratiate yourself with the queen, persuading her to welcome you back to Qjara, even after your sins of heresy and profanation against Saditha and Zaius!"

"And worse," the dripping leader chimed in, "you now subvert our princess as well, spiriting her off from her parents, slinking about the city in her wake! You even creep into the palace by night to seduce her with Goddess knows what plot or poison!" He shook his sword high, regaling his fellows with true Zaiuslike fanaticism; the other temple warriors responded in kind. "Treason upon treason," he ranted, "crime upon crime, and all by the hand of an unclean foreigner—a miserable, reprehensible outcast!"

"Enough!" Conan growled with sufficient ferocity to silence them all. "I am no friend of Sark and its gods, nor is your princess! You and she have more in common than you know! If you want to turn out Khumanos and his idol, there may be good reason. I would consider helping you—"

"Lies, and more lies!" Hassad howled. "Now he seeks to beguile us, as he has already done to our rulers and our divines! Death to him, I say—"

"Hold, by all the imps and demons of Earth and the first Seven Hells!" Again, Conan's oath and aspect were fierce enough to halt the onslaught of words. "If you really must kill me, then I say again . . . have at me! You there, Ismir, will do nicely!" He snarled forth a laugh at them, his teeth flashing whiter than his rusty-dark blade in the gloom. "But first I charge you, submit to the will of your goddess! If your champion does not slay me, consider it her sign that my words have merit, and consent to parley with me, at least before hewing at me further! May Saditha grant that this duel is fairer than the last!"

"Well enough, it sounds reasonable!"

"Make short work of him, Ismir."

Swiftly the two combatants came together, and swords clashed in the night.

CHAPTER 15
Consecration

By the topaz light of dawn Conan was abroad in the caravan quarter. Surly from lack of sleep, yet without any visible wounds, he readied his camel and traps. Exalted Priest Khumanos awaited him, along with those of the original idol-bearers who were the least sick and disabled. They soon were joined by a squad of Qjaran city guards and volunteers, some mounted, some afoot, who proceeded out with them through the city gate.

Stopping only to fill their waterskins and camel-gullets at the riverside, the band headed southeast over the desert. They followed the trail of worn, dusty bones that marked the age-old caravan route.

Thus began their search for the two other idol-bearing processions sent northward by

Anaximander, King of Sark. The parties' precise whereabouts were not known, nor was their survival assured, for it had been many days since Khumanos had received word from them. At the very least, he advised Conan, the idols could be found; it was unlikely that thieves or scavengers could make off with more than a small part of their constituent metal.

Conan felt less certain, knowing how easily something sizeable, such as the Ship of Stone or the royal expedition of Pronathos, could become lost in these immense, trackless wastes. Yet he kept his peace and plied the desert vigilantly, organizing the horse- and camel-riders as a search screen, scouting out waterholes, and making sure the footborne party stayed within a survivable march of them.

He used the route projected by Khumanos as the backbone of his search. He did so based on an antique and questionable map whose parchment was worn through in places, and in most other places illegible from overuse and overexposure. The least likely limbs and ribs of terrain he scouted out himself, sometimes roving for an entire day up desolate side canyons, often forsaking his camel in order to scale vantage points whence he could survey vast expanses of desert. In time the backs of his hands were burnt as black as those of Khumanos, his lips perpetually pursed against blowing dust and hot, moisture-stealing zephyrs, and his eyes sealed in a habitual squint. Before his gaze, bleak desert terrain unrolled like an endless shroud of corpse-canvas—blotched and bleached, scorched and frayed, desolate.

The first party of idol-bearers was intercepted some eight days' march out of Qjara. Conan, crouching atop a needle-pointed crag swept ceaselessly by a moistureless breeze, spied them hauling their oblong burden caterpillarlike into the mouth of a red-walled gorge far ahead. By the time his advance party reached them, they had trundled the wheeled idol a mere thousand paces further up the wadi—yet even at the offer of water, provisions, and physical help soon to arrive, they refused to quit their toil. After the briefest rest they resumed their labor, inching the caissons forward at a pathetic rate through soft, resisting sand.

To Conan, their continued effort amounted to madness; he knew better than to squander his strength in trying to assist them. Their physical condition was even worse than that of Khumanos's bearers—marred with the same rashes, sores, toothlessness and hairlessness, and further compounded by thirst and starvation.

To the Exalted Priest, when he arrived, and to the equally remote, vacant-eyed priestling who commanded the party, Conan urged that the idol be abandoned. In the name of mercy—of simple humanity, the gruff Cimmerian argued—it would be better to haul the laborers themselves home in litters, nurse them to health, and let them become living idols to their god Votantha's power and compassion.

But the two holy men scarcely seemed to hear

him. The looks they returned wore the dull, unquestioning glaze of fanaticism; and the toilers themselves seemed eager to bend their bodies once more beneath the cruel juggernaut. So Conan shrugged and fell silent. With the help of fresh labor from Qjara, the work was resumed—by humans only, since horses and donkeys would not let themselves be hitched to the hulking burdens. Even so, the idol proceeded on its way northward, and the remaining searchers resumed their trek.

Two days later, the third segment of the idol was found by an outrider, in a broad, dry valley that formed the lowest pass in an eastward-running mountain chain. The cargo lay at a standstill; of its six wheels, no less than three were broken; its human drays were in deplorable condition as well. Sickest and most hideously deformed of any of the bearers, they huddled helpless in the shade of the draped idol. Several of their number already lay dead of thirst and hunger; Conan, hardened as he was, dared not ask them if cannibalism had yet occurred.

Their leader, a young, dusky-skinned acolyte, said he had gone forth twice in search of water. Failing to find any after a day's walk, he returned dutifully to aid his suffering followers. Now he sat cradling the head of one, a dying female whom the rescuers' water came too late to save. Looking into his gaunt, seamed face, Conan saw leagues of hardship etched there, with voids of untold toil and suffering reflected in eyes that, though dimmed by thirst, could still squeeze out tears of compassion.

This young priest was the first of Votantha's followers who seemed capable of normal human feeling. Yet even he was subject to Khumanos's quiet, forceful will. Taking his junior aside, the elder priest knelt before him muttering admonitions or prayers, and made a pass or two with the mystical amulet he wore on a cord about his neck. From that interview the priestling came away silent and dull-eyed, accepting without protest Khumanos's order to move the idol onward.

With diabolical foresight, the Exalted Priest had bidden his slaves drag along one of the caissons from the idol segment in Qjara, placing it in service as a supply cart. Its two wheels were now used to brace up the stalled idol, while a third wheel was repaired using broken parts from the others. In a single day the procession was underway again. Incredibly, the depleted slaves joined in with their replacements to get the behemoth underway. To Conan's eye, the miserable wretches seemed to experience an unholy surge of vitality as they set their starved, bony shoulders to the wheel.

And so, in less than a fortnight they returned to Qjara. Yet Conan felt unsure whether his journey was in truth the urgent act of mercy he had deemed it. Might it not have been greater mercy, after all, to let the poor sick wanderers perish in the desert, rather than prolonging their labors under Khumanos's diabolical sway? But among the priests and toilers there was no uncertainty, no lapse of faith. And the folk of the city received them gladly, joining them in lavish preparation for the idol's triumphal entry to Qjara.

According to Khumanos's carefully planned ritual, the idol's parts were to enter the city simultaneously by three separate gates—with the caravan quarter evidently not being considered part of the city proper, but as an outer yard or bailey. That arrangement suited the town, which had but three gates of sufficient size to admit the massive chunks of holy drayage. The pieces were to be borne inward along the broad avenues in three separate processions, coming together in the Agora at the city's heart. There they would be assembled for the first time, to be consecrated before the eyes of the sacred gathering.

Afterward, by Queen Regula's decree, there would be a ritual wedding between the goddess Saditha and the newcomer Votantha. The foreign god, by the temple's doctrinal efforts, had been popularized as a sort of physical and spiritual likeness of the dead hero Zaius, really a resurrection of him in immortal guise. By Regula's decree, the city's worship would be divided evermore between the two gods.

An odd concession to the church and king of a foreign city, this . . . yet Conan surmised that Semiarchos and Regula would never have undertaken it if they did not believe it would enhance their family's power, and enshrine them more grandly in their city's history. They knew that Sark lay far to southward, and that it was unlikely that Anaximander would play any large or lasting role in Qjara's affairs. Whereas the rearing of a male god like Votantha seemed certain to skew the city's traditional balance between throne and temple . . . strongly and swiftly, in favor of enhanced royal power.

So, Conan reflected, it could mean the end of the One True Goddess, and the rapid end of Qjara's quaint appeal for a wayward Cimmerian—unless the traditionalist rebel faction, of whom he had intimate knowledge, should succeed in opposing the change. He had no certainty that they had been able to spread their message during his absence, or how many strong voices and stronger arms they had won to their side. He agreed with them, personally, but as a foreigner he had been told it would be best if he stayed out of the debate.

At present, controversy did not seem to be afoot in the town. The mood among the citizens appeared pious and festive, more suited to a wedding than an armed clash. The three white-draped segments of the idol were soon raised upright, lashed to the reinforced platforms of heavy war-chariots, which could be rolled forward by manhandling their long wooden wagon-stems. In this lofty stance the fetishes waited outside their respective city gates, gazed on with awe and reverence as they were readied to be drawn inside.

The meaning of these elaborate preparations intrigued Conan. If, like most rituals, it had some practical purpose, it was by no means clear. To be sure, the idol was too large to be transported in one piece . . . but why cross the desert by three separate routes, and approach the town from three different directions? And why send such a large effigy? Indeed, was there need for an idol at all . . . ? In Conan's experience, the most powerful religious faith dwelt not in any graven fetish, but in the hearts and minds of living men.

Doubtless there was some subtle purpose in it, and in keeping the pieces separate until the last possible moment. Pageantry clearly had a role: the mystery of the draped statues, and the grand processions passing through all quarters of the city, drawing multitudes in their wake to witness the climactic unveiling and joining—all of it seemed very clever. Conan wondered what crowning effect Khumanos might be holding in reserve for the moment of the idol's completion and consecration. Thus far, he had seen only vague hints of Votantha's power; was it possible the shadowy god himself would make an appearance, or send some tangible manifestations to his worshipers?

After the last procession trudged up to the city gate, there was little time left to reel in gossip or contact friends. On the very next morning the ceremony was to be held. Couriers had brought word of the survivor's approach, so most things were in readiness; the remaining details kept Qjara in a fervor of preparation.

Conan found he could not gain an audience with Afriandra, nor even creep to her room by night to meet her. She was said to be sequestered in the inmost sanctum of Saditha's temple with the younger priestesses, ritually cleansing their bodies and spirits for service as bridesmaids to the One True Goddess.

And so, after helping with the sick and weak survivors, providing for the health of his over-worked camel, and again beating the dust out of his clothing and belongings, Conan found the afternoon far advanced. He barely had time to conduct some personal business with his armorer, regarding revelations of his own that he planned to make on the festive day. He did not trouble Khumanos again for payment, judging that the priest would not deem the bargain complete until the idol was wholly within the city wall. Instead he consumed a lavish supper, drank his fill, and lay down in his stall at the caravansary to dreams which were far from peaceful.

The next day, under the merciless morning sun, massively laden chariot wheels grated through the streets of Qjara. Paced by throngs of joyous, chanting citizens, they ground at a slow walk toward the Agora and the holy temple. The idols standing upright in the groaning wagons towered over the heads of the worshippers, and over those town buildings that were made squatly of whitewashed clay. Since Conan walked with Khumanos and his idol via the Trellis Gate, these humbler buildings were soon behind him, with the barracks, granaries and palaces of the temple quarter looming tall on either hand.

As usual in these southern lands, Conan's own

stature gave him an advantage in the crowd. He made a imposing figure in his bulky cloak, escorting the black-skinned, cadaverous priest as he walked behind the statue and its bearers.

Since the idol's parts were still shrouded—wrapped in their travel-soiled canvas windings as well as their fringed white canopies—only the vaguest surmise as to their true shape was possible. The composite idol would scarcely be human-shaped, Conan had decided, since each of its three segments looked so top-heavy—unless the god Votantha was represented as brandishing spear and shield, or wrestling a snake, or engaged in some other space-consuming activity. But then, the evident sameness of the idol's parts suggested a three-sided symmetry that would hardly lend itself to a human figure . . . unless it were a three-armed, three-faced, semi-human monstrosity.

These matters did not seem to trouble the faithful; thus far Conan had heard no blasphemous speculation as to the idol's physique. Eager celebrants pressed up to the fetish and pushed it along for short distances, as if touching the cedar chariot-stem or steel-clad wheel would bring them good luck. With the casual aid of so many bystanders, the massive conveyance groaned forward almost of its own volition, with no need for any drillmasters' shouts or workmanlike precision.

The original bearers of the idol—those still capable of standing—were present, and greatly revered by the city-dwellers. They seemed to feel compelled even now to bend their frail bodies against the shoulder-high wheels, or to lay thin, scabrous hands on the shuddering chariot-frame, and so complete the last miles of their agonized journey. Their contribution to the forward motion of the idol was small, surely, compared to that of the stronger, huskier guards and farmers who had been assigned the task by Saditha's priesthood.

Conan noted that the survivors of the first batch of bearers seemed little recovered over the term of his absence. In truth, they looked even more decrepit than before, as if wasting away from some disease. These pilgrims, like the idol they served, had been robed by the priesthood in long, fringed shawls of fine white cloth, which mercifully covered the blotched hairlessness of their scalps and the worst irregularities of their faces and limbs. In all, this touch of discretion made the parade a prettier sight.

Yet to Conan it raised uneasy questions. In recent weeks, he had encountered bearers from three different groups, widely separated across the desert. During the privations and exertions attending their rescue, it never occurred to him to question why all seemed stricken by the identical scourge. With the variations in their routes, the conditions of their toil, and the length of their exposure to the desert, he wondered, shouldn't there be more difference in their physical aspect and sufferings?

Bad water was now ruled out as a cause of their illness, surely—and diet, since the groups had provisioned themselves at different isolated farms and oases along their routes. Further, if the source was some ancestral plague, it would likely have affected the Shartoumi slaves and the Sarkad troopers differently, instead of marring both groups with the same weals and lesions. What eerie malady was it, Conan wondered, that afflicted only the pilgrims in this holy cause, and all of them in like degree . . . with the possible exception of Khumanos and his fellow priests?

Now, as he strode behind the idol at Khumanos's side, an explanation smote him with the force and clarity of an icy bath. The one thing the groups had in common was the idol itself; all three parts formed of the same metal . . . that oddly warm, oddly glowing stuff . . . which the priests walked and slept apart from, but which the slaves hugged and sweated against by day and cowered under by night. The poor wretches never strayed far from their god, even here in Qjara, while recuperating from their ordeal. Surely, Conan realized, the holy emblem they clung to with all their hearts was what was slowly killing them.

These thoughts swirled in the Cimmerian's brain as the idol came into the Agora; then all was washed aside by the rushing tide of new impressions. Here the entire city of Qjara stood waiting—far more, it now seemed, than had come to witness his duel with Zaius. The alabaster idol of the One True Goddess had been carried forth through the broad archway of her temple; immortal Saditha now gleamed in the noon sun with her silver spear pointing toward heaven. She faced the spot at the center of the vast court where Votantha's effigy would soon be completed.

Beside her, under their gaily colored pavilion, the royal family stood like a diminutive wedding delegation awaiting the groom. King Semiarchos and Queen Regula, resplendent in many-colored robes, radiated sublime confidence to all. By their side, young Afriandra headed a train of priestesses clad similarly to herself, in bridesmaids' gowns of filmy, frothy stuff, wreathed and garlanded with lavish blossoms from the palace gardens. On either flank of the goddess and her royal servants stood the temple warriors in full array, armorless as always, but with backs straight and swords belted at their sides in vigilant readiness.

To Conan's eye, Afriandra did not now look haunted—nor troubled, nor even restless; she seemed to accept her place in her Goddess's nuptials with solemn grace. Among the temple warriors, the northerner thought he recognized two or three who had set upon him in the palace courtyard; but they too stood firm and unblinking, making no visible protest to the ceremony. Conan marveled at the transformation, wondering whether the priest Khumanos's strange persuasive powers had somehow magically been extended to the Qjaran court.

Now the idol in its chariot grated over the sun-bleached paves of the Agora, down a path cleared for it by awed, respectful crowds. Now it halted—likely because the other chariots were once again late in arriving. But there, over the heads of the watchers, loomed a second statue—to Conan it looked bundled and misshapen, like an ill-preserved mummy brought forth into the light of noon. If the festive crowds streaming from the Market Way were any indication, the third chariot would soon arrive from the Old Gate.

Khumanos chose this moment to turn his steps toward the idol of Saditha, where King Semiarchos and Queen Regula waited in attendance. Conan went beside the priest, helping him part the milling crowd; the Cimmerian gathered that, for his promised pay, he was expected to guard Khumanos and his property within the city walls—though if the Exalted Priest ever truly needed his protection, he would find that Conan, too, could shave a bargain and honor only its precise terms. For now, his main interest was in keeping his employer alive long enough to get paid.

The two passed among the spectators, into the space the temple guards held open before the idols and the pavilion; there Khumanos merely nodded curtly to his royal hosts. He scarcely paused as Queen Regula commenced her oration.

"Honored and exalted guest, Khumanos of Sark, we cherish the blessings you bring us. To wit: a wealth of holy tradition from the South; a splendid monument; and a virile husband for our lonely Goddess, to rule beside her in wisdom and justice! Know, O Exalted Priest, the gift shall be given mutually. A new idol of our Goddess is to be prepared . . . it will be carried southward over the sands to your kingdom of Sark as an emblem of our two cities' eternal unity—"

"Yes, splendid." Khumanos did not really acknowledge the high priestess's speech, nor even wait to hear it. Instead he strode out into the open space and waved toward the other idols, the second of which had just edged into view beyond the pillared portico of Saditha's temple. "Proceed!" he called out to them.

The two acolytes who had led the idols northward were nowhere in sight, Conan saw. Two Sarkad guard officers now commanded the trundling chariots, and they evidently heard the Exalted Priest's order. With gestures and gruff commands, they urged their respective parts of the effigy forward into the open space.

Regula, in her role as high priestess, seemed somewhat taken aback by Khumanos's lack of diplomacy. She left off orating in mid-sentence, turning to watch the three statues converging on the center of the plaza.

"Don't forget the shrouds and wrappings," Conan muttered in Khumanos's ear. Most of all, he was curious to see the idol's shape—though even he thought the priest's abrupt, high-handed manner a little strange.

The southerner ignored him as well, motioning to the nearby laborers to roll their segment of the idol more swiftly. They did so—although some of the Qjaran volunteers backed away from the burdened chariot, wiping their brows as if from the withering noon heat. The tall, bundled masses were all three in plain sight now, inching steadily toward an invisible point at the center of the Agora.

"That canvas will have to be cut away before the pieces of the statue are joined," Conan reminded Khumanos again. He palmed the hilt of the knife under his tunic for the task. "Didn't you mean to unveil them first?"

"There is no need," the priest said, not bothering to look back at him. "Behold."

Struck by the priest's earnest tone, Conan turned to regard the nearest chariot. A faint burning smell had been gathering in his nostrils for some moments; now, looking closely, he saw the cause. The fine white drapery over the idol seemed to be darkening in places, as if charring—sending out wisps of smoke under the bright sun. Here and there it parted, peeling back from the brown underlying canvas.

Then, with a sudden puff of ignition, it was alight. The statue, tall atop its chariot, became a pillar of racing flames and pale smoke as its shroud and canvas wrappings were consumed. Across the Agora, two identical fires blossomed simultaneously. The explosions were noiseless, but the sighs of amazement from the crowd drifted to Conan in breathless waves.

It must be some petty spell or alchemic fakery, he decided. This, then, was Khumanos's crowning spectacle, meant to impress the crowd with his foreign god's power. The bearers did not seem to have been harmed, nor the chariots, nor even the cables that held the statues vertical.

But now, as Conan watched the windings on

the nearest piece of the idol curl and drop away from its soot-blackened contours, the shape that was revealed made him uneasy. It was not human, not even remotely so; rather, it looked sinuously plantlike in nature.

It was molded as a broad wedge, clearly, with two flat sides meant to fit flush against the idol's other segments; the side that was elaborately featured and molded suggested the statue's overall shape. From the base, which was rounded like the bole of a weathered oak, the stalk rose straight and powerful, striated by long, shallow ridges. The top branches bulged forth not in a graceful treelike taper, but stubbily and strongly, like a pollarded elm. The two limbs, short and thick, terminated not in foliage but in two rounded, melon-sized fruit. Remarkably, each globe, though its seamed surface had no visible eyes or other facial features, was pierced by what could only be the representation of a gaping mouth. Jagged-toothed and unpleasant, these orifices seemed variously to be snarling or biting.

The sight of the thing—as the last, smoking shreds of its wrapping fell away—caused a hush to settle over the crowd in the Agora. It certainly did not resemble the kind of hero-god the Qjarans expected, as their dubious murmurs showed. And yet the other segments of the idol, judged by their scorched silhouettes across the Agora, were similar or possibly identical to this one.

The shape of the undraped idol tugged at dark threads of awe and menace running deep into

Conan's soul. Thoughts and impressions he could scarcely seize hold of flitted through his awareness. The shape resembled something, surely. . . . He thought of the carving, the petroglyph on the flank of the solitary rock standing in the ruins of Yb, the City in the Waste. It had depicted some kind of tree with howling heads on it, to be sure. . . .

It gave him a sense of eerie familiarity. That place and this one, now . . . the broad, open expanses themselves bore a certain resemblance, it seemed to him—except, of course, for the crowds of people in the Agora, and the proud, unruined buildings around the periphery. A vision came to him of the city wall of Yb, with the human figures graven on its inner surface. Woman, man, and child, their shapes frozen there like living shadows burned into the very stone . . .

Thinking further, Conan remembered how Khumanos had gone alone to visit the monolith in the city, and had bowed before it as if to worship it. No wonder he did so, if it was an image of his native city's god! Conan remembered puzzling over what relation the pictogram had to the fate of the ancient city . . . and to that of its blighted, degraded descendants, who now dwelt among the tumbled rocks of the streamside canyon.

Khumanos . . . the priest was suddenly absent from Conan's side, gone to urge the faithful back to their task of moving the idols, since the uncanny fires had died. But Khumanos, Conan knew, had braved great pain and risk to move the effigy to Qjara in three separate pieces, and by widely separated routes. Why then, he wondered again, go to such extremes to keep the pieces from coming together too soon? Would something sinister happen when they joined?

What indeed? Had the city of Yb, too, been favored with a visit by the great god Votantha? Had the place been aided by it, or destroyed? He thought of the evil repute of the southern priest-kings and their blood-drenched deities, and of Khumanos's cold, inhuman disregard of his own followers' illness and suffering. Everything seemed to point a certain way, the signs and omens were there . . . he bethought himself then of Afriandra's power, and of the grim, fiery nature of her recent visions.

As he wondered, half-paralyzed by the elusiveness of it all, the idols began trundling again—turning in place this time, their chariot-tongues wheeling around to face outward so that their cargoes could be rolled backward, just another twoscore paces, and then butted up against one another to make the idol whole.

The maneuver went smoothly under the priest's direction—the chariots grating and creaking under scores of ready hands, the eyeless, smoke-blackened mouths pivoting as if to broadcast their mute message of warning and woe over the heads of the crowd. The turn was accomplished and, with scarcely a pause, the vehicles rumbled inward, moving toward their common destination.

As they did so, a further odd impression grew

in Conan's awareness. The central expanse of the Agora was now bare of onlookers, with no obstacle standing between the advancing chariots. And yet at the focus of their movement, near the unmarked place where the three segments of the idol would join together, strange flashes and shimmerings seemed to occur—brisk swirls of dust, and glassy heat waves rising and rippling more sharply than elsewhere in the courtyard. As he watched, he fancied he saw faint, ethereal channels of disturbance cut through the air—pale lines of radiance extending straight from each idol to the common center, to join there in a haze of simmering phantom energy.

Much of it was the heat, he sensed; his body and limbs were heavily garbed and protected, but on his face and hands he could feel furnace waves radiating from the statue nearest him. No surprise, in truth, since the idol had already incinerated its winding-cloth. Some of the laborers engaged in pushing the body of the chariot seemed to have drawn back from the intensity of the heat, leaving only those who leaned against the wheel rims and the chariot's long wooden tongue to do the job.

"Wait!"

The voice that rang out across the Agora was a lone, youthful one; yet it bore a firm and urgent note of command. It was Afriandra's—the princess, stepping forth from her row of bridesmaids, threw out her challenge to the those assembled.

"Enough! Halt this travesty of a wedding! Our Goddess needs no husband . . . no foreign tyrant, at least, to overshadow her rightful rule of Qjara! You can see the idol," she appealed to the crowd. "It is no civilized god! It is not man, woman, or even beast, but an unholy monster! We priestesses of Saditha enjoin all her faithful followers to halt this ceremony, and to cast out the evil foreigners who have instigated it!"

So saying, she tore the wreath of flowers from her brow and dashed it to the ground. During her recent cloistering in the temple, she must have spread her message to the other priestesses—for most of them, including Sharla, joined her, stripping off their bright garlands with defiant, dancerlike gestures.

Afriandra's royal father and mother, standing behind her at the bronze goddess's side, failed to react at once; presumably her stridency took them by surprise. The onlookers, too, seemed uncertain what to do—especially since, of all the vast crowd, the princess's words and gestures could only reach those in fairly close view of her. Of these, many were distracted by the movement of the idols and by the strange, luminous effects that were now taking clearer shape at the center of the Agora.

For although most of the Qjaran laborers had stepped back from the chariots, the juggernauts still inched forward through the efforts of a few dozen white-draped survivors of the original journey from Sark. As they did so, the scintillations of the mysterious force linking the statues intensified, growing with the proximity of the three metal castings. Its eerie sheen held the bystanders' stares, especially when it seemed that some vague, ominous shape was coalescing at the center of the three streams of radiance.

These distractions left Princess Afriandra one principal set of allies—the temple warriors who now, in near-unison, clapped hands on the hilts of their swords. With a ringing cry they strode forward from their places beside king, queen, and bronze goddess. Conan silently congratulated the princess for joining with them—though he misdoubted whether their zeal against foreigners might, as before, be vented on him as well as the Sarkads. Clutching the hilt of his knife, he waited to see just what action the temple fighters would take.

Attention was abruptly drawn away from them by the high priest Khumanos striding out again into the Agora. Standing rigid, with palms raised toward the point of convergence in a ritual gesture, he commenced an invocation.

"Votantha, Lord of the Desert," he intoned, "we summon thee to receive our sacrifice! The rituals are complete—the spells are spoken, the feast is laid. Nothing more can hinder thee from descending to our plane and striding forth across the earth in all your primal power. Come thee hither, O Ravenous One! Possess your holy idol, and may our offering satisfy your all-consuming mouths!

"In return, Lord Votantha, we ask only that you bless our humble city of Sark. Send plentiful rain, that those of your worshipers who survive this millennial day may flourish and sustain your tribute in the centuries to come, until next we make sacrifice. This and nothing more we beseech of Thee, Great Votantha, immortal Tree of Mouths."

CHAPTER 16
Judgment

Exalted Priest Khumanos, having spoken, lowered his palms. He turned back toward the fringe of the crowd and strode to it, making no further attempt to urge or direct his idol-bearers.

Conan now guessed with grim certainty that the sacrifice the priest referred to was Qjara—the entire city, populace and all; they were to be scorched and blasted by some unthinkable force, even as Yb had been wiped from the map. He felt mightily tempted to take his Ilbarsi knife and find out whether this villain Khumanos had a heart—yet that was pointless, if the priest had no further part in the unfolding of the spell. And in truth, the idol segments now seemed to grind forward by some mysterious magnetism of their own, half-dragging with them their fanatical but feeble bearers.

Conan saw with foreboding that the lines of energy between the three parts of the idol waxed stronger as the heavy castings moved together. In the brilliant sun, the mystic emanations now shimmered like narrow rivulets of fire above the stones of the Agora—sinuous webs of liquid lightning, tirelessly reaching and questing toward one another. Before the onlookers' astonished eyes they pulsed and flowed together in the vacant place where the idol would be reared.

In that spot, building and coalescing like a mirage over the featureless pavement, there took shape an image . . . roughly what the idol would look like, Conan saw, but larger and still growing. Votantha, the ancient god of Sark and of countless dead cities, feared and worshiped as an austere and almighty Lord and Commander. Votantha, known in His true form to His most trusted initiates as the sacred, undying Tree of Mouths.

Made of living, swirling energy, the spectre grew and intensified, fattening each moment with power drawn rootlike from the three converging channels. Its base was a tangled turbulence of fire-streams, twining and joining like the gnarled tentacles of an ancient oak; its trunk rose thickly, a massive conduit of energy coursing skyward. As for its head, or heads . . . the top part soon blossomed forth in a spreading, multiplying mass of bluntly ill-shaped protuberances. These numbered far more than the six that were represented on the idol; eyeless and faceless, each hideous globe bore only a snarling, hungry-looking mouth with which to gape down and menace the onlookers.

Seeing these mouths gain hideous reality, Conan somehow imagined them exhaling plumes of smoke and flame. He even thought he could feel their hot breath on his face, separately from the ever-intensifying heat of the idol. At the same time, there commenced in his ears a thin, distant snarling or wailing, eerie and half-illusory. It was the raging of the demon-heads—the merest precursor, he guessed, of the howling chaos that would issue forth once this many-headed ghost grew to its full, godlike power.

At the horrific spectacle, one of the rebellious temple guards stirred himself to action. Brandishing his sword and striding into the path of the advancing idol, he harshly commanded its bearers to halt.

But as he shouted the order, he or his weapon must have been touched by the half-visible current of energy that twined ever more strongly into the towering mirage. There came at once a blinding flash; the warrior's body stiffened, haloed by flaring tongues of light. Mere instants later he twisted away and crumpled to the pavement, a wilting husk of scorched bone and feathery ash. The power of the god Votantha had consumed the young hero as a candle flame would devour a gnat.

Amid the murmurs of horror at the guard's death, two of his fellow warriors stepped forward in his place. Careful to avoid the fire-streams, they advanced toward the point of convergence, waving and shouting to all three slave-gangs to halt. But at a certain moment they must have approached too close—for without warning, living fire blossomed in the air about them. It shimmered there an instant, gloating and consuming; then, like the first guard, the two warriors crumpled to earth. Their bodies lay incinerated, their swords and helmets melting to puddles of smoking slag on the paves of the Agora.

Their fellow warriors held back in shock; only Conan found in himself the resolution to follow in their steps. Clad in the dark, hooded cloak, he made a grim, imposing figure. Yet few eyes shifted to him from the snarling, writhing menace above their heads—until Conan, with a twisting flourish, wrenched off his cloak and flung it aside.

Beneath it he wore bright armor—helmet, breastplate and greaves of purest gleaming gold—the lost mail of Pronathos, or of some far older hero, that he had found in the bow of the Stone Ship of the desert. The costume drew stares and exclamations of surprise as, girded in it, he strode forward past the foully smoking remains of the temple fighters. Countless eyes watched him draw his heavy knife; then, growling a savage oath, he moved toward the shimmering specter of the Tree of Mouths.

The Ilbarsi blade, though black and pitted with corrosion, was still a good weapon—a well-balanced hunk of steel that would hold a superb edge. Yet for battling against incandescent gods it might not be the best tool; Conan sensed this as it grew hot in his hand. The steel seemed to draw and channel the living energy that pulsed around the phantom before him; holding the knife raised, and sensing that in another instant it would scorch or immolate him, he flung it in desperation at the hellish tree.

It never reached its target; mere inches from his hand it melted—yes, and vaporized in midair. Its hard substance hissed away to nothingness, like water droplets flung into the bed of a blacksmith's forge.

Such heat . . . a mere mortal could scarce imagine it, except in the seething hearth of the sun! And yet from it Conan learned something vital. His gold armor—this soft, ornamental frippery that would not stand in battle before a well-cast javelin—protected him from the god's fierce energy. Those parts of his body it masked—the front parts, from neck to groin and knee to ankle—felt cool and unaffected by the bone-piercing glare of the mirage, enabling the rest of his skin to better tolerate the heat. Flicking down the gold visor of his helm, his eyes gained relief, along with his singed eyebrows. Now, if only he could find a suitable weapon . . .

A movement behind Conan drew his attention—followed at once by a clashing on the pavement close at hand. Whirling, he found the source: Khumanos. The priest had, evidently, crept up behind him, bearing a long sword which now lay on the stones of the Agora. A fine weapon, if an antique one—of gleaming bronze and iron, crusted with its own share of heavy gold. Where Khumanos had obtained it, there was no guessing—nor why he had let it fall from his hand, instead of trying out his skills of butchery against the weaponless Cimmerian. The Sarkad stood frozen now with one hand near his chest, looking pale and wide-eyed with what could be fear—uncharacteristic for him—or possibly amazement. His hand clutched the thong he always wore around his neck, though Conan saw no sign of the amulet usually tied to it.

Taking up his newfound broadsword, Conan regarded Khumanos balefully. He ought to try its balance by hacking the priest in twain, even if the rascal was unarmed. But in any event a more dangerous enemy loomed. Turning, he stalked toward the glowing, writhing phantom of the demon-god Votantha.

The sword was well-found, he could tell at once, as perfect for the task as his golden armor. The bronze blade did not draw in the baleful energy that pulsed and swirled around the ghostly image of the god; its gold-crusted hilt remained cool in Conan's grip. Whether the blade would have an effect on the being's filmy substance was the next question. Darting in quickly to brave the heat, he swung the weapon in a mighty stroke against the trunk of the monster-tree.

The effect was vaguely satisfying. Although the blade passed almost unimpeded through the spectre, there was faint resistance, as of tough cobwebs parting before a housemaid's broom. The dim tracery of the god's shape blurred in iridescent lines that seemed to swirl and try to reweave themselves.

Overhead, from the tree's hellish fruit, a louder howling meanwhile issued, as of muted rage and pain. An Conan ducked back out of the heat, several of the monstrous heads lashed down to growl and grimace at him, searing his arms and throat with their hot, growling breath; he seized the chance for further sword-play, slashing through the hideous appendages with more free-swinging strokes. The tree writhed and snarled in frenzied pain even as the hovering shapes dissolved before his eyes.

Darting in and out by swift turns, Conan continued to strike and slash at the god's ectoplasmic form. Though the thing did not bleed or die, its violent reactions hinted that he might be hurting or at least distracting it.

Yet it continued to wax and grow, drawing ever more power from the idol's segments as they came together. They were barely a dozen paces apart now, pushed by the frail, diseased remnant of Khumanos's slaves.

Meanwhile, some Qjarans, notably the temple warriors, eagerly joined in. Lacking the armor to get close, and not daring to risk the cindery fate of their comrades, they turned their efforts against the idol-bearers, dragging the pathetic creatures away from the chariot-stems and hurling them to the pavement, to keep them from moving the monuments forward. Princess Afriandra and her priestly bridesmaids joined in this melee, as did some onlookers; Conan, glancing aside from his own sweaty labor, even saw a band of youths, under Ezrel's lead hurling stones at the toilers.

But deterring them from their mission was not easy, for the heat from the idols themselves was intense. The giant castings now glowed fiery green, pulsing and shimmering with the same eerie light that coursed along the fire-streams; even the chariots beneath them smoked, their paint and wood beginning to roast from the unnatural heat.

Yet the Sarkad and Shartoumi pilgrims in their white shawls seemed able to bear the heat with supernatural vigor. Hurled down, they scrambled up from the pavement and back to their toil like parched, animated skeletons—and the ordinary humans opposing them found it hard to dart in near enough to snatch one from his labor without being blinded by heat, or suffering lurid, painful burns.

But the fight was irrelevant; Conan felt sure that, even without a single mortal hand to move them, and without chariot wheels beneath, the sections of the idol would still grind together across the Agora, drawn inexorably by the power of Votantha's coming. His own task of pruning the Tree of Mouths seemed equally hopeless, as its massive trunk continued to thicken, and new heads blossomed from its top faster than he could hew them off with his sword.

He felt himself growing weak, finding it harder to look into the blaze and breathe the hot, acrid air. The tree's mounting din tormented his ears, and its devilish heat gnawed at him—issuing mainly from the rounded bole at its base, which had become little more than a dome of living fire. Here, he sensed, the seed of Qjara's destruction was being incubated; from it would issue the true, living god to bestride the earth, once the three pillars of the idol clashed firmly together. Yet he could not reach the fiery hemisphere with his sword, any more than he could touch the flaming ball of the sun with outstretched fingers. The heat was too intense; he could not even throw his weapon, since he needed it to beat aside the bolts and gusts of fire that surged each moment at his unarmored vitals. In spite of his warlike fury he was now being forced back from the ravening tree, step by grudging step.

Then danger engulfed him. A host of the snarling heads, whose stalks seemed each moment to grow longer and more fiendishly agile, swooped down about him with nimble enough reach to surround him. Their howls dinned in his ears and their fiery breath beat at him mercilessly, threatening to sweep him off his feet and scorch him to a cinder.

Desperately he swung his sword, trying to hack or beat the hideous visages away; frantically he darted, like a spider trying to escape a flaming hearth. The monsters' fiery tongues licked the sweat from his skin and curled past the edges of his armor; the thongs and baser metal bindings of his mail burned away, letting vital parts of it clatter to the pavement. Flames engulfed him and lapped scorchingly at his limbs, his throat, his unprotected loins—

A blare of sound erupted around him. The heads drew upward in a blast of flame and a chaos of grating, bellowing cries. The attack by the Tree of Mouths broke off; as Conan edged away, he saw why.

From the base of the monstrous tree, transfixing its gravid ball of swirling fire, there now projected a long metal shaft—a thick, sagging spear-haft. Around it the mystic fire seemed to dim and fade, as if being eaten away. A ragged hole yawned in the luminous body of the spectral plant, a void which seemed to suck in more and more of the collapsing image as Conan watched.

Overhead, the noxious trumpetings already sounded more mournful than fierce, seeming to diminish in volume. Before him the ghost-image sagged, as if drained of the glowing energy that was its lifeblood. Fading, dying . . .

Conan wondered at the origin of the great spear, which seemed to have caused it all; though miraculously unmelted in the heat, it was of some soft, pliant metal . . . lead, most likely. A stray suspicion made him glance up over his shoulder at the bronze idol of Saditha; with a shiver, he confirmed that she now stood unarmed, her spear hand raised empty as if in salute.

It was nearly over. The spectre of the god had slumped and diminished to a mere shrub-sized desert mirage wavering in and out of existence. Around it on three sides, the chariots bearing the god's metal monuments suddenly burst into flame, ending their forward motion. As fire consumed the wooden axles, one of the great statues fell sideways to the ground, smashing the paving stones beneath it; the bases of the other two merely thudded to earth amid scatters of flaming ash. Behind them, their teams of faithful bearers knelt down aflame, their worn-out bodies having been reduced to mere papery husks of skin and sinew. Soon nothing remained of the pilgrims but feathery ash and charred bone. By then their howling god had vanished.

Conan, meanwhile, snaked out of his armor to get the last bits of smoldering undershirt away from his skin. Afriandra brought a many-colored robe from the royal pavilion to cover his nakedness. "Your vision came true," he ruefully told her. "Luckily, the gold armor protected me . . . and the sorcerous flames must have lost their power with the god's death. My burns are all but vanished . . ."

Abruptly they turned their attention to Khumanos, who had come creeping from the margin of the crowd. The priest no longer wore his hard, aloof bearing; now he knelt over the gleaming blade Conan had used to attack the Tree of Mouths.

"The Sword of Onothimantos," he said in wonder, his fingers plucking at the empty thong around his neck. "It is whole again—and I—" As he looked up from Conan to the princess, tears suddenly sprang into his eyes. Then, with an air of stricken humility, he turned toward the idol of Saditha. A moan issued from his parched throat, and he pressed his face into his hands, sobbing.

"Other spells have lost their power this day," Conan observed. Afriandra made no answer; instead she knelt beside the despairing priest to comfort him.

"A day of miracles!" a female voice declared close behind him. "A glorious, unforgettable day—on which our Goddess manifested her divine physical presence . . ." It was Queen Regula, speaking for the ears of the crowd ". . . and rescued her city from an insidious menace."

"By slaying her would-be husband at the altar?" Conan wrapped himself more securely in his regal cloak as he turned to ask the question.

"Indeed, yes," the arch-priestess rallied. "She exercised that sacred choice which belongs to every woman. In doing so, she spared her followers the harsh rule of a insensitive patriarch."

"They would have found Votantha's rule harsh indeed—" Conan grimly affirmed, "—though brief." He gazed up at the Goddess. "It was Saditha's idol, then, who cast the spear?"

"Oh, without a doubt," the queen assured him. "I myself was not blessed with the sight—I had stepped back under the royal pavilion, so my view was obstructed. But there are many in the crowd who will attest to it, I am sure—dozens, hundreds!"

"Then it must be so." Conan nodded in frank acceptance. "Anyway, other things hint at a godly hand . . . for instance, this blade I plied against Votantha." He picked up the weapon Khumanos had called the Sword of Onothimantos.

"And the provision of yourself to wield it," a hearty male voice added. It was Semiarchos, striding up to join his queen. "Once an outcast, now a dauntless hero in golden armor—did you find that suit poking about in the desert, by any chance?"

"Aye, O King. It is the last of the treasure from the Stone Ship. I found the remains of your uncle's expedition too—but not the wealth it carried." Conan gestured down at the armor plates lying on the paves. "I had the clasps and buckles mended by an armorer, to bring it to you as proof of my discovery. But it has suffered from the fight—"

"No matter! It is a rare find, and you are doubly deserving of it—but if you sell it to me, I will pay you handsomely—"

"Methinks its finding was more the work of our Goddess than of any mortal hand," Queen Regula interrupted, "since it served our side so well in this day's battle. To think of this sword and armor, brought together from such eldritch and unlikely origins, to be used in our defense by one who was reviled and shunned, branded a heretic and then exiled from Qjara—"

"I was never one to harbor a grudge," Conan announced. "I am ready, if you will, to accept your apology for my former shabby treatment at your city's hands-"

"No apology is called for," the queen

promptly assured him. "Clearly, all that came to pass was a part of the unfolding of the One True Goddess's great scheme, in which we mortals are but helpless pawns." She adjusted her capacious royal robes about her statuesque body. "My remarks were merely intended to show how far-reaching are the Goddess's powers—and how mysterious, or even astounding, their results can sometimes be."

"Oh, but Regula, my love," Semiarchos protested, "you must give the northerner some credit." He showed kingly tact in aiding Conan, who was scowling at the queen's dictum. "If the poor fellow is but an unwitting tool of Saditha, he proved at least to be a keen and ready tool—a noble implement of firm, strong mettle! Surely the Goddess would want us to reward him and acknowledge his efforts."

"Oh, indeed," the high priestess concurred, studying Conan thoughtfully. "His lesson of selflessness and endurance could be most valuable to our followers. In point of fact—assuming, of course, that he is willing to serve the temple and learn the rudiments of priestly devotion—he could someday be elevated to quite a high place in Qjara, even comparable to that of our late hero, Zaius." Her gaze flickered furtively from Conan to the princess. "In truth, it might be possible to raise him very high indeed—"

"Many thanks to you both," Conan said hastily, "but my plan is still to leave Qjara." He gazed down at Afriandra where she knelt beside the priest Khumanos. Careless of her surroundings, she cradled an arm around his quaking shoulders, hearing his confessions and sharing his tears.

Then Conan resumed speaking, glancing around the half-circle of citizens who, attentive to the dealings of their rulers, had drawn near. "I can tarry here awhile to help you clear away these evil fetishes—which I, after all, had a hand in assembling." He gestured to the segments of the idol, which still glowed and smoldered an algal green. "Such abominations should be carted off into the desert, I would say, and buried—far apart, and positioned so that your city is no longer at the center of their dire influence." He acknowledged the king's nod, which brought with it a scattered cheer from the onlookers.

"In any event," Conan resumed, "I can remain at your service until the arrival of a caravan northward. Then, after we have agreed on a price for yon armor—the mystic sword, too, would make a fine new weapon for your goddess, though it is a bit ill-weighted to my hand—why, then I can outfit myself and ride to Shadizar in style!"

Epilogue

Eventful days had overtaken the city of Sark. First came the announcement of the holy mission to Qjara; amid the drought and its related hardships, this was treated as a serious attempt to regain the favor of the great god Votantha. It entailed levies of laborers and troops for the pilgrimage, as well as the demands of King Anaximander's diplomatic visit to the north.

Then came news of volcanic eruptions in the mountains beyond the Shartoumi sea—and presently, vast plumes of smoke and ash could be seen, darkening the southern sky for weeks on end. The volcanoes were followed by a period of earthquakes in the same district—they must have been severe, since their shocks were felt even in the squares and palaces of Sark itself.

Then, finally, there was the rain. It came without warning, pattering down from heaven on a gray, featureless morn, and continuing uninterrupted day after day in a light, steady drizzle that promised to fill the rivers and cisterns without excessive danger of flash floods or landslides. It was a divine blessing, a benison of godly kindness that reaffirmed the people's faith in life itself. Where before they had crept and staggered through the streets, now they danced. Euphoria visited the town; although food reserves remained slim, the people celebrated and made plans for larger plantings and harvests in the coming season.

King Anaximander let them enjoy their leisure for the time, at least. While this rain curtailed their labors, there was no need to apprise his subjects of the heavier demands and duties he would be placing on them, of their roles in the improved order and military expansion he envisioned for this new age of prosperity. There would be time enough to scourge them into line.

The king himself was feeling almost amiable these days—although he had received no direct word from Qjara. That was a concern; the pair of acolytes he had designated to watch over the city had not yet reported back. Possibly they had perished or been struck mad or blind at their god's apparition. To be sure, if the delay was due to mere error or tardiness, the personnel involved would live to regret their malfeasance.

As far as any direct evidence of the god's visit was concerned—with all the quaking and smoke-belching that had been going on of late, it was difficult to tell. Some of the temblors and heat lightnings in past days could easily have been echoes of Votantha's titan footsteps and fiery bolts. Anaximander liked to think so.

The king wondered, too, about the volcanoes' effect on his ancestral mines and the volcanic forges in the southern district—though with any luck, that was a problem his descendants would not have to worry about for the next thousand years.

So, in spite of these minor concerns, Anaximander felt certain the mission had gone as planned. The rain was a sure sign—a sprinkling of Votantha's beneficence, as soft and warm as the blood of kings and paupers. A sated god, he reasoned, was a generous god; it made him feel sanguine about his city's future.

Then, as if to assure him further, the token of tribute arrived from Qjara. It came on a six-wheeled mule wagon, brought by carters and footmen who cringed and abased themselves suitably before taking leave. The lackeys would have a surprise on returning home—the gift had obviously been dispatched from the city just before the time of Votantha's coming. The scroll accompanying it, traced in Khumanos's neat hand, was sealed with the royal sigils of that buffoon Semiarchos and his arrogant taskmistress, Regula.

It was a bed—a frame of heavy bronze, the metal skillfully turned and leafed with gold. A fine down mattress was sent along to cover its central webbing of knotted hide stays. A suitable gift to homage a king, indeed. Softer than Anaximander's customary sleeping pad, it smacked of self-indulgence. But then, this ceaseless rain had put a damp chill in the air, and there seemed no reason not to enjoy a bit of luxury, for the time at least. The king ordered the bed assembled in his sleeping chamber.

The most splendid thing about it, perhaps, was its unique embellishment. On all four bedposts, strange fist-sized gems were mounted—translucent stones that glowed in the room's dimness with a deep green luminosity all their own. Anaximander found it fascinating the way reflections crisscrossed between them—holding his hand close, he could almost feel the steady, penetrating warmth of their inner energy.

The new Exalted Priest, who came to bless the gift, halfheartedly professed to share the king's enthusiasm. This was another fresh young acolyte—the most spineless, sentimental one yet. He was soon dismissed when the king announced his intention of retiring early.

Anaximander let his female body servants undress him; but when one of them perched shyly on the new bed, he cuffed her aside. He sent them all away, even the buxom pair who customarily waved chilly palm fans over him; then he stretched himself luxuriantly on the soft, silk-covered bolster. This night he meant to sleep deeply and warmly indeed.

PLAY

HYBORIAN WAR

IMPERIAL CONQUEST IN THE AGE OF

BE A PART OF THE LEGEND

Hyborian War, is an epic play-by-mail game which brings to life the Age of Conan the Barbarian. Rule a mighty Hyborian Kingdom with its own unique armies, leaders, and culture — authentically recreated from the Conan series. Cimmeria, Aquilonia, Stygia, Zamora ... choose your favorite kingdom from over thirty available for play.

Play-by-mail with other rulers across the nation.

Every two weeks, your game turn will be resolved at our game center. After each turn we will mail you a detailed written account of your kingdom's fortunes in the battle, intrigue, diplomacy, and adventure which is HYBORIAN WAR.

Be a part of the Conan legend! Forge by your decisions the tumult and glory of the Hyborian Age. Your game turns will be simple to fill out, yet will cover a fantastic range of actions. Send forth your lords and generals to lead the host. Now turn the tide of war with the arcane magics of thy Wizards. Dispatch your spies and heroes to steal fabled treasures, kidnap a mighty noble, or assassinate a bitter foe! Rule and Conquer! The jeweled thrones of the earth await thy sandaled tread.

FIND OUT MORE WITH NO OBLIGATION. WRITE US FOR FREE RULES AND INFORMATION. REALITY SIMULATIONS, INC. P.O. BOX 22400, TEMPE, AZ 85285, (602) 967-7979.

Turn fees are $5, $7 or $9/turn depending on the initial size of the kingdom you choose. The game is balanced with individual victory conditions. So, no matter what size kingdom you start with you have an equal chance of winning. Slower turn-around games available for overseas players.

ASK US ABOUT OUR DUEL-MASTERS™ GAME ALSO!